Praise for *Has Anyone Seen*

"Is it too soon to joke about COVID-19? In his new novel, Christopher Buckley tests that proposition, and his answer is a darkly funny, if decisive, *no*. . . . This romp is simultaneously thought-provoking and (for those of us enmeshed in current events) refreshingly escapist."

—Matt Lewis,
Washington Free Beacon

"Christopher Buckley isn't simply a marvelous humorist but also a corrosive observer of the American republic. Fresh from his novel *Make Russia Great Again*, Buckley scores once more with *Has Anyone Seen My Toes?*, a hilarious account of the travails of an aging screenwriter who is hunkered down in a coastal South Carolina town during the Covid pandemic with his second wife, Peaches, and his stepson, Themistocles."

—Jacob Heilbrunn

"Buckley delights in exploring the intersections of plausible and absurd as they arise in an off-kilter mind that resembles the author's for all its allusive gymnastics and silliness. . . . This is Buckley at his comic, mischievous best."

—*Kirkus Reviews*, starred review

"This is one of Buckley's funniest books—there's a big laugh on nearly every page, often more than one—and, perhaps unexpectedly, it's also one of his most compassionate. A delight, with bite."

—*Booklist*, starred review

"A laugh-out-loud take on the writerly life."

—*Publishers Weekly*

"The writing is lively and funny, as Buckley finds the ridiculous in much of the ordinary aspects of life, during a pandemic or not. . . . He has found all the bubbles that need bursting in our current preoccupations. If you're ready to laugh at pandemic absurdities, this is the book for you."

—Marissa Moss,
New York Journal of Books

"*Has Anyone Seen My Toes?* is mirth when we need it the most from one of our great satirists. . . . The pandemic has muddled our minds and Buckley captures these moments of inanity with comedic brilliance."

—Drew Gallagher,
Free Lance–Star

"In *Has Anyone Seen My Toes?*, Buckley has captured the zeitgeist of the pandemic in his own hysterical way. In so doing, he gives readers the chance to cleanse themselves of COVID cobwebs and another excuse to laugh."

—Joe Westerfield,
Newsweek

"A hilarious novel about life during the pandemic when one's health is the least of one's worries."

—Terri Schlichenmeyer,
The Bookworm Sez

ALSO BY
CHRISTOPHER BUCKLEY

HAS ANYONE SEEN MY TOES?

A Novel

Christopher Buckley

Simon & Schuster Paperbacks

New York London Toronto Sydney New Delhi

Simon & Schuster Paperbacks
An imprint of Simon & Schuster
1230 Avenue of the Americas
New York, NY 10020

Excerpt of "In the Tree House at Night" from *The Whole Motion: Collected Poems 1945–1992* © by James Dickey. Published by Wesleyan University Press. Used with permission.

First Simon & Schuster trade paperback edition June 2023

SIMON & SCHUSTER PAPERBACKS and colophon are registered trademarks of Simon & Schuster, Inc.

For information about special discounts for bulk purchases, please contact Simon & Schuster Paperbacks Special Sales at 1-866-506-1949 or business@simonandschuster.com.

The Simon & Schuster Speakers Bureau can bring authors to your live event. For more information or to book an event, contact the Simon & Schuster Speakers Bureau at 1-866-248-3049 or visit our website at www.simonspeakers.com.

Interior design by Lewelin Polanco

Manufactured in the United States of America

1   3   5   7   9   10   8   6   4   2

ISBN 978-1-9821-9804-6
ISBN 978-1-9821-9805-3 (pbk)
ISBN 978-1-9821-9806-0 (ebook)

For KK

Those things do best please me
That befall preposterously.

—A Midsummer Night's Dream

HAS ANYONE SEEN MY TOES?

CHAPTER 1

He shuffles to the bathroom scale and steps onto it with the enthusiasm of a man mounting the gallows. He imagines metallic groans, the sound of springs straining to their limit, the creak of timbers about to crack. But how can this be? It's a high-tech scale, probably engineered by people whose native language is German and wear white laboratory gowns. It was a *hint-hint* present from his wife, Peaches. It tells you not only how much you weigh but also how much you weighed yesterday, and how many calories you can consume today in order to weigh less tomorrow. But all this is academic, for he cannot see the numbers, owing to the protuberance of his belly. Nor can he see his toes. Are they still there? He wriggles them. It feels as though they are, but that could be phantom limb syndrome, where you think you feel body parts no longer there. He cranes his head forward, as if trying to peek over the crest of a hill. Good news. The toes are there. But leaning forward on the scale shifts his weight, causing havoc in the scale's delicate high-tech sensors. His weight fluctuates like a stock price on a day of wild market volatility.

Finally, the number stabilizes. Cue auto fat shaming. *Did you really eat an entire family size bag of Reese's peanut butter cups? After eating an entire supreme frozen pizza? You disgusting person. You pig.*

"Family size," "supreme"—labeling of distinctly deceptive American coinage. The embedded falsehood in "family size" is that this rucksack-like bag will be shared with the family. "Supreme" meanwhile connotes excellence and mastery, as in the Supreme Being, the highest court in the land, Julia Child's signature chicken. Why shouldn't a pizza loaded with pepperoni, sausage, prosciutto, onion, black olives, anchovy, jalapeño, and mushroom take its rightful place in the Valhalla of Supremacy?

On the bathroom floor by the scale, he sees an empty plastic wrapper perforated with bite marks. This sad relic contained the urgently needed Pepto-Bismol chewable tablets. This, too, has become a daily ritual: the 3 a.m. ingestion of pink bismuth to calm the roiling gastric seas. How has it come to this? Can everything be blamed on the pandemic?

He descends the staircase in a bathrobe and slippers. The day's next defeat awaits him in the kitchen, but already he can feel the pounding rhythm—if it can be called that—of hip-hop booming from the Sonos speakers. SONOS. The name connotes a Greek deity, though he suspects it stands for "Sporadically Operating Network of Sound." Whenever he wants it to play Bach or James Taylor, it refuses to cooperate. When his stepchildren want it to play rap, it works. At the moment, it is bellowing at him:

"Oop, oop, we in da poop. Don' wanna be, don' lookit me, oop, oop . . ."

His stepson, Themistocles, has yet again neglected to turn his music off before tumbling into the arms of Morpheus. Themistocles is, yes, an unusual name for an American lad; as are Clytemnestra and Atalanta, as two of his sisters are called. Another sister is more prosaically named Polly. Peaches's first husband was Greek. On the arrival of their fourth child, Peaches finally put her foot down.

Now begins the ritual search for Them's iPhone, from which the hellish din is issuing to the eight or however many Sonos speakers. He decides that the name cannot be an acronym. Sonos was surely a god of the underworld who tormented mortals with eternal unrest.

There is no point in attempting to roust Them from his sleep to ask him where his iPhone is. Them is uniquely gifted. He cannot be awakened by human device. As a child, he slept through a 7.4 earthquake. An exchange of nuclear weapons would not disturb his slumber.

A concavity in the sofa cushions indicates with a high degree of probability that the iPhone might be wedged between them. It is. Success. But such swift victories as this are rare. One morning, it took him half an hour to locate it. Them had left it in the freezer while rooting for a midnight snack.

He silences the hip-hop. He knows Them's passcode, thank God. He briefly contemplates deleting his hip-hop playlist of 2,204 songs, but decides against it. Them can be very creative at payback. The last time he deleted one of his playlists, Them programmed his stepfather's iPhone to shriek "*Allahu akbar!*" Them dropped him off at the airport, waited ten minutes, then phoned him. Caused quite the sensation as he was going through the TSA line.

Blessed silence. His rattled tympanic membranes make out the early morning chitter of birds, larks of varied feather rising from sullen earth at break of day to sing hymns at heaven's gate.

But now comes the day's third defeat. Lifting the carton of orange juice, he feels an unbearable lightness. Someone has drained it dry and replaced it, empty, in the fridge. Even the

most impartial jury would convict Them on grounds of circum-
stantial evidence. Or would they, if they knew of his talent for
retaliation?

Normally, he wouldn't care about the OJ. But he's reading a
book on the Napoleonic Wars and last night came upon a lurid
description of scurvy: rotting gums, teeth falling out, skittering
about the deck like pebbles. The admiralty solved the problem
by giving ship crews limes, from which we get the word *limeys*.
He wonders if its near homonym *blimey*, Brit for expressing surprise or alarm ("Blimey, not another story in the paper about
Brexit"), is a variant. He must look this up.

Etymology is a passion with him. He is known to accost
strangers and ask, "Did you know that *mayonnaise* is one of
the few words in the English language of Carthaginian origin?"
Peaches and the four children have heard the etymology of mayonnaise so many times that they have developed an aversion to
the real thing. He is aware that his wife and stepchildren do not
share his ardor for word origins. He does try to restrain himself,
but it's not easy. Only yesterday, he learned the word *petrichor*
and had to epoxy his lips shut, he so wanted to share it with
them. The pleasant smell that accompanies the first rain after a
dry spell. From the Greek *petros* (stone) and *ichor* (the fluid that
supposedly flows in the veins of the gods in Greek mythology).
Is this a great word, or what?

The day's fourth existential defeat presents itself at the
mailbox, where he goes to fetch his morning paper. A snake of
impressive dimension has coiled itself around the post of the
mailbox. He gets that this is South Carolina. Still. Until he married Peaches, he lived in latitudes where retrieving the paper did
not entail risk of reptilian envenomation.

He cannot discern from its markings what variety of snake

it is. South Carolina proudly boasts all five of North America's venomous species. Whichever it is, this one appears to have a theatrical bent. It has coiled itself around the post, head facing out, forked tongue protruding, as if posing as a caduceus, the ancient symbol of healing. (From the Greek *kerux*, "herald," but this is not the time for etymology.)

Honestly. The news these days is depressing enough without having to risk your life getting it. Nor does he relish becoming an item of local news himself.

RETIREE DOING BETTER
AFTER COPPERHEAD BITE

Their friend Stonewall was bitten by a water moccasin. By the time he got to the ER, his leg was "so swole up" they had to cut his pants off. They injected him with antivenom (cost: $10,000), but this had the unfortunate side effect of stopping his heart. (The ultimate undesirable side effect.) Turned out Stoney is allergic to antivenom. Nearly a decade later, his leg still occasionally throbs. Stonewall has become a more reliable predictor of rain than Weather.com.

"Shoo," he says to the snake, a feckless choice of words that moreover, makes no impression on it.

"Look," he says in a manly way, "fuck off." More assertive than "shoo." But the snake remains unimpressed.

He is acutely conscious of the absurdity of his situation, standing here rotundly at the end of the driveway in slippers and bathrobe, trying to get a dialogue going with a passive-aggressive serpent of theatrical bent. Right about now the guys working on the new house down the street will be arriving. He must resolve this situation before they show up. How humiliating would that be: an old Yankee fatso in slippers and bathrobe dithering before a snake? One of them will drive up in his F-150, festooned with NRA, Nam Vet, Semper Fi, and MAGA decals. He'll slow, take in the absurd spectacle of fatso Yankee and snake; grin, ask, "Y'all need some assistance with that?" He'll rummage in the back of his pickup for the appropriate tool—machete, nail gun, M-16— and efficiently dispatch the snake. "Mind if I keep it? My dogs love snake." Please. By all means.

But no one comes. He decides there is no dishonor in ceding the field of battle to a potentially lethal three-foot-long snake. This surely falls into the category of "pick your own fights." He can read the news on his iPad. Still.

As he turns to begin his craven retreat, he notices that a sign has been planted on the neighbor's property. He walks over to see what it says. A public service announcement, perhaps? "Danger: Snakes!" But no:

REELECT BOBBY BABCOCK CORONER

He was not aware that coroner is an elective office. He does know that the word derives from the Anglo-Norman French *coruner*. The coroner was the officer who safeguarded the king's property, most important, his crown.

Since marrying Peaches and moving in with her here in Pimento, he's made an effort to keep up with local elections for mayor, sheriff, country commissioner, and such. He takes democracy seriously. Look what happens when you don't. Jury duty can be a bore, but it's the least we owe the men who froze at Valley Forge during the bitter winter of 1777–78.

As he walks to the house, he wonders: What qualifications does one look for in a coroner?

He can't recall seeing any other coroner-related campaign signs. Perhaps this Babcock person is running unopposed, but feels he should have some signs so folks won't think he's taking reelection for granted. Or maybe Mr. Babcock likes seeing his name in big letters on people's lawns.

He continues his way to the house, keeping an eye peeled for other uliginous creatures. (Very useful word down here, *uliginous*: "swampy," "slimy," "slithery." Faintly onomatopoeic.)

What qualities would he look for in a coroner? Some medical knowledge would be in order, so the coroner could determine if the deceased died of foul play. Doesn't the smell of bitter almonds suggest cyanide poisoning? (Or is it arsenic? He must look this up. Just the sort of thing a coroner should know.)

What else? Punctuality. In TV crime shows, they're always saying, "We mustn't move the body until the coroner gets here." So punctuality would definitely be an asset. Who wants to sit there all day with a body, waiting for a dilatory coroner? Not him.

"Where the heck is that coroner? It's been over three hours now."

"He doesn't appear to be in any great hurry."

"Serves us right. Everyone said, 'For God's sake, don't elect Bobby Babcock. Ol' Bobby would be late to his own inquest.'"

The more he thinks about it, the more he realizes you don't want just anyone as coroner.

CHAPTER 2

Pimento is excited to have its own Hippo King. It opened a few weeks ago, and ever since, the line for the drive-through has stretched out onto the highway. Aged Boomers are quipping, "Just like Woodstock!" Sheriff's deputies are out every day, directing traffic and putting up cones. Not to detract from HK's excellence, but the lines are in part due to all the restaurants closing because of the pandemic, or as folks here call it, "the Kung Flu." He himself calls it "the coronavirus."

He takes his place at the end of the line. There must be thirty cars ahead of him. Today is the first time he's been back. He was here on opening day, but it was a disaster. When it came his turn to pick up his order at the window, the man handing it to him sneezed. The man was not wearing a face mask. Neither was he himself wearing a mask, because why would he need a face mask in the drive-through lane? This was no ordinary "achoo"-type sneeze. This was a "thar she blows!" Icelandic geyser–type nasal eruption. He had never seen a human being sneeze with such violence. How careless of him not to anticipate that being showered with millions of lethal airborne droplets is part of "the HK experience." *This week only, Hippo King customers will receive a fatal side order of coronavirus—at no extra charge!*

He thought, *Well, that's it. I'm a dead man. And what will they say at my memorial service? "He died as he lived, stuffing himself with Hippo burgers."*

All thought of food abandoned, he screeched into an empty space in the HK parking lot, pulse pounding, and called Dr. Paula, his concierge doctor. Another uniquely American concept: fork over a $7,500 annual retainer, in return for which your doctor will actually take your call. Imagine—a doctor who'll take your phone call. What'll they think of next?

His wife, Peaches, is disdainful, indeed contemptuous of the arrangement. She views concierge doctors as mercenaries in white coats. He thinks this may have to do with her upbringing. Peaches is the youngest of eight. Her mother is not a Christian Scientist but might as well be. The children had to go to school unless they had fevers of 101 or were vomiting or bleeding. Mother did not believe in allergies. "Nonsense!" she declared. Then one of her kids was stung by a wasp and turned blue and couldn't breathe. Even years later, she insists that his brush with death was "probably due to something else." Peaches inherited her momma's stoic ethic. When her own youngest, Polly, came home from soccer one Friday with an oddly angular forearm, Peaches ignored it until Polly's whimpers became unignorable. At the ER, the nurse took one look at the arm and said matter-of-factly, "It's broken."

It must be stressed that despite this incident of appalling negligence, Peaches is a loving and attentive mother. Since that unhappy episode, she has moderated her "Put on your big-girl panties and deal with it" philosophy. Of the four children, Polly is the one who comes home least often. But she lives in Boston. The restaurant where she worked had to close owing to the pandemic. She's writing a cookbook based on the television series *Game of Thrones*. On her last visit home, she made a lamprey pie. It was not improved by his launching into a detailed description of how Romans punished their servants by throwing them into pools full of lamprey, to be slowly nibbled to death.

Another reason Peaches disdains Dr. Paula is her website.

"Why shouldn't she have a website?" he said. "Everyone has a website. Our plumber has a website."

"She looks vampy," Peaches sniffed. (Translation: Dr. Paula is an attractive woman of a certain age.)

"Darling," he said, "I'm not paying Dr. Paula seventy-five hundred dollars a year to have sex with me."

"You better not be, or she'll be treating you for missing testicles."

His darling is very feisty and possessive. He finds this endearing. Peaches is all he ever wanted in a wife. He hasn't had an adulterous thought since they found each other a decade ago on the set of *Swamp Foxes*. Stipulated: fidelity comes easier in one's sixties now that the command center has relocated back to the brain after a half century's residence in the aforementioned testicles.

"She was the chief resident at Baptist Memorial," he pointed out.

"Uh-huh," Peaches said. "And now she takes care of rich retiree golfers for seventy-five hundred dollars a year."

"I'm not rich and I don't golf," he says, mentally appending a "touché."

He found Dr. Paula through Jubal Puckett. The Pucketts are their best friends here. Jubal had been to one specialist after another for a back problem. "I had so many damn CAT scans, PET scans, MRIs I was radioactive. I was setting off the damn alarms in airports." He was about to go the Mayo Clinic when someone told him about this concierge doctor in nearby Purrell's Inlet.

Jubal had never heard the term "concierge doctor," but Purrell's being a lot closer than Minnesota, he figured he'd give it a shot. By this time, he'd spent more than $7,500 on co-pays alone. And what do you know: Dr. Paula had him back to deep-sea fishing in two weeks.

So when his own doctor dropped dead of a heart attack while training to run a marathon, Jubal pressed him to try Dr. Paula. Outside her office he saw the gleaming, late-model Mercedes S-Class with a Keep America Great bumper sticker. He reminded himself that he had not come to debate politics. He has long despaired of his adopted state's unquenchable devotion to President Trump and has learned never to initiate a political conversation.

Dr. Paula turned out to be even more attractive than her website photo, exuding a MILFy sexuality.

"I thought *Swamp Foxes* was great fun," she told him.

He sighed. *Swamp Foxes* is his least favorite topic of conversation.

"Isn't that how you know Jubal?" she asked. "Wasn't it filmed at his plantation?"

"It was, yes."

"Well, I thought it was a hoot and a half."

"Kind of you to say so."

He refrained from launching into his usual lamentation about the villainy of the producer and director who sabotaged his screenplay. Over the years, he's become a local version of the Ancient Mariner, buttonholing strangers to tell them the saga of *Swamp Foxes*.

"You need to let it go," Peaches has told him more than once.

Jubal had correctly praised Dr. Paula's warm bedside manner. And he very much appreciated her nonjudgmental attitude when it came time for him to mount the scale. She did not say, "Whoa!" or start humming Henry Mancini's "Baby Elephant Walk."

"Are my toes still there?" he asked, by way of signaling his awareness that his body mass index was less than ideal. "It's been a while since I've seen them."

Dr. Paula laughed. She took out an expensive-looking Montblanc pen and poked each little piggy. "One, two, three . . . yup, all ten, present and accounted for."

He braced for a lecture about diabetic amputation, blindness, and other assorted horrors associated with obesity, but she did not reprove. During the prostate exam, he asked what had brought her here from Charlotte. (He did not particularly care, but he finds that making mundane conversation with the person whose finger is inserted in his rectum mitigates the inherent awkwardness.) She replied that the "rat race" and "traffic" had gotten to her. And she had always wanted to be a "country doctor." Between the Mercedes and her office suite, which resembled an airline first-class lounge, Dr. Paula is a different breed of "country doctor" than, say, Dr. Quinn, Medicine Woman.

"So," she said, snapping off the latex gloves. "Do we want to address the weight issue, or are we okay with it as is?"

"I didn't always eat this much," he said. "But with the pandemic, I seem to have defaulted into comfort-food mode." He thinks: *Defaulted? Dude. You did a swan dive into the deep end of the mac and cheese.*

Dr. Stone nodded sympathetically. She said that in her opinion, much of the research into "so-called obesity"—so-called! He could have kissed her—is grant driven and frankly politically motivated. She smiled in a cheeky way and said, "Well? Do we *want* do something about it?"

He felt he should at least pretend.

"I guess we could."

He left with prescriptions for several "promising appetite suppressants." He recognized the prefix in one: "amphet-." He hadn't taken speed since writing the screenplay for *A Bubble Off Plumb*, the movie that launched his career. But maybe appetite suppressants would give the current screenplay a boost. It's been moving at the pace of a Galapagos tortoise.

A week later, he was in the Hippo King parking lot, hyperventilating and wiping nasal jetsam off his face.

"He was handing me my Enormo Burger Combo and sneezed all over me! I'm covered in aerosol droplets!"

"Okay, let's calm down," Dr. Paula said. "Take a deep breath."

"That'll make the droplets penetrate deeper into my lungs!" he moaned.

"What it will do is make you relax. By the way, I love that you're calling me from Hippo King."

"This is not the time for a lecture!"

"Are you taking those meds I prescribed?"

"Yes."

"And you're still going to the HK. Interesting."

"Dr. Paula," he said. "I did not enroll in a field study. I'm calling to tell you that I have been assassinated by a food handler!"

"Got it. Okay, I'm going to call in a scrip for you. For Lysoloquine. It's very effective. It'll be ready for you at the pharmacy by the time you get there. Do *not* drive there at ninety miles an hour. Promise? Everything's going to be fine. If you start to show any symptoms, call me and we'll deal with it. Okay? I'll call the manager of the HK and see if their employees are Covid tested."

Dr. Paula reported back that the HK manager swore on the Bible—"up, down, and sideways"—that all his staff had been Covid tested. And that he would instruct them henceforth not to sneeze on the customers.

Two weeks have gone by, and he's still among the living. He hasn't developed symptoms. And by gum, he's hungry. So here he is, back in the HK drive-through lane, finger on the window up button in case the guy in the window so much as twitches.

It does seem strange that Dr. Paula's appetite suppressants haven't suppressed his appetite. His mouth is watering like a monsoon. His mask has become a face diaper. But no wonder, for word on the street is that HK's new Hippomongous-Burger Combo is to die for. (Maybe literally.) And that the forty-eight-ounce Mudshake is a thing of beauty. Each one contains three pints of ice cream and an entire package of crushed Oreos. And get this: they serve it to you *upside down*. To demonstrate how compacted it is. Themistocles said that a drive-through lane server accidentally handed a customer his burger combo upside down, with calamitous result. The HK drive-through A-team strikes again.

Twenty cars between him and mouthgasm. This must be what it was like waiting to get the last chopper out of Saigon.

The nightmare thought intrudes: *What if they run out of Mudshakes?* This cannot be dismissed as mere paranoia. If someone had predicted, "There won't be toilet paper," he'd have laughed. Now he's ordering toilet paper from Amazon. And where is it coming from? China.

He said to Peaches, "Let's hope it's not made from repurposed bat wings." He thought this witty, as the pandemic is thought to have been caused by Chinese bats at a "wet market." (Horrible concept.) But it could have been a plot by the odious

Chinese—and the Deep State—to make President Trump lose the election. Fox News is not discounting this theory.

Peaches did not find his remark witty. She said, "Can we please not talk about toilet paper at the dinner table?" Peaches masks her ukases as questions, to make them sound less like czarist edicts.

He responded that currently, 90 percent of conversations in America concern either toilet paper or bleach. You can't keep up with the TP memes on the Internet. Bathroom tissue now qualifies as breaking news on TV. He's tracking his shipment of Chinese toilet paper from Guangzhou to South Carolina.

"It just left Oakland," he says.

"What did?" Peaches said.

"Our toilet paper, darling."

Peaches groans. But she's played right into his hands.

"You scoffed when I ordered those N95 masks in February," he reminds her. After hearing the word "pandemic" on the news for the tenth time, he went on Amazon and ordered a box of twenty N95 masks. Peaches rolled her eyes and accused him of being hysterical. A week later, she was doling them out to her inner circle like communion wafers. Now he's monitoring a shipment of toilet paper as it makes its way across the Pacific. Who knew? Even at the height of the Cuban Missile Crisis, there was toilet paper. Which was a good thing, since everyone was having digestive issues.

The HK line is moving, but oh so slowly. These are the times that try men's stomachs.

He finds himself thinking about the coroner election and wondering what other qualifications one looks for. Bedside manner. You don't want a coroner with attitude. Someone who breezes in and grunts, "Where's the stiff?"

BEREAVED PERSON (*sobbing*): In the bedroom.

CORONER (*petulantly*): *Which* bedroom? Look, I don't have time to play Clue.

At the same time, a coroner shouldn't have to act as though Grandpa's death is the worst tragedy to befall mankind. He shouldn't have to moan, "Why? *Why?*" and shake his fist at the ceiling, as if expressing existential rage at an indifferent deity. But he should at least feign sympathy. You don't want someone who shrugs and says, "He's toast."

BEREAVED PERSON: Shouldn't you at least examine him?

CORONER (*shrugging*): I'd say it's pretty obvious he offed himself. His head's in the oven.

BEREAVED PERSON: But . . . it doesn't make sense. He was such a cheerful, happy person. Only yesterday he sounded so excited about the party next week for his sixtieth birthday.

CORONER: Just goes to show. You never know what's really going on inside someone's head.

BEREAVED PERSON: But what about that bruise on his forehead?

CORONER (*expressing mild curiosity*): Eh, he probably banged it stuffing himself into the oven.

BEREAVED PERSON: But—

CORONER (*visibly annoyed*): Look, if it's that big a deal to you, I'll give him a once-over at the morgue. Jesus Christ!

BEREAVED PERSON: What?

CORONER: Is the clock over the sink right?

BEREAVED PERSON: I think so.

CORONER: I've got a massage at one thirty. I gotta go. Sorry
for your loss.

Also, you wouldn't want a coroner who drums up business
for himself on the side.

*"You can pick up the death certificate at my office. Or for thirty
bucks, I could mail it to you. I don't take American Express. Cash
would be best. Have you picked out a funeral home? I wouldn't
trust my loved ones with some of them. They sell the bodies and
put mannequins in the coffin. Gallagher's on Broad is the only reliable one. Tell them I sent you and they'll knock ten percent off
burial, fifteen off cremation."*

What a nightmare! The more he thinks about this, the more
he realizes how important it is to have the right person in that job.

But, whoa—he's now just three cars from the Order Here
kiosk. *Time to concentrate*, he tells himself. *Focus.* He reminds
himself to take his meds. Dr. Paula said to take them with food
so they won't make him jittery.

How many Mudshakes can he order without self-disgust?
He calculates. One for right away, here in the parking lot. One
for the ride home. Two to put in the freezer. Themistocles will
want one. He's got 24/7 munchies. How many is that? But
wait—Atalanta is here for the weekend, and she'll want one.
(She moved to Atlanta, causing address confusion. Her mother
keeps sending her mail to Atalanta, Georgia.)

The line inches forward. He rehearses his order out loud. As
a screenwriter, he often says lines out loud.

"Good afternoon," he says to himself. "I will have two
Hippomongous-Burger Combos. And five, no, make it six Mudshakes." He adds, "And that's all," to make it sound less glut-
tonous.

Only one car in front of him now. Show time. In the rear-view mirror he sees a lawn sign by the HK exit, wobbling in the slipstream of passing cars. It's hard to read backward, but he makes out:

HARRY CHAMBLESS FOR CORONER

So, someone is running against Bobby Babcock.

"The race to decide who will be Pimento County's next coroner got down and dirty last night during the third of five planned debates between incumbent Bobby Babcock and challenger Harry Chambless.

"Chambless accused Babcock of being 'terminally tardy,' saying, 'By the time Babcock arrives on the scene, rigor mortis has set in and you're lucky if the corpse doesn't smell.'

"Babcock fired back that Chambless, who owns a local funeral home, has 'the bedside manner of an Ostrogoth.' And further charged that Chambless 'typically shows up at the deceased's home, reeking of ardent spirits and humming Chopin's funeral march, off-key.'

"Chambless attempted to deflect that charge with humor, saying that Babcock was 'dead wrong. Get it?' He did however admit that occasionally he'll hum Chopin's funeral march, saying, 'most folks find it kind of soothing.' As for the ardent spirits, he said it was embalming fluid. 'Which indeed does have a strong smell.'"

Boy, they play rough down here. He wonders what kind of campaign ads they're running. Will Babcock go for a soft-focus "Morning in America" tone? The Babcock family holding hands as they walk through a field of tobacco—wheat might be safer—bathed in golden, late-afternoon sunlight, their golden retriever, Styx, scampering after them?

"Growing up, I used to dream about being Pimento County's coroner. Thanks to y'all, that dream became a reality. Over the last four years, I've signed the death certificates of, gosh, must be over four hundred Pimentoans. Each one of them was a loss to our community. Well, most of them, anyway. In some cases, I determined there was more going on than what met the eye. That led to some folks going to jail. Reckon I won't be getting their votes on November 3. But I'm hoping I can count on yours.

"I'm Bobby Babcock, and you bet I approved this message."

"Good afternoon. Welcome to Hippo King."

A female voice is asking if he wants to try their grits and gravy.

"No!" he says vehemently, as if she's offering a sheep eye or testicle. "I have not come for grits and gravy!"

"All right, sir," says the voice, professional despite his violent rejection. "What would you like, then?"

The HK menu is four feet wide and seven feet high. It's—encyclopedic. How is he supposed to process all this? He feels a vortex of anger building in the cars behind him. *Focus*, he tells himself.

He locates the Extreme Burger. Now his eyes are drawn to an immense amount of fine print beneath. *What's this—footnotes?* "Nutrition Facts." *Nutrition? Right. Who thought that up?*

"Calories: 1,700." Oh dear.

He feels a telepathic cyclone of hatred for him gathering in the cars behind. Any second now, someone is going to honk. In his rearview mirror, he sees cigarette smoke being furiously exhaled out windows, like dragons' breath.

This could get ugly. But he reminds himself: this is the South. People are nicer here than up north. They're polite. These folks would stop their car and deal with a minatory snake for you, asking only in return to keep it for their dog.

Fine, but how long before their patience runs out? How long will they wait uncomplainingly in an already interminable HK drive-through line for an obese Yankee to make up his damn mind about what he wants to eat? (His Connecticut plates will give him away. He *must* get around to reregistering the car.) They're probably thinking: *Those Yankees sure take their time deciding how many Extreme Burgers they can stuff down their gullets before their bellies balloon into the steering wheel and pin them there like stuck hogs.*

The nightmare unfolds in all its ghastly vividness. He'll become another of those sad, morbidly obese people who live out their pointless lives recumbent on the sofa, their flesh eventually melding with the upholstery, requiring them to be surgically separated from it before they can be hoisted—by crane—from their dens of gluttony. The ignominy. Won't that make Peaches and the children proud?

EMTS SUMMONED TO HK TO REMOVE RETIREE FROM CAR AFTER HIS STOMACH EMBEDS ITSELF IN STEERING WHEEL

Not the kind of media coverage to gladden the hearts of HK's corporate suits. They doubtless prefer Hippo King–related news items, not to mention paramedics and morbid obesity. They'll issue a statement apologizing for the inconvenience to the customers in the cars behind him, and point out that HK's menu features a "wide variety of tasty low-calorie salads."

"As it happens, next week we'll be unveiling a highly nutritious new menu item we're calling our 'Green New Meal'—a delicious, heart-healthy smoothie made from kale, spinach, kelp, and pine bark nuggets. It's colon-cleaning good!"

"Sir? May I take your order?"

The voice in the kiosk has taken on a sterner tone. But so has the coroner's race.

"We're talking to Bobby Babcock, who's running for reelection this November as Pimento County coroner. Thanks for coming on WPIM."

"My pleasure. Tickled to visit with y'all."

"So, Bobby, I guess you've seen all sorts of things in your time as Winyah County coroner."

"You can say that again, and twice on Sunday."

"Tell us about some of them."

"Heck, hardly know where to begin. Well, there was this one fella, a Yankee retiree. He must have done his clothes shopping at the big 'n' tall stores. But we love our Yankee retirees, whatever size they come in. Anyhow, this individual, well, I guess he just liked to eat. But don't we all? Anyhow, he was going through the drive-through at the HK and he musta had himself a hearty lunch, 'cause his stomach just . . . expanded into the steering wheel. Pinned him good. That was something, I tell you."

"Lord, that sounds just awful."

"It was not pleasant; I will say that much. The EMTs—I can't say enough about our paramedics here in Pimento. They are flat-out the best in the business. That's not to take anything from our EMTs up in Purrell's Inlet or Itchfield. Anyhow, they did what they could. They finally managed to pry the guy out, using those Jaws of Life, those hydraulic deals they use. But the poor fella's organs got compressed. It was a sad thing. You do see sad things in my line of work. But you can't let 'em get to you. It fell to me to call his wife and inform her what had happened. You can imagine how she felt, poor woman. That was one tough phone call."

"I bet it was. Okay, let's take some calls from our listeners. Purrell's Inlet, you're on the line."

"Sir? Would you like to order at this time?"

"Oh. Sorry. Sorry. Salad. Do you have salad?"

"Yes, sir, we do. Would you like the chicken BLT salad or the side salad?"

"The side."

"Creamy ranch or balsamic vinaigrette?"

"No dressing."

"That'll be one dollar and twenty-nine cents. First window. Thank you for choosing Hippo King." She sounds relieved to be done with him.

On the drive home, he wonders what tone Chambless's ads take. Is Harry going high or low? He'll have to address the "Ostrogoth" bedside manner thing. (What *is* an Ostrogoth? Were they the ones who sacked Rome? He must look this up.) He'll also have to address the "ardent spirits" business. That embalming fluid explanation sounded a tad glib. Pimentoans aren't likely to vote for a lush who staggers into the place of bereavement stinking of bourbon and humming Chopin.

Scene: family gathered around Grandpa's deathbed. Quietly weeping.

Gentle doorbell chimes.

Harry Chambless enters the bedroom, hat in hand, tiptoeing, face drawn, the very paragon of empathy.

HARRY (*whispering*): I am so very sorry for your loss. Please accept my most heartfelt condolences.

BEREAVED WIDOW: Herbert was a wonderful man.

HARRY (*putting his arm around the widow's shoulder*): He was. Pimento has lost a giant.

WIDOW: Can I offer you a drink? Highball?

HARRY: Bless you, no. I have not partaken of alcoholic beverages since the first Bush was president.

WIDOW: But they say you . . .

HARRY (*smiling, shaking his head*): No, no. Those were lies. Terrible lies, told by a terrible man. Now, darlin', why don't you sit down and let me go about my duty. I won't take long, I promise. How peaceful he looks. Rarely have I beheld such serenity in all my years of coronating.

WIDOW: He does look serene, doesn't he?

HARRY: Now, I've got to put this here thermometer up his rear end, so's I can determine how long he has been deceased. Then I'll just have a sniff to see if there's a smell of bitter almonds, so's to establish he wasn't poisoned. Not that I have the least suspicion of that. Who would poison a man so beloved as him?

WIDOW: You do whatever you have to do, Harry. We all love and admire you so. I'm just grateful it's you and not that hot, steaming mess, Bobby Babcock.

HARRY: At times like these, wouldn't you prefer to see your dear departed in the hands of a competent, sober professional, instead of those of a chronically tardy, inept drama queen like Bobby Babcock?

I'm Harry Chambless, and I sure as heck approved this message.

One thing's for sure. It's going to be an exciting campaign.

CHAPTER 3

Five rivers flow into the Atlantic near Pimento. That's a lot of confluence. The place has seen more than its share of history.

The nineteen-year-old Marquis de Lafayette landed here in 1777 to join in the American fight for independence against the British, who had killed his father during the Seven Years' War. Francis Marion—"the Swamp Fox"—was from near here. Pride in him runs rightly deep. Every other street, square, and (aptly) swamp is named for him. His hit-and-run guerrilla tactics kept General Cornwallis pinned down in South Carolina, preventing him from joining up with Clinton in the north and annihilating Washington's army.

It's said that the very first European settlement in the New World took place here. "It's said" invariably guarantees that what follows is in fact *not* the case. And sure enough, the very first European settlement in the New World did not take place here. Pimentoans nevertheless continue to aver that it did; or at least that it might have. If you can have "alternative facts," why can't you have "alternative history"? At any rate, he's now lived here long enough that he, too, wants it to be true.

Driving across the bridge over the Greater and Lesser Pimento rivers, he'll say, "The very first European settlement in the New World might have been right there." He'll wait a beat and add, "Though to be honest, we're not a hundred percent sure. Still, kind of cool, huh?" People generally don't know how to respond to this theoretical Möbius strip, but to be polite, they'll sometimes grant that, yes, it is, indeed. Kind of cool.

Now that he's warmed them up, he'll point to another spot on Whohah Bay, into which the five rivers debouch, and say, "Now *there*—over there—is where Lafayette landed, in 1777. And that we *do* know for a fact."

This will elicit an "Oh?" or "Huh," a signal that he must now explain who this Lafayette person was. Alas, surveys routinely reveal that two-thirds of high school students think Adolf Hitler was Winston Churchill's vice president. After Washington, Jefferson, and Lincoln, more places in America are named for Lafayette than anyone: seventy-five cities, towns, or villages; seventeen counties; eleven city squares; and twenty-five avenues or streets. When General Pershing arrived in France in 1917 at the head of the American army, he went to Lafayette's grave in Paris, where the marquis reposes beneath earth from Bunker Hill, and declared, "Lafayette, we are here." Lafayette is probably the only French person Americans have wholeheartedly loved, other than Brigitte Bardot.

Now that his passengers are wondering why they agreed to come for a weekend, it's time for the pièce de résistance, as the marquis might say.

"See that house? There?" he'll say. "*That* was the home of Bernard Baruch."

Silence. "Who?" No matter. Now he can launch into his précis about the great financier. (Still with us?)

Born in Camden, South Carolina, in 1870, Bernard Baruch was the son of an immigrant Prussian who served as a Confederate surgeon in the Civil War. Canny young Bernie did not linger in burned-out, ruined postbellum South. He got out of there and went north. By age thirty, he'd had made his first million on Wall Street. He advised six U.S. presidents and was close to both Franklin D. Roosevelt and Winston Churchill. He and Churchill passionately argued at the post–World War I Versailles conference against making Germany pay ruinous reparation payments. If people had listened, World War II might have been avoided. In old age, Baruch spoke out against nuclear weapons at the UN: "We are here to make a choice," he said, "between the quick and the dead." Quite.

He tries not to prattle on at too great a length, but if his listeners are still awake, he also tells them this:

In March 1944, with D-Day approaching, President Roosevelt's blood pressure was so off the charts his doctors told him he'd be dead in a month if he didn't take a break. His friend "Bernie" offered him his estate here, Hobcaw Barony, as a place where he could rest and rejuvenate. Roosevelt arrived pale and coughing and left a month later tanned and relatively fit. The ground-floor bedroom where he stayed is mostly as he left it, except for the framed front page of the local newspaper a year later, with its somber headline: "Roosevelt Is Dead."

All this he learned when he first came to Pimento a decade ago for the filming of *Swamp Foxes*, the movie based (loosely, as it would disastrously turn out) on his screenplay about a patriotic group of prostitutes who set up shop here during the Revolution in order to raise money for Francis Marion and his patriotic guerrilla fighters. He pitched the idea as *The Patriot* meets *The Best Little Whorehouse in Texas*. The ladies charm their British officer clients into divulging intelligence over pillow talk, which they pass along to the Swamp Fox. A bawdy comedy, a romp, all in good fun. Many happy endings leading up to one very happy ending: America winning its independence. What a great movie it should have been. Now, the very name *Swamp Foxes* sends him into the fetal position, muttering. His only consolation—no small one—is that he'd have never met Peaches if it hadn't been for the movie.

It was shot at a nearby plantation named Itchfield, owned by Jubal Puckett, he of the bad back healed by Dr. Paula, medicine woman. The plantation has been in Jubal's family for seven—or eight?—generations. His ancestors made fortunes growing indigo and rice, thanks to the thousands of enslaved people who worked in miserable conditions of brutality, heat, reptiles, insects, pestilence, and disease.

Jubal maintains the "stately" (as the brochures say) plantation house, with its trademark allée of (also stately) live oak trees dripping with Spanish moss. In addition to the regular tourist trade, Itchfield can be rented out for weddings, parties, conferences, and moviemaking. During the season, buses bring tour groups from as far away as Charleston. Despite its blushful reputation, *Swamp Foxes* has been good for Jubal's business. People like to see where movies were filmed. Jubal does entertaining impersonations of the tourists: "Is this the room where Lafayette got the epic blow job?" When the movie came out with its NC-17 rating, Jubal deftly sidestepped local outrage, shrugging and saying, "Heck, I didn't know it was going to be a titty movie." His wife, Angie, remarked in her throaty chortle, "I don't know if I'd call it art, but it paid for the tree surgery." Itchfield's stately live oaks took a whomping from Hurricane Harriett. Local evangelicals said that the storm was God's judgment on Itchfield for being the location of a debauched film, and that it was only due to his infinite mercy that it was spared total devastation.

When Peaches married him, just after *Swamp Foxes* was released, she acquired a new status as wife of "that Yankee pornographer." She no longer bothers to point out that her husband's wonderful screenplay was hijacked by the producer and director. By now, no one really cares. Except for him. Whatever. As the saying goes, the dogs bark, the caravan moves on.

Perhaps unconsciously looking to rehabilitate his local reputation, he's recently conceived an idea for a movie based on FDR's stay at Hobcaw.

German intelligence learns Roosevelt will be staying at the house of "the rich Jew Baruch" right on the Atlantic Ocean. A chance like this will never come again. They devise a plan to parachute in a team of elite commandos who will seize Roosevelt and put him aboard a U-boat and take him to Germany. Hitler will use his prize hostage to get the Allies to call off the invasion and sue for peace. This screenplay will write itself.

Fade in.

Exterior. Night. The Reich chancellery, Berlin. Hitler's headquarters. Swastika banners everywhere.

A staff car with motorcycle escort pulls up at the entrance, heavily sandbagged because things are not going well for the thousand-year Reich. Everyone is on edge about the upcoming Allied invasion.

Admiral Canaris, head of the Abwehr (German intelligence), emerges from the car, tightly clutching an attaché case that looks like it contains something very hush-hush. He strides up the steps of the chancellery, to the staccato click of the guards' heels.

Interior. Hitler's office. Heavy, severe furniture. [Think Restoration Hardware meets S&M dungeon.]

The führer looks terrible: pale, clammy, twitchy. We sense that his breath is dreadful, but no one is about to offer the führer a breath mint. [Historical note: Hitler's vegetarian diet made him chronically flatulent.] His quack doctor has been giving him a witches' brew of pills and injections. To make matters worse, his mistress, Eva Braun, is driving him batty with demands for first-run Hollywood movies, which are not easy to obtain, inasmuch as the Hollywood studio heads are all Jewish. But this will change when the Third Reich runs Hollywood, along with the entire world!

Admiral Canaris makes his way to the führer. In the outer office, he sees Reichsmarschall Hermann Göring, an obese, porcine morphine addict, slumped in an armchair, staring into the fireplace with glassy eyes.

Göring has been telling the führer that there won't be an Allied invasion. And if there is, he'll deal with it. War isn't hell if you're zonked on opioids.

But the führer is worried and he could use some good news right about now. Und here comes the head of the Abwehr, with his attaché case.

Hitler's German shepherd, Blondi, snarls at Canaris, who protects his genitals with the attaché case. He takes out a top secret dossier and places it on the führer's desk.

Hitler reads.

[English subtitles.]

> **HITLER** (*not looking up*): "Hobcaw Barony"? What kind of name is that?
> **CANARIS**: A seaside estate in South Carolina, *mein Führer.*

HITLER (*peevishly*): Yes, yes, but why is it called by this silly name?

CANARIS: I believe "Hobcaw" means "the Land Between the Waters." It's what the local tribe of Indians called it before the Americans devised a Final Solution to the Indian question. The land later became the estate of an English baron. We will rename it after the war.

HITLER (*reading*): This operative of yours, code name "Pork Chop." He is reliable?

CANARIS: He is our top agent in South Carolina. He reports that the local tobacconist in Pimento—also a silly name—has received a large order for Lucky Strike cigarettes in anticipation of "an important visitor." Roosevelt's brand of cigarettes. Pork Chop assesses that the important visitor is Roosevelt, a close friend of Baruch.

HITLER: It is a disgusting habit, smoking.

CANARIS: Quite so, *mein Führer*. But if I may draw your attention to—

HITLER: He also drinks, Roosevelt. Martinis.

CANARIS: Yes. He likes to mix them himself, for his guests.

HITLER: Disgusting.

CANARIS: Agreed, but if I might draw the führer's attention to—

HITLER: He eats meat.

CANARIS (*stifling a groan*): Correct again, *mein Führer*. Meanwhile—

HITLER: Between the tobacco, the alcohol, and the meat, he will not live long, Roosevelt.

CANARIS: Doubtless you are right, *mein Führer*, as always. Meanwhile, I believe fortune has presented us with a unique opportunity.

HITLER: Kidnapping the American president? Risky.

CANARIS (*muttering under his breath*): So was invading Russia.

HITLER: What's that?

CANARIS: I said I rush to agree with you. Your perspicacity dazzles. Yet I believe that here is a risk we cannot afford *not* to take.

HITLER: Have you run it by Göring?

CANARIS: I didn't want to wake him. He looked so peaceful with his mouth open.

He sent twenty pages off to his agent in New York.

"Love it," Winky said. "But isn't it kind of similar to the Jack Higgins movie?"

"What Jack Higgins movie?"

"*The Eagle Has Landed.* Huge best seller; hit movie. The Germans find out that Churchill's going to be spending the weekend at a village on the coast. They put together a scheme to kidnap him and bring him back to Germany in a U-boat. Everyone was in it. Michael Caine. Robert Duvall. Donald Sutherland . . ."

His mouth is open as wide as Göring's. WTF? Now it makes sense: the whole time he was banging it out, he had this feeling of déjà vu. Boy, is this embarrassing. Now Winky will think he's sunk to the level of plagiarizing famous movies.

He croaks, "Please tell me you don't think I was *consciously* plagiarizing a famous movie."

"Of course not." Winky laughs. "I can't remember my PIN half the time." It's kind of her to equate forgetting her PIN with his stealing—even if unconsciously—the plot of a novel read by half the world's population and a movie viewed by the other half. How could this *happen*? He is mortified, baffled. If he had a pistol, he would shoot himself. Winky would be able to dine out for the rest of her life. "Then I heard this *bang*."

"So, how are things down there?" she says, politely moving the conversation away from theft of intellectual property. "New York's a ghost town. Actually, it's kind of nice, though I really shouldn't say that."

"Someone sneezed on me."

"Omigod. Are you okay? Did you get infected?"

"No. I'm still here. Plagiarizing Jack Higgins movies."

"Oh, stop. It's no big deal."

"I've put on so much weight people are calling me Bubba the Hutt."

"Hilarious. I can't fit into any of my clothes. Not that I need clothes. I haven't been out of my pajamas since March. So, great to hear your voice. Give my love to Peach."

"Wait. I've got another idea."

"Okay."

"Vengeful shark terrorizes small coastal town in South Carolina. Title: *Gone with the Finned*."

"Love it," Winky says.

CHAPTER 4

It does surprise him from time to time to think that here he is, ten years later, living a stone's throw from the scene of his worst professional experience. How did that happen? The Yiddish proverb says, "Want to make God laugh? Tell him your plans."

He'd been on the set of *Swamp Foxes* for two weeks, every day yearning more and more to be somewhere else. He was barely speaking to the producer and director, who had drawn so many mustaches on his Mona Lisa that she looked like Joseph Stalin. Marvin, the producer, kept telling him to "trust Brian's vision." Brian, the director, kept reminding him that Marvin's movies had grossed half a billion dollars. "But it's *my* script," he kept saying. To which Brian replied that he thought of it as "*our* movie." When one day Kim Kardashian arrived on the set—"Relax," Brian said, "it's only a cameo"—he realized the game was over. There was no point in further resistance. But yanking the eject handle was not an option. That would mean forfeiting his executive producer fee, earmarked for his divorce settlement. To make his happiness complete, the air-conditioning in his trailer kept malfunctioning. In a South Carolina swamp in June, air-conditioning is a fundamental human right, not an amenity. Plus, it made throwing tantrums problematic. A Hollywood tantrum on the set, done correctly, ends with the tantrum thrower declaring, "I can't work this way. I'll be in my trailer."

Itchfield Plantation's owner, Jubal, was having a grand time playing host to the crew and cast of *Swamp Foxes* on his historic property. He was especially attentive to the "Marionettes" (as in Francis Marion), the dozen ladies who, as Marvin Entertainment's press release put it, "portray the pulchritudinous patriotic prostitutes of Parnassus Plantation." (The hyper-alliteration should have been an early warning sign.) Jubal took the girls shopping in Charleston, on sunset boat rides along the Wandoodree River, deep-sea fishing, on picnics. He couldn't do enough for them.

He was glad to have Jubal around. He was a cheery soul, a good old boy of the first rank. His bonhomie was implacable. You could tell him you'd just been diagnosed with stage 4 cancer and had two weeks to live. He'd pat you on the back, hand you a beer, and say, "Well, damn. In that case, there's no time to waste. Let's get this loco in motion!" And within hours, you'd find yourself strapped into the chair of his deep-sea fishing boat, reeling in an eighty-pound tuna, your death sentence all but forgotten. You had to love the guy, really.

"Brian," he said one morning in his stifling trailer after the script person delivered new pages. "What the fuck?"

"Marvin and I agreed that the scene needs to be bigger."

"Marvin and I agreed" was code for "It's *our* movie. Not yours."

He flipped through the pages. His strategic reserves of outrage were depleted. Still.

"An orgy? Brian. He's the Marquis de Lafayette, not Dirk Diggler."

Brian shrugged. "He's nineteen and French. Are you telling me he doesn't want to get laid?"

"Not to get all historical, but the Marquis de Lafayette didn't come to America to get his knob polished. He came to fight the British. Why? Because they killed his father in the Seven Years' War. Not, as you keep calling it, the Hundred Years' War. Again, I apologize for making an actual historical reference. I'm just pointing out that the marquis risked losing everything by coming to America. Royal favor. His fortune. His life. And not to nitpick, but he was devoted to his wife. I stipulate that this perhaps made him unusual for a Frenchman. Nevertheless, you've now got him in bed with *six* tarts?"

"Lot of people joined the revolution to get laid, pal."

"No, Brian. I demur. Abbie Hoffman and Jerry Rubin may have joined the revolution to get laid. The Marquis de Lafayette joined the American Revolution to avenge his father. Not to split hairs, but there's a difference."

"Where's the harm in letting the guy get his oil changed before going off to wherever the fuck he went?"

"Saratoga Springs."

"Right. There."

Brian is a talented director, but he knows nothing about anything. His ignorance is so comprehensive it aspires to greatness. Brian might, in fact, be among those who think Hitler was Churchill's vice president. And if Brian calls him "pal" one more time, he's going to drag him by his fucking ponytail and throw him and his Canon EOS into the Wandoodree River, which at this time of year is a uliginous bouillabaisse of alligators, snapping turtles, and water moccasins.

Into this happy milieu arrived one morning a white Jaguar convertible, top down and two blondes in the front. In his memory, Angie had one hand on the steering wheel and with the other held a Martini glass. This is a false memory, but as Peaches says, "She might as well have been. Angie came out of her momma's womb holding a cocktail."

The ladies debouched from the car. The driver, the aforementioned Angie, smiled and extended her hand.

"Angie Puckett. What a pleasure to meet you. Jubal has done little else these past weeks but talk about you."

He processed. *Puckett . . . Jubal . . . as in . . . Mrs. Puckett?* Much as he wanted to reciprocate with "And Jubal has done nothing but talk about *you* these past weeks," he was hampered, as Jubal had not once in two weeks mentioned his wife's existence.

"We were going to bring flowers," she said, "to strew in your path. But we couldn't find quite the right color. And we so wanted to make a favorable first impression."

Scarlett O'Hara and Auntie Mame, with a dash of Bette Midler, whom she physically resembled. She talked as if doing a scene. Was this an impromptu audition for a bit part in the movie? (A frequent occurrence on movie sets.) But he quickly realized it was just her, playing the role she was born to play—herself.

She touched him gently on the hand, the way Southern ladies do, and cooed, "I *love* that you named the house Parnassus. So much more elegant than Itchfield. I've been trying for years to get Jubal to rename it. Itchfield. Sounds like a *flea* powder. But he says it would be rewriting history. I tell him, 'Who *cares*?' But that's my Jubal. Immutable, never mute."

Her friend said, "Angie. Leave the poor man alone. Can't you see he's about to fall asleep on his feet?"

Angie segued into Bette Davis mode. "I *thought* it was an interesting point."

"It wasn't."

"This," Angie said, "is my erstwhile friend Paige. But her fellow inmates at the correctional facility called her Peaches, so why don't you."

"I'm a big fan," Peaches said in an embarrassed tone.

"Oh. Thank you."

"I loved *One of Our Whales Is Missing*."

What does one say? Nothing. But that meant remaining silent, smile frozen, as the lady explained why she loved the movie, written by someone with whom he shared a first name.

"Where do you get ideas like that?" she asked.

His smile tightened into a DIY face-lift. He shrugged, to show that he himself was at a loss to explain his genius. He put a quietus on his misery with "You must be looking for Jubal."

"I must say," Mrs. Puckett said. "He certainly has taken to the life cinematic. How *are* we going to keep him down on the plantation now that he has seen the bright lights?"

"It's been great having him around. He's been a huge help."

"That's my Jubal. A river to his people."

"Let me go find him." *Before you do, in the hayloft, rehearsing lines with Indigo Sal.* He trotted off into the warren of trailers and grabbed a production assistant. "Find Mr. Puckett. Stat. Tell him his wife is here."

"They're getting him. He's dealing with"—*Indigo Sal's brassiere*—"a tree issue."

"A tree issue. Did you hear that, darling? The glamour."

"We're getting ready to shoot the scene where the British colonel—the bad guy—is going to hang the girls from the live oaks."

"Dear me. That is a tree issue. Why is this colonel being such a pill?"

"He's found out that the ladies are funding Marion and his guerrillas. He's sent an ultimatum: If Marion doesn't surrender, he'll hang the girls."

"Tell me no more. I feel faint."

Jubal arrived, out of breath but braying hellos. He bestowed a moist connubial smooch on Mrs. Puckett and gave Peaches a bone-crushing hug.

"I hope we're not interrupting your tree issue," Angie said.

"Tree?" He recovered quickly. "Nah." He grinned exuberantly. "It's all good. All great. Fan-tastic. So, whatch'all doing here?"

"We're on our way to Charleston, for lunch and a bit of retail therapy. I had a question about the chairs for the veranda."

Mr. and Mrs. Puckett huddled to discuss wicker, leaving him and Peaches standing awkwardly.

"Would you like to see the set?"

"Sure. Great."

He led her through the hamlet of trailers and trucks to the famous live oaks–lined allée dripping with Spanish moss. Production assistants on cherry pickers were looping hangman nooses over the branches.

"God." Peaches recoiled. "That's horrible."

"That's sort of the point."

"What happens?"

"Sure you want me to spoil it?"

"I'm not going to see it if it ends with women hanging from trees."

"It's a brothel. All endings are happy."

Peaches grunted in an exaggerated Southern accent, "Well, that's a load offa *my* mind."

As they walked beneath the trees, he tried to figure out a

way to tell her before she started in again about how much she loved a movie he didn't write.

"They're magnificent, these trees," he said.

"These plantations were built on misery. The rice fields were the worst kind of slave labor. When I was little, my nanny, Eunice, a big Black woman—*huge*—told me the Spanish moss was tears the trees were crying on account of the awful things they saw. Her great-grandfather was born a slave. Sorry. Didn't mean to go Debbie Downer on you. They *are* beautiful, the trees."

"Between your tears and my hangman nooses, this is starting to feel like Desolation Row."

"I'm sure your movie's going to be great."

"I'm glad you liked *One of Our Whales Is Missing*."

"I did. I—"

"If I happen to run into the guy who wrote it, I'll pass along your compliments."

It took a half second to register. Peaches turned plum.

"Aw, *shit*. Really?"

He smiled and nodded. "Kind of funny, actually."

"No, it's not. Give me a hand."

"Hmm?"

"Lift me up."

"Why?"

"So's I can stick my head inside that noose."

He told the story in his toast at the rehearsal dinner a year later.

CHAPTER 5

Before the Civil War, or "The War of Northern Aggression" as some here call it, Pimento was home to many great plantations like Itchfield that provided the world with over half its rice. And much of its indigo. He does not know what percentage of the world's indigo, exactly, but he has been meaning to look this up. It's on his to-do list, but as an item, it lacks urgency. No one is panting to know. Indigo has been moving down, rather than up, the list. And now, this coroner election has pushed it even further down. At this point, there's frankly no telling when the indigo question will be resolved.

He and Peaches live in a neighborhood called Aqueous Acres, a tract of land bordered on one side by the Greater Pimento River and on the other by the very great Atlantic Ocean. "Aqueous" refers neither to the river nor to the ocean, but to the thirty-eight lakes that the developer scooped out of the ground in order to provide every buildable lot with a "water view." He tells prospective buyers, "Heck, we got almost as many lakes as they do in Minnesota!" Aqueous Acres cannot truthfully claim hydro-equivalency with the Land of 10,000 Lakes, but no one seems to mind.

The alligators certainly don't, nor do the turtles, and there is an abundance of both here. The latter comes in three varieties:

snapping, bog, and river cooter. He'll see a lump up ahead on the road, which soon reveals itself to be a turtle that has injudiciously chosen to pause there, perhaps in hope that the strange, enormous things bearing down on it at great speed won't notice it.

He has benevolent feelings toward turtles, so he'll stop the car, get out, and carry it—they're generally about the size of a medium pizza—to the nearest lake. There being thirty-eight of them, it's never a long trek, and it leaves him with the glow of a Boy Scout who has earned his Turtle Rescue Merit Badge.

One time, as he was reaching for the door handle, Peaches said, "That's a snapping turtle. I wouldn't mess with it."

He replied that he had lived here long enough to know the difference between a snapping turtle and a bog or river cooter. Peaches said one day she was in the local ER for an ankle injury when a man was brought in with a snapping turtle clamped on to his hand.

"They don't let go. They have to cut the head off. It's not real pleasant." The turtle, whatever kind it was, was left to fend for itself.

Their house is on the ocean, which is nice but a mixed blessing during hurricanes. To get to it, you drive over a levee bordering a large, swampy wetland that is home to an impressive number of creatures whose ancestry is measured in tens of millions of years. He calls it a "gator community."

Gators and their ilk hibernate here. In late February, early March, comes the Great Awakening, followed by the Great Slithering. The time of going barefoot or in flip-flops is over. Now is the time for sturdy footwear and ankle protection and watching where you put your feet.

One day Peaches returned from walking the dogs with an iPhone photo of a creature that defied taxonomic classification.

It looked like the spawn of a land crab and scorpion that had mated in nuclear waste. It lifted its single claw at Peaches in a defiant posture. The message was clear: "Do not fuck with me." Peaches did not.

By early April the nights are so cacophonous with frog-croak that it would impress Aristophanes, who wrote a play featuring frog onomatopoeia. Before bed, he takes the dogs out so they can do their duty. He'll stand and listen to the amphibian concerto. "Loud" is not adequate to describe it, nor does the sound lend itself to quaint toad phonetics like *jug-a-rum*, *jug-a-rum* or *ribbet*, *ribbet*. It is a deep, primal sound that makes him intensely grateful to be located above it on the food chain.

While he ruminates ontologically, the dogs are usually not doing their duty, but rummaging at the nearest new home site. They'll return, tails wagging, with disgusting remnants of fast-food wrappers protruding from their mouths. Sometimes they bring things that were recently alive—moles, toads, crabs. They have not yet returned from nocturnal foraging with a snake, and for this he is grateful. He has imagined that scenario and it makes him twitch. He retains a still-vivid memory of a long-ago night in Maine, when his yellow Lab showed up with 113 porcupine quills embedded in his face. He and the vet counted them, one by one.

Aqueous Acres boasts something few communities can or would care to: singulars of feral Hungarian pigs. Paradoxical as it sounds, "singular" is the collective noun for a group of pigs. Remember Mr. Baruch? About a century ago, he imported some for the hunting pleasure of guests at Hobcaw Barony. It seemed a splendid idea at the time. Mr. B is long gone, but his pigs live on. Do they ever. They litter three times a year. (Litter, as in reproduce.) Professional hunters are called in every now and then to cull the population explosion, but it's a pointless exercise.

Their greatest pleasure in life—or perhaps second greatest, after the thrice-annual rutting—is to swarm nocturnally over Aqueous Acres, rooting for grubs. Nature has provided the pigs with snouts that are more efficient at earth moving than John Deere's finest backhoes. Plantings and flower beds are turned into hellscapes, as though an army of giant bad golfers has come in the night and left thousands of divots in its wake. If General Sherman had seen what these pigs could do, he'd have enlisted them for his marches through these parts.

In addition to the gators, turtles, snakes, and Mr. B's pigs, Aqueous Acres also features a variety of sharks. Young Themistocles is an avid surfer and paddleboarder. He recently beheld— *beheld* seems the right word—a six-foot-long bull shark leap into the air, clear of the water, like a submarine-launched cruise missile. Why, one might ask, would a bull shark perform an aquabatic display more typical of Shamu the Orca? Them's theory is that it was feasting on a "bait ball," those tight, spherical arrangements of small fish one sees on computer and TV screensavers—and got so darn excited he just had to make a gesture. More cynical than Themistocles, he suspects that it was not gastronomic ecstasy, but a malevolent urge to give the humans bathing nearby a moment to remember.

After seeing one too many promotions on TV for Shark Week, he was inspired to compose a doggerel.

> *I like to watch people get eaten by sharks,*
> *I cannot explain, but I do.*
> *Be still, oh my heart, for this Monday's the start*
> *Of Shark Week, which is not for the meek.*

For days on TV, there'll be blood in the sea.
Imagine my glee. Can you hear me shout, "Whee!"?
If once I was wary of things wet and scary,
I now, more and more, am attracted to gore.

Sharks are not the only entertainers on the beach. One day while he was walking the dogs, a neighbor lady ran up with an air of urgency. "No, no," she said. "Don't let them in the water." She pointed to a by no means inconsiderable alligator, lying contently in the surf, perpendicular to the shore, as if waiting to catch the right wave.

"We get a couple of them every spring," she explained. "They come out of the swamp and go in the ocean, to get rid of the lice."

One uliginous seeker of saline lice-detox measured thirteen feet. Even Peaches, who pooh-poohs at his whimperings about being eaten, conceded that thirteen feet *was* impressive. A photograph of the saurian beachcomber made the front page of the *Weekly Pimentoan*, accompanied by an article reminding readers to run in a "zigzag or circular pattern" if being chased by a relic from the Mesozoic era, since they can outrun humans on a straightaway.

As he tells these stories to visiting Yankee friends at the dinner table, spouses exchange nervous looks. *You told me they live in a nice neighborhood, not Jurassic Park!* Peaches rolls her eyes and says to pay no attention to her husband. And the weekend proceeds pleasantly, the only tragedy being the regular cocktail hour attack by the Divine Wind squadron of kamikaze gnats. No one has been eaten by a prehistoric reptile or oceanic apex predator. Things could be worse. He once checked into a cabin on an island in Australia's Great Barrier Reef to find a note on the welcome basket asking him to keep the door closed "at all times" because "Our Komodo dragons do love their fruit!" *Their* fruit? This struck him as a novel concept in hospitality management: leave the guests to fight it out for the complimentary fruit basket with giant lizards.

CHAPTER 6

His passport is not where it should be. He has looked every-where, yet it remains nowhere, and its nowhereness has now become maddening. He's starting to feel like a character in an Edgar Allan Poe short story. He is fastidious to near-OCD levels about keeping things in their proper place.

Peaches does not join in this obsession. She's constantly losing things. She has never once put her car keys, wallet, credit cards, earrings, lipstick, or other necessities in the same place. It's as if they're in a witness protection program, so no one, including herself, will ever find them.

In fairness, it must be said that his darling juggles many balls. It makes him dizzy just to watch. There are her four children, her seven siblings, her ninety-five-year-old mother, her many friends, and her job. Peaches supervises online auctions of assets seized by the federal government. An interesting niche. On any given day, Peaches will be overseeing bidding on a jacket made of ostrich feathers ("Estimate: $8,000–$12,000") that belonged to a disgraced presidential campaign manager; or a twin-engine Cessna ("All seats except the pilot's have been removed") used to smuggle cocaine and fentanyl.

It's not that he needs his passport. He's not going anywhere. No one is. There's a pandemic on. The only countries that allow

Americans aren't places Americans want to go. It's more the idea of not having his passport that's gnawing at him, like Poe's telltale heart, beating beneath the floorboards. He suspects his anxiety may be related to his World War II screenplay, which has scenes of the Gestapo banging on people's doors and demanding to see their papers. "*Your papers are not in order. You will accompany us to headquarters.*" Where nothing good ever happens. But the Gestapo is not, to his knowledge, currently active in Pimento, South Carolina.

When he can't find something, he immediately suspects foul play.

"No one took your passport," Peaches says.

He concedes that there is no logical reason someone would steal his passport. Their devoted housekeeper, Nathene, is not a member of a criminal network trafficking in purloined passports. Nor would the kids have any use for his passport. If Themistocles wants to punish him for deleting his playlists or some other affront, he'll serve vengeance electronically. "*Allahu akbar!*"

And yet: the passport is gone. Emphatically. Defiantly.

He likes the maxim, "If you can't solve a problem, make it larger." He doesn't understand it, but it sounds wise.

He logs onto the U.S. State Department website, to report that his passport is missing. *You're doing the right thing,* he tells himself. *At this very moment, your passport could be in the hands of ISIS, or a Colombian drug lord, or one of Putin's assassins, the ones who go about putting nerve agent in people's underwear. What if something awful happened, and you hadn't reported it missing?* He imagines the knock on the door. Not the Gestapo, but the FBI.

"*Sir, did you report your passport missing?*"

"Well, er, I was going to, but my wife said it must be here somewhere."

. *The agents exchange grave looks.*

"Sir, are you aware that Trenton, New Jersey, has been destroyed by a nuclear bomb?"

"I did hear something about it. Why?"

"The people who planted the bomb used your passport to enter the country."

Wonderful. Now he's an accessory to mass murder. No question—he's absolutely doing the right thing.

He finds where you tell the State Department that your passport is missing, and in the Comments box writes that he thinks it might have been stolen during a trip to California. But wait. Will this make the feds suspect that he left his baggage unattended? Major federal no-no. He deletes that and writes that he last remembered having it on a trip to California. Better. Less self-incriminating.

He clicks on Submit, invalidating his passport. He feels greatly relieved. Now they cannot blame him for destroying Trenton. If ever he visits Trenton, he can hold his head high. He can tell Trentonians that it was his diligence that led the FBI to thwart the bomber. The FBI will thank him for reporting his passport stolen. They'll probably give him a commendation. Wouldn't *that* show Peaches? "Told you someone stole my passport. In addition to the commendation, there's a reward. I'm going to give the money to turtle rescue." Turtle rescue is one of their local charities. Turtles hatch on their beach. Sweet things, turtles.

Well done, he tells himself. But this is no time for resting on laurels. Now he has to get a new passport, which requires going to the UPS Store to have his photo taken. That will mean taking off his face mask and inhaling God knows how many airborne Covid droplets. The State Department probably doesn't accept passport photos of people looking like train robbers. Then he'll have to go to the post office and fill out forms and breathe more nasty Covid spores.

What if they ask for his birth certificate? The kind "with raised seal"? Fastidious as he is, he has no idea where that might be. Maybe if he springs for the extra fee for expedited service they won't insist on the birth certificate. He's always suspected that they don't take you seriously unless you're willing to pay the extra fee.

"Well, what do we have here? Another passport applicant who doesn't need expedited service."

"Cheapskates. I hate them."

"What say we put his application at the bottom of the pile? That way, he'll have his new passport by August."

"Yeah. August 2028."

They roar with laughter. Disgraceful. And they call themselves "civil" servants? What's happening to this country?

He prepares to set off, full of foreboding. He'd better make a photocopy of his driver's license. They're sure to ask for that. He lifts the cover of his printer. There, open and facedown, is his now-invalid passport. *Fuck!* Now he remembers: he had to make a copy of it, months ago, for some reason he can't even recall.

He'll have to tell Peaches. That would be the honorable thing to do. But she'll lord it over him. It'll be months before he can lecture her again about always losing things. Maybe best to not mention it. For now. He slinks off to the UPS Store. His new passport photo won't show him smiling, that's for sure.

At the UPS Store he removes his mask and holds his breath while the woman takes his picture. There's a problem with the camera. Wonderful. He's turning blue from lack of oxygen. She solves her camera problem just as he's about to pass out.

At the post office, he fills in the form. It asks for occupation. It feels like an existential question. All his life he's put down "writer." But he hasn't sold a screenplay in years. What will he say if they ask, "What have you written lately?"

A year ago, back when people still traveled, he and Peaches went for their interview with Homeland Security to get Global Entry cards. The agent asked him, "What do you do?"

"Not much, really," he replied truthfully.

"Retired?"

"Well, I still do some writing." He started to tell him about his FDR kidnapping screenplay. The agent's eyeballs glazed. He changed the subject by asking if he knew that *mayonnaise* is one of the few words in the English language of Carthaginian derivation.

"Sir," the agent interrupted, "what do you want me to put down?"

"Let's go with 'retired.'"

"Works for me."

Thank God he remembered. If he puts down "writer" instead of "retired," it'll set off alarms at Homeland Security.

"This application by the guy in Pimento. Anything about it strike you as fishy?"

"Now that you mention it, yeah. A year ago, he applied for Global Entry. Said he was retired. Now he's a writer?"

"That's what I was thinking. Doesn't add up."

"Pimento . . . Pimento. It's ringing a bell . . ."

"Wait a minute. Isn't that where Bernard Baruch lived?"

"The famous Wall Street financier and adviser to six U.S. presidents?"

"Yeah. Him. What was his house called? It had some weird name. Hobnob . . ."

"Hobcaw. Hobcaw Barony."

"Holy shit. Where the Nazis tried to kidnap Roosevelt."

"Well, well, well. And now Mr. Writer needs a new passport. What a coincidence. Fucker's getting ready to flee the county."

"Where's he gonna go? No one's letting Americans in. Only the shithole countries."

"Wanna give it to the FBI?"

"So they can claim credit? Fuck, no. I say we sit on his application. See what his next move is."

"Yeah. Sweat the son of a bitch."

He sits in his car in the post office parking lot, breathing into a smelly old Hippo King bag as he speed-dials Dr. Paula.

"Now what have you done to yourself?" she asks. He explains that he's having a panic attack. She says she'll call in another prescription but makes him promise not to drive after he takes the new pills. Meanwhile, the HK bag that formerly contained a two-pound Enormo Burger (with cheese) is making him hungry.

He thinks it through. He and Peaches won't be traveling abroad until the pandemic is over. So he doesn't need the passport. But at some point, the world will presumably reopen for business—assuming anyone's still alive—and the first thing Peaches will want to do is travel. His darling lives to travel. She's always arranging trips.

"Guess where we're going? To the Arctic Circle in Finland, to see the Northern Lights!"

"Oh? Well, great."

"What's the matter? Aren't you pleased? You've always wanted to see the Northern Lights."

"I don't have a passport."

"What? I thought you got a new one."

"I applied for one."

"And?"

"Seems they've put a hold on it."

"What? Why?"

"Unclear. It may have something to do with my involvement in the FDR kidnapping plot. Don't worry. I'm dealing with it."

What a mess. And all of his own making. At times like this, he thinks of the *Exxon Valdez*, the supertanker that ran up on the rocks in Prince William Sound, spilling 11 million gallons of oil, unleashing a tsunami of goo on the populations of seals, otters, salmon, and seabirds. The captain had left the third mate, a man named Bob, in charge of taking the ship out to sea. On reaching the bridge after his ship grounded, the captain said to him, "Damn fine job, Bob."

Damn fine job, Bob, he tells himself.

CHAPTER 7

He can't remember what he put down under "occupation." But Dr. Paula's latest prescription has given him a wonderful burst of energy and mental clarity. He's busier than ever. He certainly doesn't feel "retired."

Even if the State Department relents and issues him a new passport, where is he going to find time to gad off to the Finnish Arctic Circle to stare at Northern Lights and reindeer? There's way too much on his plate. The coroner race; the article he promised *Etymology Today* on English words of Carthaginian origin; settling once and for all what percentage of the world's indigo was produced here. Meanwhile, Peaches has asked him to paint white stripes on the porch stairs, so her nearly blind ninety-five-year-old mother won't end her life on them. That is not a can that can be kicked down the road. He's got enough trouble as it is without being blamed for killing his mother-in-law. And if all that weren't enough, he's decided to proceed with his FDR kidnapping screenplay.

So what if Jack Higgins (net worth $86 million, according to Google) wrote a novel about a Nazi plot to kidnap Winston Churchill. What does that have to do with Roosevelt? *The Eagle Has Landed*—a title, ahem, brazenly filched from Neil Armstrong—takes place in November 1943. And the plot failed. So it is entirely plausible that Hitler, having been thwarted at nabbing Churchill, would want to kidnap Roosevelt in March 1944. What was Winky thinking, trying to talk him out of such a great premise? She'll change her tune when she reads the finished screenplay. She'll be cooing. He can hear her already. "I love it. It's so much better than that Higgins dreck. You'll end up with a net worth way more than eighty-six million. I'm sending it to Spielberg."

In the midst of this frenetic activity, he's falling behind on another pandemic project: reading Proust.

When the sheltering in place began back in March, he decided he was finally going to read Proust's *Remembrance of Things Past*. Over the years, he's made several attempts to read this 4,277-page cinder block. To be candid, his motivation had more to do with guilt than with actual desire. He was tired of hearing himself lie, "Proust? Oh, yes, it's next on my list." Really, who believes you when you say that? They're thinking: "*I can't believe he* still *hasn't read it. What a philistine!*"

On his first attempt, he made it to page thirty. As Mark Twain said about a book by Henry James, "Once you put it down, you can't pick it up." He forced himself through another twenty pages. He kept saying to himself, *Something has to happen.* But nothing happened; only hawthorn blossoms. Lovely as they are, hawthorn blossoms are only interesting up to a point. Proust's sentences went on and on and . . . never ended. Somewhere in those seven volumes is said to be a sentence of 958 words. Some scholars say it's the longest sentence in all literature. James Joyce said that Proust's readers finish his sentences before he does. Evelyn Waugh told Nancy Mitford, "I am reading Proust for the first time and am surprised to find him a mental defective."

Years passed. Proust remained on his bookshelf, gathering dust. Meanwhile, he continued to find himself in the company of people who swoon at the mention of Proust, people who referred to him as "the incomparable Marcel."

One night in Washington, DC, he found himself at a dinner party hosted by a great Georgetown hostess. (A formidable breed, truly.) It was very glittery. Among those present were the French ambassador; a big-deal biographer; a big-deal columnist; a daughter of Winston Churchill; the head of the National Gallery; the head of this; the head of that; the Secretary of Something; and the Deputy Undersecretary of Something Else. Five minutes into dinner someone mentioned Proust. That was the signal for the French ambassador to launch into literary orgasm. Soon everyone was joining in. Except him. What did he have to add to this Proustian fête? *Rien.* Then they all began speaking in French. His was at the level of "The pen of my aunt is lost," which is of limited utility unless you have an aunt who is always losing her pen.

The elegant lady seated next to him—another legendary Washington hostess—took pity on him and translated for him. "At that end of the table," she elegantly whispered, "they are discussing Proust's Dreyfusism."

He nodded with sham knowingness, as if to say, "*I would join in, but as you are no doubt aware, my views on Marcel's Dreyfusism have been known to arouse duels.*"

"At that end," she continued, "they are talking about the notebooks in which he wrote the first chapters. They were a gift from the wife of Georges Bizet."

Again, he nodded. "*Ah, the notebooks. Yes. Invariably, one turns to the notebooks.*"

In the lull occasioned by the arrival of the soufflé, he drained his glass of Montrachet and said to the whole table, "Do you recall Monty Python's All-England Summarize Proust Competition?"

To judge from the silence, the answer was no. (Or as the incomparable Marcel would say, *Non.*) But it was now too late to retreat. Flushed with Montrachet, he soldiered on.

"The judges were all local cricket players. Plus Omar Sharif and Yehudi Menuhin. The contestants had fifteen seconds. To summarize all of Proust." *Maybe you had to be there.*

The hostess put him out of his misery by asking the French ambassador what he made of President Chirac's speech about hypercapitalism at the G7.

The next day, he blew the dust off his boxed edition of the C. K. Scott Moncrieff and Terence Kilmartin translation. Lifting the damn thing took both hands. He positioned himself in an uncomfortable hard-backed chair, propped his eyes open with toothpicks, popped thirty milligrams of Adderall, and went to it. His days as a philistine were over. *Finis.*

An eternal week later, he'd reached page 456, *and still nothing had happened.* The Adderall made him jumpy. He barked at the children. "Quiet. Can't you see Dad is reading Proust?" He frog-marched himself through another fifty pages before hurling volume whatever across the room. From now on, if anyone wet themselves over the incomparable fucking Marcel, he would quote—verbatim—the rejection letter Proust got from the editor: "My dear fellow—I may be dead from the neck up, but rack my brains as I may, I can't see why a chap should need thirty pages to describe how he turns over in his bed before going to sleep." Quite.

Now, decades later, he has decided to give it one last shot. He still feels guilty about not having read a work that many smart people regard as the greatest novel ever written. Why they think this, he does not know, but when nature hands you a pandemic, what excuse, really, do you have for not reading Proust? "I didn't have time"? *Oh, yes you did. Philistine.*

He knows from his past attempts that intention alone will not suffice. He must have a strategy. And it won't do to sit in another ass-breaking chair, with his eyes pronged open like Malcolm McDowell's in *A Clockwork Orange* and his heart going *rat-a-tat-tat* from amphetamines.

He hits on a solution: He'll *listen* to Proust. While doing something to occupy his hands. But what? Flower arranging? Origami? Basket weaving? Pottery? Knitting?

While searching one day on Amazon for an X-Acto knife, the screen fills with pop-up ads for balsa-wood models. Eureka! Model airplanes! As a boy, he spent endless happy hours, fingers sticky with glue, assembling balsa-wood models of Fokker Triplanes, Sopwith Camels, P-51 Mustangs, B-17s, and Messerschmitt Bf 109s.

Peaches will approve. Her grandfather was an American ace in World War I. He shot down eleven Huns. (Claimed twelve.) His family nickname was "War Bird." The ancestral home in Sophia Springs is a museum of memorabilia, including a large bullet-holed chunk of fuselage from a downed German Fokker.

It all fits. It was the Great War that finally got Proust to sit down and fill Madame Bizet's notebooks. (Ah, the notebooks.) In September 1914, a month after the guns of August sounded the first volleys, he walled himself off from the outside world in his cork-lined room on the Boulevard Haussmann.

He's now actually excited about Proust. He's even started referring to him as "Marcel," which Peaches finds affected, but *peu importe.* (Translation: whatever.)

For his first model, he chooses a B-25B Mitchell bomber. A World War I plane would seem more appropriate to the occasion, but there is a reason for the B-25. Many years ago, he was at a dinner, seated next to an elderly, rather dashing man who introduced himself as Jimmy Doolittle.

Jimmy Doolittle? As in Doolittle's Raiders? *Thirty Seconds Over Tokyo?* Here, in the flesh, sitting next to him, was the iconic American hero who in 1942 led a squadron of sixteen B-25s off the deck of the aircraft carrier USS *Hornet* to deliver the American response to Pearl Harbor.

His balsa-wood plane arrives. He tees up volume one of *Remembrance* on his iPad. Like Proust's masterpiece, balsa-wood models of World War II bombers consist of many, many parts, which, like the incomparable Marcel's interminable sentences, require intense focus and endless patience. In less time than it takes hawthorns to blossom, he wants to hurl the iPad and B-25 out the window and curse the day he met Jimmy Doolittle. But he keeps at it, cursing and listening as he tries to get two halves of an engine nacelle to stick to each other.

> *I would stop by the table, where the kitchen-maid had shelled them, to inspect the platoons of peas, drawn up in ranks and numbered, like little green marbles, ready for a game; but what fascinated me would be the asparagus, tinged with ultramarine and rosy pink which ran from their heads, finely stippled in mauve and azure, through a series of imperceptible changes to their white feet, still stained a little by the soil of their garden-bed: a rainbow-loveliness that was not of this world. I felt that these celestial hues indicated the presence of exquisite creatures who had been pleased to assume vegetable form, who, through the disguise which covered their firm and edible flesh, allowed me to discern in this radiance of earliest dawn, these hinted rainbows, these blue evening shades, that*

precious quality which I should recognize again when, all night long after a dinner at which I had partaken of them, they played (lyrical and coarse in their jesting as the fairies in Shakespeare's Dream) *at transforming my humble chamber pot into a bower of aromatic perfume.*

He puts down the two stubborn and still unattached sections of the engine nacelle and hits pause. Was that passage about . . . asparagus? He abandons Doolittle and fires up Google.

The words "Proust" and "asparagus" yield more than 300,000 hits. Has he stumbled onto something here? The commentary is impressive. PhD theses appear to have been written about Proust's asparagus. One literary blogger suggests that "In two sentences," Proust "gives us a charming peek into a mind completely engaged with the world, capable not only of lovingly attending to the myriad details of which the things around us are composed, but of transforming these things through a triumph of imagination at once intensely personal, subversively multiversal, and urologically jocose."

He cannot find "multiversal" in the dictionary, but he is blown away by "urologically jocose." This has to be the first instance since writing was invented in Mesopotamia six millennia ago that *urologically* and *jocose* have been annexed.

Does the urological community know about this? As it happens, he has an appointment next week with his urologist. He'll ask him. Or is that not a good idea? His urologist's taste in novels probably runs more to Jack Higgins than to the incomparable Marcel. One doesn't want to alienate one's doctors. They can take it out on you in so many ways. "*Let's do another colonoscopy, just to make sure.*"

This asparagus passage—and the Talmudic commentaries

on it—have stimulated his own urological jocosity. He's been reading Julian Barnes's book about Samuel Pozzi, the Belle Epoque gynecologist. Pozzi is famous today for the striking portrait John Singer Sargent did of him, showing him in a lustrous red dressing gown. Pozzi was a colleague of Proust's brother, a urologist who performed the first successful prostatectomy in France. His colleagues dubbed the procedure a "Proust-ectomy." *Très* urologically jocose. Anyway, he now has more than enough material here for small talk with the urologist as he's snapping on the latex gloves.

He's feeling very Proustian. He must know more.

Proust *père*, he learns, was a prominent epidemiologist, which seems an interesting detail to learn during a pandemic. Proust *fils* was raised Catholic, became atheist, and ended a mystic. He had asthma. As a child, he spent a lot of time indoors, with the curtains drawn. When he started in on the book, he turned into an eremitical shut-in. The cork-lined walls dampened the clatter and din of wartime Paris. Until then, Proust was generally regarded as pointless, a dilettante and social climber. It was Madame Bizet, mother of one of Marcel's school chums, who had provided him with an entrée to the haute monde.

"It was high time to decide what sort of books I was going to write. But as soon as I asked myself the question, and tried to discover some subjects to which I could impart a philosophical significance of infinite value, my mind would stop like a clock, I would see before me vacuity, nothing, would feel either that I was wholly devoid of talent, or that, perhaps, a malady of the brain was hindering its development."

Thus he describes his writer's block in *Swann's Way*, the opening volume of his monument. The block crumbled when he remembered biting into a small cake—the madeleine that launched a thousand (and more) pages. He was off and running, filling Madame's Bizet's notebooks with descriptions of his own struggle to become a novelist. He became the Karl Ove Knausgaard of his day.

He was an outsider (and outlier) in four distinct ways: Jew, gay, artist, invalid. Despite these exotic compass points, his sensibility remained moderate. He was an atheist but opposed the ferocious anticlericalism current. He alienated from the society he had once worshipped but rejected socialism. He defended Dreyfus, the Jewish military officer framed by the anti-Semitic French army, but remained politically centrist. Like Whitman, Marcel contained multitudes.

As Bertie Wooster might put it, he also had a "Tabasco side." He derived sexual gratification by sticking pins into starving rats in cages as they tried to eat each other. It was the French, after all, who came up with the saying *Chacun à son goût*. (Translation: Whatever spins your wheels.) His new literary hero was certainly a man of many parts.

Has the asparagus thing come to the attention of the R & D departments at Chanel and the other *parfumiers*? Surely. They're French. For a time he worked at a luxury lifestyle magazine, where his duties included attending "fragrance launches." He never knew what to say to the fragrance execs, other than variations on "Boy, does that smell great." Now he wishes he'd known about Proust and the asparagus, a fragrance begging to be launched. *Asperge, by Proust. Irresistible. Urologically jocose.*

CHAPTER 8

He keeps a notepad by his bed so he can write down things that come to him in the night. Years ago, he had an idea in his sleep so stunning that it actually woke him up. There was no notepad, but the idea was so amazing he knew he'd remember it in the morning. On waking, he remembered that he'd had an amazing idea. And nothing else. Ever since, pen and pad have been at the ready. Each morning, he checks the pad, as a Maine lobsterman does his trap, hoping something marvelous has crawled into it.

This morning he sees scrawled:

Heimlich's Maneuver

WTF? But then he hears violins, trumpets, cymbals, drums, the whole orchestra, rising to a crescendo. It's the title of his screenplay! Heimlich is the German commando tasked with snatching FDR.

It's going to be a challenge, in more than one way. American movie audiences tend not to root for Nazis, especially when they're kidnapping American presidents in wartime. Heimlich will have to be if not likable, at least not completely detestable. He sees him as a tough, combat-hardened warrior, beneath whose heavily decorated chest beats a fundamentally decent heart. He hasn't committed any atrocities. And some of his best friends are Jewish, though oddly they all seem to have disappeared. He knows nothing—like Sergeant Schultz of *Hogan's Heroes*—about the concentration camps. And if he did, he'd be appalled. He's not into whole Aryan superiority thing, though he's really good-looking in an Aryanish way. (Think Matt Damon.)

He's a great leader. His men worship him. He gets the job done. But now, in the spring of '44, he's burned out. And frankly, he is unimpressed with the way things are going. Declaring war on the United States four days after Pearl Harbor? What genius thought that up? Invading Russia with winter coming on? Wunderbar. Stalingrad? Don't get him started. Yes, the führer got Germany back on its feet. But the Second Coming of Frederick the Great he is not. It would not ruin Heimlich's day to hear that Hitler choked to death on an eggplant or got bitten by his Alsatian, Blondi, and bled out. Meanwhile, the only thing he can do is go on doing his job. He'll stick it out. Not for Hitler. For . . . Brunhilda? Hildegard? Angela? Elise? *Ja, für Elise.* The fräulein he left behind in . . . Frankfurt? Dusseldorf? Bonn? Aachen. *Ja,* dear old Aachen, where . . . his beloved Auntie Greta—Gerta?—is hiding an entire Jewish village in her attic.

Now, Heimlich has been handed his toughest assignment yet: parachute into South Carolina—wherever that is—to kidnap the American president and bring him back to the Fatherland on a U-boat. Piece of cake. The high command has clearly lost it.

Being a fundamentally decent sort, he's not thrilled at the idea of manhandling an elderly, ailing, and differently abled man, even if he is the enemy president. It just feels wrong. There—he's said it. This is not why he joined the Wehrmacht. Shooting

French, Belgians, Dutch, Poles, Englishers, Americans—he has no problem with that. It can be very satisfying, and, on occasion, fun. This? Not so much. But if it will bring about an end to the war, he'll do it. *Für* Elise. *Und für* Auntie Gerta.

He's very excited that his commando now has a name. Heimlich is one that Americans can relate to in a positive way, as they associate it with not choking to death. Heimlich's "maneuver" will be some brilliant—and totally unexpected—thing he does in act 3. He might save FDR from choking on a bratwurst aboard the U-boat. That could work. He could have a line of dialogue suggesting that this is actually how the maneuver was invented. The audience will say, "I didn't know that. Cool." Roosevelt could thank Heimlich for saving his life, though naturally he's still kind of pissed off about being abducted. He'll offer Heimlich a Lucky Strike. They have a smoke together, and discover that maybe they're not so different, after all. (Though admittedly they come from pretty different backgrounds.) It could be the proverbial "start of a beautiful friendship." (Great line. He must write it down.) FDR and Heimlich become—friends. Buddies. But they have to conceal their gemütlichkeit ("warmth and fuzziness") from the U-boat captain, a real by-the-book (*Mein Kampf*) hard-ass kraut whose idea of a great time is torpedoing hospital ships then machine-gunning the survivors in the water. Captain . . . Kreeg. Perfect.

Now he's got most of act 3. He could throw in a bit of counterfactual history, the "what-if" genre where, say, the South wins the Civil War, Lee Harvey Oswald's gun jams, or a failed casino owner is elected president of the United States. It's all coming together.

In the real world, a policeman in Minneapolis has cruelly murdered a Black man named George Floyd. *Damn fine job, Officer Chauvin.* Riots are breaking out all over the country. And now troops—actual soldiers—are shooting tear gas and rubber bullets at peaceful protesters in Lafayette Park, which is named for the marquis. And the next thing you know, the president of the United States is standing awkwardly in front of a church, holding up a Bible, like some rookie crossing guard on his first day on the job. What happened to "It can't happen here"? It's happening. For this the marquis risked everything? He must be rolling in his grave.

Or not, actually. During the French Revolution, the marquis was in charge of the troops in Paris. A mob gathered in the Champs de Mars (where the Eiffel Tower is now). He ordered his men to fire on them, killing dozens. It didn't help. Things went downhill fast. So, the good marquis's remains might in fact not be in a position to rotate in his grave. But he must channel this energy going on in America's streets. It will give his screenplay a bracing, contemporary feel.

Day. Interior. The Eagle's Nest, Hitler's retreat in the Bavarian Alps.

Hitler is holding forth, boring everyone comatose. But no one wants to be seen nodding off in the middle of one of the führer's interminable monologues.

Goebbels and Himmler listen raptly. Göring, in his customary opioid haze, is slumped in an enormous armchair.

[Historical note: after the war, Göring will tell his American interrogators Hitler's monologues were the principal cause of his morphine addiction.]

[*English subtitles.*]

HITLER: My physician, Dr. Morell, says I am in superb physical shape. He has never seen someone of my age in such perfect condition. I have the organs of an eighteen-year-old.

HIMMLER: You look fantastic.

GOEBBELS: A thousand-year führer, for a thousand-year Reich!

HITLER: Write that down. In addition to the physical exam, he also gave me a cognitive function test.

GOEBBELS (*appalled*): Do you mean to say that Morell questioned your mental ability?

HIMMLER (*outraged*): I question *Morell's* mental ability!

HITLER: At the beginning of the exam, he told me five words, which I was to repeat back to him in the same sequence at the conclusion of the exam. I remembered them perfectly.

HIMMLER: What were the five words?

HITLER: Adolf, Hitler, is, the, führer.

HIMMLER: Incredible. I could never remember all that.

GOEBBELS: Genius. Superhuman.

GÖRING (*stirring*): What's that? Eh? Time for lunch, is it? What are we having? Please, no more fucking vegetables.

Door opens. President Franklin Delano Roosevelt is wheeled in by two horrible-looking SS thugs.

HITLER: Ah, Herr Roosevelt. How good of you to drop in. I believe you know Reichsminister Goebbels, Reichsmarshall Göring, and Reichsführer Himmler?

FDR (*jauntily*): I've not had the displeasure.

HITLER: Please, have a sit. But I see you are already sitting. How jocose I am today! So, what were you saying about having nothing tó fear but fear itself?

It's pouring out of him onto the laptop. His fingers can barely keep up.

Roosevelt refuses to go along with Hitler's insidious scheme to get D-Day canceled. Hitler has the SS drug his martinis. Still FDR refuses. Hitler's mood ceases to be jocose. He tells Roosevelt, "The view here is excellent. As you see, we are in the mountains. Perhaps you would like to admire the view from . . . the balcony?" His meaning is clear. The SS goons are going to dangle him upside down from the balcony.

Roosevelt delivers an incredibly eloquent soliloquy on the theme of the Fifth Freedom—freedom from being dangled from balconies by Nazis.

Hitler's face curdles with rage. Himmler nods at the SS goons. Then, suddenly . . .

Shots! Gunfire! But where is it coming from?

The ceiling is perforated by bullet holes. *Ping-ping-ping.*

Hitler and his inner circle shout variations on "*Was zum Teufel?*" (German: "What the hell?")

The SS goons manhandling President Roosevelt drop to the ground, dead, bullet holes in the exact center of their nasty Nazi foreheads. Whoever's shooting, boy, are they good.

A dozen American commandos crash through the roof. They land one by one in Hitler's living room. As they do, their parachutes drape various pieces of furniture, turning the Eagle's Nest's ugly interior into a Christo installation. (Symbolizing the triumph of art over tyranny.)

Himmler and Goebbels cower behind furniture. Göring smiles woozily and waves "welcome" to the visitors, but is unable to lift himself out of the armchair to greet them properly.

Goebbels clumps about on his clubfoot. Himmler takes cover behind Hitler. (Not a good career move.) Hitler watches in horror as one of the commandos fires a burst from his machine gun at the enormous portrait of Hitler over the fireplace, ruining it. Hitler dives into the dumbwaiter shaft. We hear his screams as he crashes, floor by floor, all the way down, landing in the kitchen in a loud clash of smashed Third Reich–themed china.

The commandos form a protective perimeter around President Roosevelt. Their faces are blackened with camouflage greasepaint.

FDR beams with pride and satisfaction. He inserts a fresh Lucky Strike cigarette in his holder and says, "Well, I was hoping you boys might drop in."

He stares more closely at his liberators. They're not wearing camouflage greasepaint—they're Black. All of them.

We will counterfactually learn in the end credits that Secretary of the Army General George C. Marshall—featured so movingly in the Mrs. Bixby scene in *Saving Private Ryan*—dispatched America's first all–African American commando unit to rescue the president.

Roosevelt grins. He says, "Well, I'll be. You lads have made this the second worst day in Hitler's life, after he had to watch Jesse Owens sweep the golds at the '36 Berlin Olympics!"

The commandos suppress smiles. They look at their unit leader.

FDR stares at him. "Jesse? Is it . . . you?

U.S. Army Ranger Major Jesse Owens replies, "Yes, sir."

FDR grins and shakes his head. He can scarcely believe his eyes. "Well," he says. "I've been wondering what you've been up to."

OWENS: I'll tell you all about it, sir. But first let's get you out of here.

FDR: Suits me. The view's not bad, but they can't mix a martini to save their lives.

He sits back and stares in awe at his laptop screen. He feels the sugar rush of adrenaline that comes—all too rarely—from writing something really and truly good. What a scene! It packs ten times more punch than anything that hack Jack Higgins ever wrote. And what a timely homage to George Floyd. This is counterfactual history to stand up and cheer for. In real life, Jesse Owens went from Olympic glory to jobs as a gas station attendant and janitor. But now here he is, at the head of a team of elite commandos, rescuing the president of the United States from Hitler's clutches. He can already see the reviews. "Stunning!" "Inspirational! History like never before!" "Way better than *The Eagle Has Landed*!" "Look to your laurels, Jack Higgins!"

He's done it. He's got his act 3. He's so excited he has to get up and pace. But as the endorphins settle, he considers: his movie is titled *Heimlich's Maneuver*. Where's Heimlich? Last seen, he was on the U-boat, in the middle of the Atlantic, male bonding with FDR. Why did he deliver his new BFF to Hitler? Not very friendly.

Wait. He's got it. Heimlich had to follow orders—he's a German, after all. So he delivered FDR to Hitler. But then secretly contacted the Americans. Told them where the president was.

That's it. He and Roosevelt are playing a clever game. Roosevelt feeds Hitler fake details about D-Day. And drops hints that what the Americans most fear is that "your best commander, Göring, will be in charge of German defenses." Meanwhile, Heimlich is skulking about, photographing documents in the Eagle's Nest filing cabinet, gathering great intel. When the two SS goons were about to dangle FDR from the balcony, Heimlich was behind a curtain, taking aim at them with his trusty Luger.

Problem solved. Phew. Now to get them home . . .

FDR, the commandos, and Heimlich flee the Eagle's Nest in the führer's fleet of Mercedeses. They drive to the airfield, where they commandeer Hitler's private plane. Hitler is going to be *so* pissed. His tantrum will be Wagnerian. There's going to be an avalanche coming down the slopes from the Eagle's Nest—of rolling Nazi heads.

General Marshall is glad, in his own understated way, to have the president safely back. He decorates Owens and his commandoes. As for Heimlich, he wants to have him shot. But the president says, "No, George. Heimlich is my friend."

Nothing will be said about the abduction or the rescue. The press is fed "fake news"—a new term—that the president is continuing to enjoy his recuperation at the Baruch residence. He's smuggled back to Hobcaw, accompanied by his new aide-de-camp, Heimlich (whom FDR is now calling "Hanko," to General Marshall's continuing understated fury).

The president resumes his rest and relaxation regimen. Hanko will remain at Roosevelt's side for the rest of the president's life. That's him in the background in the famous photograph taken the day before the president died. As the final credits roll, the camera pans across the photo, showing FDR, Fala, his black Scotch terrier, sitting on his lap, the little girl standing beside the wheelchair, finally settling on Hanko smiling benevolently through the window.

Fade out. There won't be a dry eye in the theater. What a movie this is going to be!

There's just one problem. How does Heimlich snatch the president away from thousands of bodyguards and get him onto the U-boat?

FDR's stay at Hobcaw was secret. Technically, that is, despite being splashed all over the front pages of local newspapers. (Pimento and South Carolina were understandably proud about their visitor.) Nor did FDR leave Washington without being noticed, a special train carrying a full complement of Secret Service, FBI, staff, two doctors, and detachment of Marines. Meanwhile, the Coast Guard was patrolling the waters around Hobcaw, while the Navy was standing by offshore, ready to drop a depth charge on any German submarine within fifty miles.

So, no, this is not going to be a "piece of cake." Or even remotely doable. Heimlich's got his work cut out for him.

This is depressing. But he has such a terrific act 3, he must figure something out.

⸻

He throws himself into research. YouTube turns up home movies taken during FDR's stay at Hobcaw. (Amazing, YouTube.) Here is charming footage of little Fala digging furiously on the beach at Arcadia, the Vanderbilt plantation next door. Here he is fetching a ball thrown by Secret Service agents; playing with a black cat; frisking about with other dogs. They look like normal pets, but they were probably undercover canines trained to sniff German spies and submarines. The more he digs, the more his heart sinks. After Hitler, FDR was the most protected human being on earth.

His gloom is temporarily alleviated by a newsreel clip of Roosevelt sticking it to congressional Republicans who've accused him of dispatching a naval flotilla to the Aleutian Islands to retrieve Fala, accidentally left behind after his visit.

"These Republican leaders," FDR says to a large and delighted audience, "are not content with attacks on me, or my wife, or on my sons. No, not content with that they now include my little dog, Fala. Well, of course, I don't resent attacks. My family doesn't resent attacks. But Fala does resent attacks. You know, Fala's Scotch. And being a Scottie, as soon as he learned that the Republican fiction writers—in Congress and out—had concocted a story that I'd left him behind on the Aleutian Islands, and had sent a destroyer back to find him, at a cost to the taxpayer of two or three or eight or twenty million dollars, his Scot's soul was furious. He has not been the same dog since."

The applause and laughter could be heard on the far side of the moon. The speech was scripted by Orson Welles, fresh from his box office bomb *Citizen Kane* and scaring the bejesus out of New Jersey with his radio broadcast about Martians landing. In the annals of presidential dog orations, the Fala speech is up there with Nixon's 1952 Checkers speech.

He's in no rush to return to the insoluble problem of how Heimlich is going to abduct FDR. He dawdles, like premadeleine Proust, musing. What if Welles had written the Checkers speech?

On the way over here, I asked Checkers how he felt about people accusing me of misusing campaign funds.

"Dick," Checkers said to me—that's what he calls me, "Dick." He said, "Look, Dick, I'm a dog. I didn't understand one word of

what you just said. I understand 'Sit,' 'Roll over,' 'Shake,' and, on rare occasions, 'No.'

"But let me say this, Dick. You may be a crook and a liar and all those other things people say you are. But that doesn't mean I should have to suffer. I like living here in Washington. I don't like you, but I like little Tricia. And Julie and Pat. They're good Nixons. Unlike you. So please, don't send me back to that man in Texas who gave me to Tricia and Julie. Sure, you could, to make people feel guilty about calling you what you are—a crook and a scoundrel. But that would be wrong."

CHAPTER 9

In the wake of the George Floyd murder in Minneapolis, HBO Max announces that it is pulling *Gone with the Wind* from its streaming menu. Within twenty-four hours, *Gone with the Wind* is the number one best seller on Amazon. HBO Max then announces that *Gone with the Wind* will soon no longer be gone. It will be back, with an introduction by a "prominent African American studies scholar," who presumably will explain why you shouldn't be watching the movie in the first place.

Floyd's murder makes him think it's time for those Confederate statues to come down. (His great-great-grandfather fought for the Confederacy.) And time to rename military bases after soldiers who *didn't* fight to preserve slavery. But is it necessary to make movie viewers sit through a tutorial pointing out that slavery was not a good thing? Don't people already know that? And isn't *Gone with the Wind* long enough as it is, at three hours and forty-one minutes?

Last week, he watched a movie with warnings of Adult Content, Violence, Profanity, Nudity, Smoking.

Smoking?

Why not have a new R rating for Racist? And WTL: Way Too Long. Oh, for the days when the Ministry of Truth left you alone with your popcorn, and the movie began with a Pink Panther cartoon short.

He's doing a lot of harrumphing these days. Probably not a good sign. It's one thing to harrumph about snakes wrapping themselves around your mailbox, but harrumphing about HBO Max and *Gone with the Wind*? Everyone is losing it these days. Yesterday he saw a Chambless for Coroner ad on TV that showed refrigerator trucks backed up outside an overburdened morgue in New York City, with a voice-over saying, "Reelect Bobby Babcock county coroner, and *this* is what Pimento can expect: chaos and corpses." This, in a coroner race?

Sidney Howard adapted Margaret Mitchell's novel for the screen. His original draft would have resulted in a movie five and half hours long, which would have made it longer than the actual Civil War. Howard was killed in a freak accident while the movie was being shot. His tractor pinned him against the barn on his Massachusetts farm. He was awarded the first-ever posthumous Oscar.

Thinking about this, it occurs to him that Margaret Mitchell also died in an accident; she was struck by a passing car. And didn't Leslie Howard—sweet, tragic Ashley Wilkes—die violently? He must look it up. Sure enough: In 1943, a commercial DC-3 carrying Howard and a dozen other passengers from Lisbon to England was shot down by the Luftwaffe over the Bay of Biscay. A book has just been published, speculating that a German spy watching at the Lisbon airport mistook Howard's traveling companion for Winston Churchill. The man was portly, wore a homburg hat, and puffed on a big cigar. The spy mistakenly deduced that Howard must be Churchill's bodyguard. He alerted Berlin. A squadron of Junkers Ju 88s scrambled from a base in France and shot down the plane. Another theory—perhaps more plausible—is that the Germans deliberately targeted Howard because of his tireless fund-raising for the British war effort.

Sidney Howard, Margaret Mitchell, and Leslie Howard—all killed. Didn't something unfortunate befall George Reeves, who had a small part in *Gone* but became famous as Superman on TV in the 1950s? Now he must look that up.

"His death at age forty-five from a gunshot remains a controversial subject; the official finding was suicide, but some believe that he was murdered or the victim of an accidental shooting."

Good Lord. Is there a curse attached to *Gone with the Wind*?

Beautiful Vivien Leigh—Scarlett O'Hara—didn't die violently, but it wasn't pretty. She suffered from illness physical and mental. Her friend David Niven said that she was "quite mad." She suffocated, alone in her Belgravia flat, lungs filled with fluid.

Rummaging in these cyber-graveyards, he also learns that she "hated kissing Clark Gable because of his bad breath, rumored to be caused by his false teeth, a result of excessive smoking." He wishes he had not learned this. If HBO Max wants to turn people off *Gone with the Wind*, they should just put factoids like this above the opening credits. In another version, Leigh didn't like kissing Gable because he would "sometimes eat garlic before his kissing scenes." The question is begged: Why gorge on garlic before doing kissing scenes with Vivien Leigh? How is he now supposed to not think of this the next time he watches Rhett take Scarlett in his big, brawny arms and tell her, "Open your eyes and look at me. No, I don't think I will kiss you, although you need kissing, badly. That's what's wrong with you. You should be kissed, and often, and by someone who knows how." Someone, say, with false teeth, who chain smokes and eats raw garlic.

F. Scott Fitzgerald was brought in by producer David O. Selznick to "punch up" Sidney Howard's script, but was soon fired and then died, age forty-four. Given his history with booze, Fitzgerald's death can't be blamed on the curse. Still. This is all very depressing.

Margaret Mitchell's original title was *Pansy*, after the novel's heroine. Probably for the best that she changed it. It's hard to imagine Rhett saying, "There's only one thing that I do know. And that is that I love you, Pansy."

The replacement title is from a poem by Ernest Dowson, "Cynara."

I have been faithful to thee, Cynara! in my fashion.
I have forgot much, Cynara! gone with the wind . . .

In Greek mythology, Zeus falls head over sandals for a beautiful mortal girl named Cynara. He whisks her off to Olympus to have his lusty way with her while his dreaded wife, Hera, is away putting snakes in Heracles's crib. Cynara soon becomes bored. (Bored—on Mount Olympus? *Girlfriend.*) She misses her mother. She escapes and goes back to her island. Zeus is not happy and changes her into a flower—but a beautiful flower, named *Kynara*, from which we get the word *artichoke*, though artichoke does not sound at all like *kynara*.

Dowson (1867–1900) was a tragic figure. At twenty-three, he became infatuated with an eleven-year-old girl. Inappropriate, except perhaps as a premise for a Woody Allen movie. His father died of a drug overdose; Mum hanged herself. Ernest became a dissolute member of Oscar Wilde's naughty circle and died at thirty-two. Wilde eulogized him as "a tragic reproduction of all tragic poetry." In so many words, really tragic.

What a crowd of phantoms.

At the moment, he's taking a break from the incomparable Marcel and reading a book about the Allied bombing campaigns in World War II. It mentions in passing that the most popular novel in Germany in 1939 was—wait for it—*Gone with the Wind*. It triggers a memory about watching a documentary years ago on PBS about Eva Braun's home movies.

In 1936, Hitler gave his mistress an eight-millimeter movie camera for her twenty-fourth birthday. Eva was a camera buff. She shot hours and hours of color Agfa stock film at the Eagle's Nest, Hitler's alpine aerie—candid, warm, and fuzzy celluloid mementoes of . . . happy times.

Here are Eva's girlfriends doing acrobatics by a lake, picking flowers and sunbathing.

Here's Hitler, reading to little children, playing with them, pinching their cheeks, urging them to grow up to be strong soldiers.

Here are dogs. Hitler's Alsatian, Blondi, and others scamper about the sunny terrace, the beautiful mountains in the distance. Eva cuddles a pair of black Scottish terriers. They look identical to FDR's Fala.

Here's Reichsminister Goebbels, grinning broadly as he realizes he's being filmed. Has something wonderful just happened, or is he just mugging for the boss's squeeze?

Here's Obergruppenführer Reinhard Heydrich, coarchitect of the Final Solution to the Jewish Question, looking tanned and fit and ever so Aryan. Hitler called him "the man with the iron heart." He meant it as a compliment.

And who's this? Why, it's Reichsführer Heinrich Himmler. And Albert Speer, the führer's architect. And here comes Joachim von Ribbentrop, the foreign minister. The gang's all here.

How different they look out of uniform, smiling and laughing. They could be travel agents or stockbrokers or dentists, out for a day of mountain air.

Here they are, eating lunch. What's this the führer is saying to the person sitting next to him about Reichsmarshall Göring?

"I looked across him at the dinner table and then I knew what they say was true, that pigs eat the flesh of their own."

Ach du Lieber. The führer doesn't sound at all pleased with the Reichsmarshall.

From 1945 to now, these films lay forgotten and unseen in the archives of the Office of Strategic Services. Technology has made it possible to lip-read what everyone is saying. Their dialogue has been dubbed in. Chilling.

On the sunlit terrace, Hitler teases Eva and her girlfriends for complaining about last night's entertainment.

"I understand you didn't like the movie," he says. "I know what you want. You want *Gone with the Wind.*"

CHAPTER 10

Breaking news! The latest tracking of his toilet paper shows that it has left the depot in St. Louis. Next stop, Atlanta.

Marvelous as this is, the TP crisis has abated. America is once again awash in bathroom tissue. The country may be divided, but everyone—Republican and Democrat, mask wearing and non–mask wearing—seems to agree that hoarding toilet paper is no way to make America great again.

When FDR's special friend Lucy Mercer drove from her home in Aiken, South Carolina, to visit him at Hobcaw, Bernard Baruch, titan of Wall Street and adviser to six presidents (etc., etc.), gave her his gasoline ration coupons. It wasn't the first time he did a Lucy-related mitzvah for his friend Franklin. In 1933, President-Elect Roosevelt quietly asked Bernie to arrange two tickets for Lucy to his first inaugural. And when the owner of the Charleston, South Carolina, newspaper continued to publish fulminating anti-FDR editorials while the president was just up the road at Hobcaw, in agonizing pain from gallstones and spiking a blood pressure of 240/130, Bernie used his remaining gas coupons to drive to Charleston to tell him to knock it off.

Bernard Baruch was a mensch, though in anti-Semitic America, it's unlikely he described himself as such. He saved his friend Winston Churchill from financial ruin, after the future prime minister made bad bets on the U.S. stock market. Baruch saw the Crash of '29 coming and kept Churchill afloat by putting him in stocks that offset his losses.

In December 1931, Churchill was very nearly killed when he was hit by a car on New York's Fifth Avenue. He stepped out of a taxi and, being English, looked the wrong way. The impact was buffered by his heavy overcoat, but the injury was serious; his convalescence lasted two months. If he'd died, the twentieth century would have turned out very differently. The reason Churchill got out of the cab was to ask directions to Baruch's apartment.

He decides that Baruch must have a significant role in *Heimlich's Maneuver*. But what actor could do him justice? In 1944, Baruch was seventy-four. In photographs of the time, he looks like a combination Wall Street elder and vaudevillian: banker dignity with Groucho Marx eyebrows. Who could convey this equipoise of gravitas and mischief?

It comes to him: Donald Sutherland.

He plunges into Sutherland's filmography. *The Castle of the Living Dead*. Hasn't seen it. *The Dirty Dozen*. Great movie. He played the goofy convict. *M*A*S*H*. Hawkeye Pierce, one of his best roles. *Kelly's Heroes*. Oddball, the spacey World War II tank commander. *Klute*. Noir detective. *Don't Look Now*. Noir-er. *The Eagle Has Landed*. Hasn't seen it, but it sounds familiar. Must be about the moon landing. Donald Sutherland as Neil Armstrong? Maybe he played the other astronaut, whatshisname. *JFK*. Directed by that wack job Oliver Stone. But a gifted wack job. *Space Cowboys*. Sweet movie. *Buffy the Vampire Slayer*? Really? *The Devil's Eyeball. The Italian Job. The Hunger Games: Mockingjay*. Atalanta and Polly are fans of that one.

Why is an actor of Donald Sutherland's stature wasting his

time on such tripe? All the more reason he'll be eager to sink his teeth into a meaty role like Bernard Baruch.

Wait—didn't he play Clark Clifford in John Frankenheimer's *The Path to War*, trying desperately to persuade Lyndon Johnson not to escalate in Vietnam, while Alec Baldwin, as Robert McNamara, keeps urging more troops and more bombing. He remembers the joke that went around after Johnson defeated Goldwater: "They told me in '64 that if I voted for Goldwater, we'd end up with half a million men in Vietnam. I did, and we do."

He tees up *Path*. Sutherland is perfect as the expensively tailored, wavy white-haired, soft-speaking Washington wise man. He won a Golden Globe for best supporting actor, beating out Baldwin. Sutherland was born to play smooth-talking presidential advisors. It occurs to him that *Path* came out in 2002, just as President George W. Bush was being persuaded by his defense secretary, Donald Rumsfeld, among others, to embark on his own path to war, in Iraq. While Bush's father's former adviser Brent Scowcroft argued passionately against invading. Did W. watch *The Path to War*?

How old is Donald Sutherland? Eighty-four. But a youthful eighty-four, assuming the photo on Google is recent. There's no time to waste. He must finish the screenplay. But first, he must do more research.

He enters "Donald Sutherland," "health," "illness," "ailing," then takes a deep breath and hits return, uttering a prayer to the gods of Mt. Google please not to tell him that the only actor on earth who could do justice to Bernard Baruch has Covid.

He opens his eyes. *Mirabile dictu!* Donald Sutherland is alive and well. Wikipedia now prompts him: "People also ask . . ." It wants him to drill deeper. "Where is Donald Sutherland now?"

He is, in fact, interested to know where Donald Sutherland is now. Somewhere safe and socially distanced, he hopes.

"Sutherland was made an Officer of the Order of Canada on December 18, 1978."

Not very "now."

"And was promoted to Companion of the Order of Canada in 2019."

It's nice that Canada is proud. Canada should be.

"He maintains a home in Georgeville, Quebec."

Of course, Sutherland would live in Georgeville, Quebec— "Population: 1,000"—not LA or some glam tax haven like Monaco. Good for him. Where is this Georgeville, Quebec? On Lake Memphremagog, a mere ten miles from the Vermont border. Population one thousand. Sounds nicely remote, pandemic-wise; unlikely to be a superspreader hot spot. Very encouraging, all this.

Wikipedia is now tugging at him to ask: "How much is Donald Sutherland worth?"

A bit tawdry. Is this what AI does? Deduce from your clicking that you're panting to know how much people are worth? On the other hand, it would actually make sense to know, since he and Sutherland will be doing business together.

"$60 million."

Not bad for a lad from St. John, New Brunswick. (Is that $60 million U.S. or Canadian? He must add this to the to-do list. Indigo again moves down.)

Wikipedia is now nudging him to ask: "Is Donald Sutherland nice?"

What a question. But might as well find out now.

"Nice guy, but scary."

What on earth is *that* supposed to mean?

"Should Donald Sutherland cross your mind at some idle moment, you will probably give a little shiver."

Who's saying this? An Australian newspaper called *The Age*. In 2002. More breaking news.

"Even though he has played nice guys in some of his most successful films, there is something unsettling about him. Something that will make him forever the soul mate of the sinister in Nic Roeg's *Don't Look Now* rather than the good dad in Robert Redford's *Ordinary People*. Like Anthony Hopkins, Sutherland is a classically trained actor who seems trapped on a treadmill of thrillers."

Fair enough about the treadmill.

"Anyway, the point is that Donald Sutherland is rather unsettling in person."

The writer seems to have forgotten what he said in his prior paragraph.

"Not because he is scary—he isn't, he's so nice that he backs out of the interview room calling out, 'Did I answer all your questions? Did I miss any?'—but because he's absolutely and proudly loopy."

So, to recap: Donald Sutherland is "unsettling." But not really. And is not scary, despite the writer telling us that he is. Wikipedia is clearly saying he's scary in order to get us to click on an eighteen-year-old interview in an obscure Australian rag. Shameless. Sutherland must have only agreed to be interviewed by this jackass to promote a movie that ended up tanking at the box office. Despite being directed by "Chinese hitmeister Feng Xiaogang."

Being unfamiliar with the oeuvre of Chinese hitmeister Feng Xiaogang, he looks him up. Among the hits he has meistered are *The Dream Factory*, *Be There or Be Square*, and *Sorry Baby*.

Now he learns that while filming an earlier movie in China, Sutherland contracted a "mouth parasite that, to this day, eats away the surface of his tongue every six months or so. He ate watermelon that had been injected with dirty water, to make it weigh more."

How awful. Poor man. But he must think strategically, not sentimentally. What if Sutherland is stricken with this god-awful recurring tongue-eating parasite while filming *Heimlich's Maneuver*?

FDR: Say again, Bernie? Didn't catch that.

BARUCH: Ahroo euy phaaa une.

FDR: Sorry, old boy. My hearing's not what it used to be. Say again?

BARUCH: Ahro*oooooo* eh ooo ph*aaaaa* unt-eh.

FDR (*whispering to Lucy*): Cupcake, has Bernie been into the martinis? Bit early in the day.

He informs Peaches of this calamitous development. She says, "Why do you care about Donald Sutherland's tongue?"

"Darling, he's playing Bernard Baruch in the movie."

"What movie?"

Is she being deliberately obtuse?

"Sweetheart," he sighs. "*Heimlich's Maneuver*? Nazi plot to kidnap FDR from Hobcaw? Hel-lo?"

She looks bewildered. And worried. She's taken to asking him, "Who's president of the United States?" It's what doctors ask if they think you've had a stroke. He refuses to play this insulting game. The first time she asked him, he said, "You can't be serious." The second time, he snapped, "Why don't you google it for yourself?" Thing is, both times he went completely blank.

Then when he remembered who is president, he wished he hadn't.

He's sure this is what psychologists call "displacement." Peaches is convinced *she's* going to get Alzheimer's. She spends hours doing crossword puzzles and brainteasers and other cognitive calisthenics on her iPad. This strikes him as preposterous. His darling's brain is a mighty dynamo. She was Phi Beta Kappa. He hasn't beaten her at chess since Grover Cleveland was president. Or was it Woodrow Wilson? Whatever.

She says apropos his screenplay, "That's great, sweetheart."

"I'm sure I mentioned it to you."

"If you say so."

Is it remotely possible that he hasn't mentioned *Heimlich's Maneuver* to her? Surely not.

"Heimlich was one of Dan Coit's professors at med school in Cincinnati," Peaches says. "He used to practice his antichoking protocol on his students. You should talk to him."

"Sweetheart," he sighs, "that's fascinating, but my screenplay has nothing to do with that Heimlich."

"Oh? Okay."

"My Heimlich is a German commando who's been tasked with parachuting into Hobcaw and kidnapping Roosevelt out from under the Secret Service, FBI, half the Marine Corps, the Coast Guard, and the Navy. And taking him back to Germany as a hostage. On a U-boat."

"Sounds . . . challenging."

"Sweetheart," he says, "you do see the problem. If Donald Sutherland is going to play Bernard Baruch, it would be helpful to know—ahead of time—if this ghastly tongue-eating parasite is going to recur in the middle of shooting. Can you imagine what a disaster that would be?"

"Yeah. That would not be good."

"So, you agree it makes sense to find out before we sign him."

"Uh-huh."

"I could just call him and ask him. But I'd kind of prefer not to start our relationship by asking him about his tongue. It would feel awkward."

"Yeah, I get that."

She looks like she's about to ask him who's president. She says, "Sweetheart, I'd love to hear more about it, but I've got to call Tituba back." Tituba is one of her numerous sisters. Their mother saw *The Crucible* on Broadway while she was pregnant with her. Many of her children are named after characters in progressive works of literature or drama.

"No problem," he says. "I'll ask Dr. Paula. She'll know."

"For the kind of money you pay her, she should," Peaches snorts, going off to call her sister.

He recognizes that his darling is stressed. She's dealing with what TV news calls "a developing situation" in her hometown of Sophia Springs. In the wake of the George Floyd murder, she and Tituba have organized a petition drive to remove from the town park a statue of somewhat breathtaking racial incorrectness: an obelisk dedicated to their ancestor, Ptarmigan "Old Tar" Spratt, or as he's called by the family, "the Colonel." After valiant service in "The War of Northern Aggression," he returned to Sophia Springs and formed the local chapter of the Ku Klux Klan. He eventually rose to the rank of grand snapdragon. Not ideal ancestry. The main problem with this one is the inscription, which claims, "Erected by his grateful slaves, in recognition of his service." This is taking "Thank you for your service" a bit far. It is conceded, even by the colonel's staunchest admirers, that it is unlikely that the monument was erected by his slaves, however grateful they may have been for his valorous attempt to keep them in bondage.

Peaches, Tituba, and the other sibs are good liberal Democrats to their toes. They have long been appalled by the statue. Now, in the wake of the George Floyd murder, they've decided the time has come to do something about it. But their petition is meeting with pockets of resistance. And now Facebook, always a calming influence and prompter of civility, is awash in spittle, invective, and death threats. Any minute now, some seventeen-year-old lumpkin with the Stars and Bars tattooed on his forehead is going to show up with an AR-15 to "protect" the statue. South Carolina Senator Squigg Lee Biskitt has yet to take a stand on the issue, as he polls well among militia groups.

He concedes that #oldtarmustgo is a more urgent matter for his darling than Donald Sutherland's tongue-devouring parasite. Instead of fussing about it, he should sit down and figure out how to get FDR onto that fucking U-boat.

CHAPTER 11

Peaches's cluelessness about the screenplay now has him wondering if caterpillars have crawled into *his* brain and are eating the wiring. How can he not have mentioned it to her? But why would she pretend he hadn't? Very strange. What joy at his age to look forward to dementia, macular degeneration, impotence, incontinence. Really looking forward to that last one. When the adult diaper ads come on during the evening news, he presses mute and recites the ending bit from Shakespeare's "Seven Ages of Man" riff:

> *. . . is second childishness and mere oblivion;*
> *Sans teeth, sans eyes, sans taste, sans everything.*

It's encouraging he still remembers it. He's read Seneca and Montaigne and other stoic savants. He's with them: the real horror would be immortality. Living forever. Imagine if you just went on and on and on. He doesn't fear death. Isn't his obesity proof? After all, it is one of the more significant morbidity factors. There are worse ways to go than a heart attack in the drive-through lane at the Hippo King, though he'd prefer not to go by getting embedded in the steering wheel and hoisted out by crane.

He doesn't feel like going home just yet, though he *must* get to work on the screenplay. His Hippo King lunch is turning to wet cement in his stomach. He'll go for a walk, or in his case, a waddle. Peaches would approve. She's always after him to exercise.

But where? Someplace landscaped. This is no time of year for tromping about in underbrush. He's depressed enough as it is without adding "Go to ER for antivenom injection" to the list.

There's a lovely cemetery nearby, All Saints Pimento. Just the place. For reasons he can't explain, he finds cemeteries comforting. One of his favorite poems is Gray's "Elegy Written in a Country Churchyard."

> *Perhaps in this neglected spot is laid*
> *Some heart once pregnant with celestial fire;*
> *Hands, that the rod of empire might have sway'd,*
> *Or wak'd to ecstasy the living lyre.*

Seneca and Montaigne advise thinking about death as a way to prepare for it. Where better than a cemetery? Not just as a place in which to muse on intimations of mortality. They're also good for clearing the head. Over the years he's worked out many a plot problem while ambulating among headstones. He's made pilgrimages. Twice, he's taken the Lexington Avenue 4 train to Woodlawn Cemetery in the Bronx to pay his respects to Herman Melville. The second time, he found that someone had left a bathtub squeeze toy whale atop the monument. Rather sweet. The dark granite marker is carved with a blank scroll, which seems odd. Shouldn't the scroll say "Call me Ishmael"? He once met the musician Moby, Melville's great-great-great-nephew, and told him this. Moby politely nodded, as if to say, "*Yeah, I'll get right on that.*"

He's been to Père Lachaise in Paris more times than he can count. It's named for Louis XIV's confessor, the former owner of these 110 acres overlooking Paris. To paraphrase Mel Brooks: it's good to be the king's confessor. Everyone who was anyone reposes in the vast necropolis: Oscar Wilde, Balzac, Edith Piaf, Sarah Bernhardt, Jean de Brunhoff, Isadora Duncan, Delacroix, Abelard and Héloïse ("It's said"), Rossini, Gertrude Stein and Alice B. Toklas, Colette, Proust. Jim Morrison attracts so many moaning bacchantes and graffiti-scrawling votaries they had to remove his marker. Oscar Wilde's tomb—a massive, ugly, Assyrian-themed stone block by Jacob Epstein—is so profusely besmooched with lipstick kisses they've encased it in plexiglass. This has only encouraged the lipstick brigade. It looks awful, like a wall in a dingy subway station. As Oscar said of the wallpaper in the hotel room where he died, "One of us must go."

On one visit to Père Lachaise, he stumbled on the grave of Gérard de Nerval. Who? Why, the French novelist, poet, and Proust "influencer," as we say now. Nerval (1808–55) was one strange duck. He used to walk his pet lobster, Thibault, on a leash in the Palais-Royal. Why? Because he said it made every bit as much sense as walking a dog. Maybe he just liked lobsters. "They're peaceful, serious creatures," he said. "They know the secrets of the sea, they don't bark, and they don't gnaw upon one's monadic privacy like dogs." (*Monadic*? You look it up. The to-do list is closed for the day.) M. Nerval hanged himself from the bars of a cellar on one of Paris's meanest streets. Oddly, he was found with his hat still atop his head.

On the other side of Paris is Montparnasse cemetery, where he laid a reverential pebble on the grave of Captain Dreyfus, which isn't easy to find. Baudelaire's there, too; so is Bartholdi, sculptor of the Statue of Liberty. You can spend a lifetime with the dead of Paris.

In England once, he went well out of his way to find Lawrence of Arabia's grave. It's in Moreton, Dorset, in a tiny cemetery not far from where Lawrence had his fatal motorcycle accident in 1935. He stood in front of the grave, hat off, thinking about a scene in Lawrence's monumental memoir, *The Seven Pillars of Wisdom*. You won't find it in the movie. In the excitement of the mounted charge on the Turkish garrison at Aqaba, Lawrence accidentally shot his own camel in the back of its head. Down he ingloriously went. In the movie, it would have caused an abrupt pivot from drama to farce. Lawrence lost the manuscript of his seven-hundred-page (Proustian) book while changing trains on his way home from the 1919 Paris Peace Conference. He spent three months of grueling twenty-hour days rewriting it, but then he did incline to masochism.

Five foot three and plain-faced, the real Lawrence was less tall and a lot less handsome than movie Lawrence Peter O'Toole. (Who isn't?) At the premiere, Noël Coward told him, "If you were any better looking, they'd have had to call it *Florence of Arabia*." In his diary, Coward noted, "I said to him afterwards that if Lawrence had looked like him there would have been many more than twelve Turks queuing up for the buggering session."

When O'Toole met his costar Omar Sharif, he said, "My dear, no one is named Omar Sharif. I shall call you Fred." Fred and Peter they remained for the rest of their lives, best of friends.

When he first met the pretty little twelve-year-old Clytemnestra, who later became his stepdaughter, he told her, "No one is named Clytemnestra. I shall call you Cake." She thought her momma's new friend very strange, but to this day, she remains his darling "Cake."

While he was thinking these thoughts at Lawrence's grave, a cat shimmered out of a raspberry bush and brushed up against his leg. The sun suddenly came out from behind the clouds, bathing the white marble in light and warmth. The cat sashayed over and lay on the marker, scratching its shoulder blades one at a time on the stone.

The gravestone is elaborate, in the form of an open book. Unlike Melville's blank scroll, this one is verbose: *Dominus Illuminatio Mea* (the Lord is my light). The deceased is identified as T. E. Lawrence, though at the time of his death, he'd changed his name yet again, this time to Shaw. The inscription continues, assertive, strident. You can hear the trumpets: The Hour Is Coming & Now Is When the Dead Shall Hear the Voice of the SON OF GOD and They That Hear Shall Live.

It seemed odd to him. He'd read a half dozen or so books on Lawrence, as well as every one of the seven hundred pages in *Pillars*, and couldn't recall a single reference to his religious beliefs. For the good reason that Lawrence had none. He asked one of Lawrence's biographers about it. He told him that the inscription was composed by Lawrence's pious, martinet mother. She was governess to Sir Thomas Chapman's four daughters before being promoted to the rank of mistress. Lawrence, their son, was born in 1888. His mother and father eventually married.

An elderly lady appeared, as the cat had, out of nowhere. They chatted. She and the cat were old friends. She said she wasn't going to be around much longer, so she'd "put just a bit aside" in her will, for its care. *So* English. She told him that as a young girl, she'd stood right where they were and watched

American soldiers who'd been wounded on D-Day limp up the road.

"You looked at them and thought, 'What these poor men have been through.'"

All Saints Cemetery in Pimento lacks the grandeur of Père Lachaise, Montparnasse, and Woodlawn, but it's the resting place of a notable American: James Lafayette Dickey, whose heart was roaringly pregnant with celestial fire. The grave marker is plain: "Poet. Father of Bronwen, Kevin, and Christopher." Below is a line from one of his poems: "I move at the heart of the world."

Almost exactly fifty years ago, James Dickey pulled off the neat but unintended trick of eclipsing his fame as a poet by publishing a best-selling novel. Nine out of ten people today might be surprised to learn that the author of *Deliverance* was also a poet; indeed, America's de facto poet laureate, by virtue of being the poetry consultant to the Library of Congress. But ten out of ten people would likely recognize the line "Squeal like a pig!" Just yesterday, in the supermarket parking lot, he saw a bumper sticker: "Paddle faster, boys—I hear banjo music!" "Squeal like a pig" was actually improvised on the movie set. Strange, to be remembered for that rather than for—

> *My green, graceful bones fill the air*
> *With sleeping birds. Alone, alone*
> *And with them I move gently.*
> *I move at the heart of the world.*

CHAPTER 12

Babcock and Chambless are going after each other hammer and tong with TV and radio ads. This prompts him to call Babcock.

"Pimento County coroner's office. Good morning."

"Good morning. May I speak to Coroner Babcock, please?"

"Is this in reference to a body?"

"Not a specific body, no."

"Sorry?"

"It's in reference to the electoral body."

"Forgive me, sir, but I'm afraid I'm still not understanding."

"I'm calling in my capacity as a voter in the upcoming coroner election. I want to cast an informed vote."

"Oh. Yes, I see. How may I help you?"

"Well, no offense, but I kind of wanted to speak to the coroner himself."

"There is a website. Let's see . . . I can never remember . . ."

"Could you tell me when the next rally is?"

"Rally?"

"I assume Coroner Babcock is doing campaign events."

"Events? There was a breakfast at the Rotary in Purrell's Inlet a couple weeks back."

"When is the next debate?"

"Debate?"

"Yes. Between Coroner Babcock and Mr. Chambless, his challenger."

"I don't believe I've heard anything about a debate."

Not much of the proverbial "fire in the belly" at Babcock campaign HQ.

"How is Coroner Babcock doing in the latest polls?"

"Well, I don't believe I have seen any polls."

The complacency is breathtaking.

"I hear he's not doing well with the nineteen-to-thirty-four age demographic group. Of course, at their age they think they're going to live forever, so it's not surprising that they don't pay attention to the coroner races."

"I'm afraid I just don't have an answer for you about that, sir. I'm sorry. I realize I'm not being very helpful. May I put you on hold for just a moment?"

A male voice comes on, braying authority.

"This is Bobby Babcock. With whom do I have the pleasure of conversing?"

The man himself. Now we're getting somewhere. He explains about wanting to make an informed decision.

"I respect that," Coroner Babcock says. "How can I help you?"

"Well, for starters, I was wondering what your reaction is to these ads Chambless is running."

"Ads? I haven't . . . what ads?"

"They're pretty hard-hitting."

"I am not aware of any *ads*. We both of us—me and Harry—have a few lawn signs here and there. And flyers explaining our positions and what have you. But that's about it, in terms of getting out our respective messages and so forth."

"What about the ad I saw on TV?"

"TV?"

"I'm referring to the Chambless ad with footage of all those refrigerated trucks outside hospitals and morgues in New York City. With Chambless's voice-over saying, 'Reelect Bobby Babcock and this is what Pimento County will look like—corpses, everywhere.' Mind you, I'm not saying it convinced me. That's why I'm calling. To hear your side of it."

"Where did you say you saw this ad?"

"Well, it must have been on a local channel. Can't think why it would have been on network television. It is a local race. Wouldn't be much point in Chambless paying to influence voters in Kansas."

"Sir, I am truly . . . I don't know what to tell you."

"My wife and I watch the evening news. I try not to watch TV during the day, unless there's a tornado warning. Which lately, there seem to be more and more of. I guess I'm as skeptical as the next person about this so-called climate change. But *something* definitely seems to be going on. We like to watch *Jeopardy!* Alex Trebek was the gold standard. Wouldn't you agree? Sundays, we try to catch *60 Minutes*, but I miss Mike Wallace and Morley Safer. Guess that dates me, huh?"

"Sir, I'm going to pass you on back to Harriett. That's the lady you were talking to before. She's going to take down your information. Meanwhile, I am going to look into this, and I promise, someone will get back to you."

"You should look into it, Coroner Babcock. I'm not from here, as you've probably gathered from my accent. Color me naive, but I had no idea coroner elections were a contact sport."

"I assure you, sir, I am more than a little surprised myself. I will be in touch."

"Thank you. I only want the best for Pimento County. As your ad says, 'Pimento deserves the best.'"

"I believe that's actually Harry's slogan, but I'm with Harry a hundred percent, far as that goes. I agree. Pimento absolutely deserves the best. And then some."

"Thank you for your time, Coroner. And may I say, without prejudicing my vote, thank you for your service."

"Thank you, sir. Appreciate the call."

He likes the cut of Babcock's jib. He sounds like a man of quality, and into the bargain, a nice guy, though niceness is not the paramount qualification in a coroner.

That afternoon, on his way back from a highly satisfying scarf in the HK feed bag, he listens to a scathing radio ad attacking Harry Chambless. Cagey of Babcock not to have mentioned it. Time to get Chambless's view.

"Thank you for calling the Arthur T. Chambless Funeral Home. How may I assist you?"

"Did you say Arthur T. Chambless?"

"Yes, sir, I did."

"Actually, I'm calling for Harry Chambless."

"Mr. Harry, yes. That would be Mr. Arthur's son."

"I see. Family business."

"Yes, sir, since 1927. Mr. Arthur's father, Mr. Leroy Chambless, was our founder. May I ask if this is in connection with a bereavement?"

"Happily, no. I'm calling about the coroner race."

"I see. How may I help you?"

"I was hoping to speak to the candidate. I want to make an informed vote."

"I understand. Of course. Yes. Certainly. Let me see if Mr. Harry is available. Would you be so kind as to hold while I attempt to locate him?"

The hold music is appropriately somber for a funeral home, leavened with upbeat fluty bits and harp glissandos to keep callers from sobbing uncontrollably while they hold.

"This is Harry Chambless. With whom do I have the honor of speaking?"

In the background he hears the thwack of a well-addressed golf ball and a shout of "*Sweet!*" Is Harry taking this call on the *golf course*? In the middle of a tight race? Not much "fire in the belly" here, either. Shouldn't he be out, pounding the Pimento pavement, knocking on doors, canvassing for votes, making his case, closing the deal? Or maybe Harry doesn't have that kind of mojo. Inheriting a business is certainly easier than building one yourself.

He explains about wanting to cast an informed vote.

Chambless replies somewhat blandly, and with a trace of annoyance. "We *do* have a website." In so many words: *Why don't you look it up yourself and let me get back to my golf game?*

"Yes," he replies with mild disdain. "I've seen your website."

"Oh. You have?"

"There's nothing on it that addresses these allegations by the Babcock campaign."

"Allegations? What allegations?"

"Well, for starters, about how you ducked military service."

"Whoa. Hold on. Hold on right there. I hold a commission in the Air Force Reserve."

"You do?"

"I sure as heck do." Some fire in the belly. Finally.

"Boy, that's disgraceful."

"Excuse me?"

"No, I didn't mean you, Mr. Chambless. What they're saying about you."

"Who is they? And what is it they're saying?"

"They're certainly not saying, 'Thank you for your service.' They don't quite come right out and say it, but they do a darn good job of insinuating that our country's wars have been good for your family business."

"What?"

"Don't shoot the messenger, now. I'm not saying I take these allegations at face value. But you can see how they might give pause to people who'd otherwise be inclined to vote for you."

"*Where* did you hear this bull?"

"It was on the radio. Just now."

"The radio? What station?"

"Sorry, Mr. Chambless. I couldn't tell you. There are so darn many channels these days, I can't keep track. I assume it was a local station. It wouldn't make much sense for the Babcock campaign to be paying for ads on satellite radio. People in Colorado don't vote in Pimento County elections."

Harry sounds flustered. As well he might.

"If you're telling me you heard this on WPIM, I . . . just do not . . . Roscoe Lachicotte owns WPIM. Him and me are old friends."

Him and me? Harry certainly isn't running on his pronouns.

"I don't know what to tell you, Mr. Chambless. But hearing is believing. It went on at some length. There was also reference to your funeral home doing a quote unquote 'brisk business in body bags.' Political ads love alliteration, don't they? I guess it helps people remember the slogans."

"This is outrageous!"

"So, your position is that these allegations are inaccurate?"

In the background he hears someone shouting, "Harry! Quit yappin'! You're up!"

"Look, I'm gonna have to call you back," Chambless says. "Something is not right here."

"I'm glad to hear that. You might want to get that message out. I'm no pollster, Mr. Chambless, but the good folks of Pimento might be reluctant to entrust the bodies of their dear departed to a—I'm only quoting—'a third-generation war profiteer.'"

Chambless rings off, cursing. The poor man's madder than a hornet. And who'd blame him?

This coroner race is getting way out of hand. A coroner race, for Pete's sake. What's happening to this country? Everyone is so angry these days.

CHAPTER 13

He sweeps the crosshairs across the kill zone and brings them to rest on the *O* of "One is nearer God's heart in a garden than anywhere else on earth." Not tonight, one isn't. The ornament was a gift from Peaches when they took up gardening. It reads less sentimentally through a scope mounted on a rifle.

The moles, or as he calls them, "the fucking moles," have once again turned his tomato patch into a hellscape. It used to look like Martha Stewart herself tended it. Now it resembles the Battle of the Somme. He has painstakingly reassembled it three times. There will not be a fourth time. Enough is enough. He did not start this war, but by God, he will end it. The (fucking) moles have feasted on their last tomato.

He'd prefer a weapon of greater heft, say a .22 or pump-action 12-gauge Street Sweeper. But the neighbors might find gunfire uncongenial in the middle of the night. Nor would Peaches approve. No matter. The air rifle is sufficiently lethal: .177 caliber, eight grains of copper-jacketed lead exiting the muzzle at 650 feet per second. *Pffffftt.* The neighbors will slumber undisturbed as the bodies pile up.

The night vision scope is very macho. It makes the terrain glow psychedelically green, as if saturated by radioactive rain. He found it on eBay. (Where else?) The seller said it's the same kind Navy SEAL snipers use. Good. Osama bin Mole won't know what hit him. *Allahu akbar, my furry little friend. Welcome to hell.*

He checks his watch: 3:30 a.m. Or as SEALs say, zero three thirty hours. He yawns. He is not normally awake at zero three thirty hours. But these are not normal times. The moles will come. Soon. From his second-floor window perch, he has a commanding view of the kill zone. He merges with his weapon, becoming one with it. One instrument, one purpose: revenge and annihilation. (Technically, two purposes.) He tries to blot out all extraneous thought, but he cannot entirely suppress the irony that his life's trajectory has taken him from his beloved Mole in *The Wind in the Willows* to *Tom Clancy's Black Ops: Objective Mole.* He did not ask for this mission. It is the mission that seeks the man, not the man that seeks the mission. However that goes. He will look it up. But not now. Later. After the killing.

Empty your mind, he tells himself. *Embrace the suck. The only reality is the mission. The enemy is—*

He's bathed in harsh light. He shields his eyes.

Peaches is standing at the light switch, in her nightie, hands on hips. He knows this pose well: *Adho Mukha Saheb.* ("Wrathful Wife," often paired with *Chaapaloosee Pati,* "Cringing Husband.")

"*Douse that light,*" he hisses. "*You're ruining my night vision.*"

"It's three thirty," Peaches says.

"*Shh. They'll hear you.*"

"Who?"

"*The moles.*"

"This is absurd."

"No, darling," he says. "*This* is gardening."

"I'm going back to bed."

"Good."

"Are you coming?"

"No. Go away."

"Do you want a glass of milk?"

"No!"

"There's Key lime pie."

She knows his weak points too well. Why fight? He's lost the element essential to any ambush—surprise. He rises stiffly from his perch, groans, and closes the window.

"Is that thing loaded?" Peaches asks.

"I can't believe you asked me that."

"Why?"

"I've been here since midnight. Three and a half hours, peering through a scope, finger on the trigger, waiting for a shot. Do you really think I would go to all that effort—*with an unloaded gun*?"

"How would I know?" Peaches says, as if he'd asked her the atomic weight of molybdenum. She slippers off to bed.

He goes to the kitchen and eats the entire Key lime pie. It's good. Very, very good. Bay-at-the-moon good. Kudzoo, their local bakery, makes them with inch-thick crusts of compacted Graham cracker, brown sugar, butter, and chocolate. He would happily eat another, but there is not another. What time does Kudzoo open? Probably not 4 a.m. Alas.

He trudges upstairs and gets into bed. He is tired, but he does not fall into the arms of Morpheus, owing to the extremity of caffeine crackling through his nervous system. At five thirty (zero five thirty, SEAL time), he abandons any hope of sleep and gets out of bed. He puts on his bathrobe and slippers and shuffles outside, braced for the bitter sight that he knows awaits him.

Sure enough, there before him lies another a scene of devastation. The moles waited for Peaches to abort the ambush. If it weren't so insidious, he might admire their foul little scheme. How clever of the little bastards to have a mole of their own on the inside. His own wife. Perfidy, thy name is Peaches.

From the look of it, the moles have done more than feast. They held a mole rave. He beholds the mutilated remains of his Early Girls, Big Boys, and San Marzanos. What plumpness, what juiciness they might have attained had they not been sacrificed on the altar of insatiate mole gluttony. There can be no going back now to the way things were. Peaches may have saved her confederates from slaughter, but in the process, she has revealed her true colors. His own wife, a mole hugger. *How* has he deserved this?

No one must know. The humiliation would be too great. For now, all he can do—all he must do—is pick up the pieces and try to move on. He'll wait to make his move. As the saying goes, revenge is a dish best served at room temperature.

Can he lay all the blame at Peaches's feet? Or is it time to face some hard truth? Would a true, combat-hardened Tom Clancy black ops sniper abort a mission because some nightie-wearing female lured him from his post with Key lime pie? Do SEALs run that training scenario at Coronado?

All day, he affects a nonchalant, even uxorious air, as if her treachery never took place. It's all "darling" this and "darling" that. At bedtime, he kisses her tenderly, tells her he'll be up shortly. He just wants to make a few notes for the screenplay. But this is not his real intention. No.

He googles. His search yields a promisingly named site called Mole-No-Mo. Pulse quickening, he reads.

"It's an appealing idea, to make one's own rodent extermination device. There are dozens of DIY videos on how to assemble some version of a propane mole killer."

Propane mole killer? Very exciting.

"Injecting gas directly into the tunnels of burrowing rodents can be an effective killer. But bear in mind that propane, mixed with oxygen and then detonated by an ignition of some source, will definitely remove pests—but not without risk."

Indeed, pumping propane and oxygen into subterranean tunnels does not sound at all "without risk." On the contrary, it sounds rather risk-full. But what a delightful image it conjures, of the ground trembling, then suddenly, violently erupting as dozens—scores—of moles, their fat little bellies distended from gorging on his tomatoes, are propelled into the sky, up, up, up . . . and fall to earth, one by one, *thud . . . thud . . . thud.*

But this delectable panorama now widens, like an IMAX screen as the curtains draw back, to reveal Peaches, standing at the periphery of the blast area, face blackened, nightie smoldering, in tatters, her hands reaching to close around his neck in the *Saheb Hasta Mañana* pose. Mole-No-Mo forthrightly admits that propane "*can* decimate your landscaping." (Along with your marriage.) Yes, one must factor this in. A final cautionary note advises, "Safety goggles and earplugs are prudent but may not protect you from fast-moving debris and larger rocks following the detonation."

But wait—Mole-No-Mo has an alternative to the scorched-earth protocol. It's called Mole X-Termination Device. He very much likes the sound of that. It involves "pumping smoke into the ground."

How to sell this to Peaches? "They don't feel a thing, darling. They just go to sleep. It's very humane."

"Humane?" No, Peaches will have none of it. "You are not pumping smoke into the ground."

Asphyxiating subterranean mole colonies could make for awkward chitchat over the cucumber sandwiches and iced tea at the next meeting of the Pimento Garden Club. *Personally, I feel closest to God's heart when I'm pumping carbon monoxide into the garden through a hose from my car exhaust. And you?*

CHAPTER 14

The Face ID function on his iPhone has stopped working. Infuriating. The phone is less than six months old. He calls Apple support in high dudgeon.

"Are you wearing a face mask?" asks the support person.

"No. I'm at home. Where else would I be in a pandemic?"

"Have you altered your facial characteristics?"

"How do you mean?"

"Glasses, facial hair, cosmetic surgery."

Facial hair? "I do have lycanthropic issues," he says. "Would that affect it?"

"Is that a medical condition?"

"You could call it that. When the moon is full, I develop copious facial hair and enhanced dentition. But shouldn't the phone recognize me the rest of time?"

"I'm not sure I follow you."

"I become a werewolf. But it's only for one or two days a month."

"Okay."

"I prefer the term *lycanthrope*. From the Greek *lukos*, for wolf. And *anthropos*, Latin for man. It sounds prissy, I know, but I find it more dignified than *werewolf*."

"Okay."

His iPhone alerts him to an incoming call from "Pimento Coroner." Why would the coroner be calling? No one's died. Then he remembers the lawn signs. They're having an election. This must be a fund-raising call. Honestly. Cold-calling taxpayers to hit them up for contributions—for a coroner race? Where does it end? He taps decline and returns to Customer Support.

"I was joking about the werewolf thing."

"Okay." So equable, millennials.

"How do we fix this? Why does my own phone no longer recognize me?"

"Sometimes if a person changes their facial metrics—"

"What does that mean?"

"Putting on weight, say. I'm not saying that's the situation in your case." He walks him through resetting Face ID.

"Is there anything else I can help you with?"

"No. Thank you."

Well, that was morale boosting. What a terrific day he's having. His wife is in league with the mole underground and his iPhone is fat shaming him. He gets that Apple would assume that everyone's facial metrics should be skinny and millennial, but this seems like very flawed programming. If all you have to do to thwart facial recognition is put on a few extra pounds, let's hope the terrorists don't learn about it. They'll be stuffing themselves with Hippo King Enormo Burger Combos and waltzing past the facial recognition sensors at airports. Terrorists of the future will weigh four hundred pounds. They'll need XXXXL suicide vests. He must write a strongly worded letter to Apple's (doubtless slim and fit) CEO, with a copy to the head of Homeland Security.

He listens to the voice mail from the coroner's office. It's Babcock himself, saying that he's calling him "back." This makes no sense. He has no recollection of speaking to Babcock. *Aha,* now he gets it: it's the new scam. Cold-callers leave a message saying they're "returning" your call. So, you—naive lamb—call them and before you know it, you're listening to a sales pitch for something called Gutter Guard. The Pimento County coroner is now engaging in this shabby tactic? What's happened to the concept of shame in this country? He's tempted to call this Babcock person back right now and give him a piece of his mind.

He tells Peaches about this outrage. She shrugs.

"Darling," he says, "does it not bother you that local elected officials are shaking down taxpayers?"

"Sweetheart, I might care, if I'd had a decent night's sleep instead of being up all night with Lee Harvey Oswald. By the way, I see you enjoyed the Key lime pie."

He knew she'd bring up the pie. But he's ready. Peaches has played right into his hands.

"For your information, darling, this morning's *Washington Post*—which I read on my iPad rather than risk death from one of your charming native venomous snakes—has an article about managing spousal anger during the pandemic. May I read you a sentence? 'Research has found that married people who had less glucose in their blood stabbed voodoo dolls representing their spouse more times than those who had more glucose in their blood.'"

Peaches processes. "So, if you hadn't eaten the entire pie, you'd be stabbing me with a pin? Is that the takeaway?"

"I am *suggesting*, oh light of my life, that we listen to the scientists. Meanwhile, I think you might evince at least some concern about the rampant corruption in our local government."

"Sweetheart, if you're that worked up about it, why don't you send a campaign contribution to whoever's running against Babcock?"

Not a bad idea. In fact, a very good one. Oh, a clever one is his darling. What a Borgia she'd have made.

In his study, he makes out a $50 check to Chambless for Coroner. In the memo line, he writes: "Babcock delenda est." Nice touch. A gloss on Cato the Elder's famous "Carthage must be destroyed." Will Chambless get it? Probably not. But the donation itself might teach Bobby "I'm returning your call" Babcock not to leave disingenuous messages on people's voice mails.

Is it enough, sending Chambless money? No. He'll write a letter to enclose with his donation—and send a copy to Babcock. Excellent.

Dear Mr. Chambless,

I am sending you this contribution in part because of your eminent qualifications to become Pimento County's coroner, but also by way of countering the outrageous conduct of your opponent, Mr. Babcock, the incumbent coroner. Allow me to explain:

Yesterday, after discovering a technological flaw that has grave, indeed dire consequences for the nation's security . . .

At the bottom of the last page, he adds a PS: *Thank you for your family's sensitive handling of Pimento's dead since 1927.*

He wonders if the letter is a tad long. He could tighten the section about Pimento's mole problem. Technically, moles don't fall within the remit of a coroner. But these remorseless, insatiable vermin could be spreading God only knows what pestilence. Look what one bat in Wuhan did. That's all the country needs right now: a mole-borne virus, on top of Covid. No, best to leave in the mole bit. There's a long paragraph on page four about the excellence of Kudzoo's Key lime pies. Somewhat digressive, but he feels it adds a folksy touch eloquent of his affection for his adopted hometown. And to judge from photos, old Harry is no stranger to Kudzoo's Key lime pies. Or to the delights of HK. Bet he's wrapped his lips around a few Enormo Burger Combos in his day.

Should he show the letter to Peaches? She's a good editor, and it was her idea to teach Bobby "Brother, Can You Spare a Dime?" Babcock a lesson by sending Chambless a contribution.

But wait. What is he thinking? Peaches is the Kim Philby of Mole World. She'll say, "Why have you got two pages in here about moles? What does a coroner have to do with our moles?" (Note the tell: "our" moles.) She'll use it as an excuse to ask him who's president.

He prints out two copies of the letter, one for Chambless, one for Babcock, and puts them into the mailbox. He feels lighter. Now he must get to work on the screenplay.

But he can't stop thinking about the coroner thing. Those fifty clams he sent Chambless aren't nearly enough to turn the tide in his favor. But there are other ways he can help.

Somber, anxiety-inducing music.

We see the front page of the Weekly Pimentoan, *headline:*

AUTHORITIES ALARMED BY "DRAMATIC RISE" IN PREMATURE BURIALS IN PIMENTO COUNTY

Camera on a coffin being lowered into a grave. We hear frantic pounding coming from inside and a muffled voice cry out: "Help! Help! Let me outta here! Helllp!"

Another front page of the Weekly Pimentoan, *headline:*

PREMATURE BURIAL SURVIVOR
"WAS ONLY TAKING A NAP"
WHEN CORONER BABCOCK
SIGNED HIS DEATH CERTIFICATE

Camera on survivor of a Babcock premature burial, nervously smoking a cigarette as he relates his harrowing tale:

It was the most horrible thing. One minute, I'm lying in my hammock, having a snooze. Next, I'm on a slab in the morgue with a tag on my big toe. That Bobby Babcock is a danger to this community. Another four years of him coronating and we won't have a community left.

Camera pans across gloomy, sepia-tone photograph of cemetery. Mossy headstones, Spanish moss everywhere.

Voice-over [Morgan Freeman, depending on budget]: Determining if someone is dead isn't rocket science. What's Coroner Babcock's excuse for the appalling increase in premature burials? Folks in Pimento are asking if it's even safe to take a nap.

Trim-looking [photoshop if necessary] funeral home director Harry Chambless with model of his patented Babcock-proof coffin, with hole in lid and aboveground bell apparatus.

HARRY (*smiling and genial, affectionately patting the coffin*): We didn't used to need these here in Pimento. But ever since Bobby Babcock became coroner, folks are terrified he's going to come along and declare them dead— without even checking for a pulse. You kind of wonder why Bobby's always in such a darned hurry. Maybe he just can't wait to resume his womanizing and boozing.

(*demonstrating*) Way it works is, if you wake up alive inside the coffin, you just yank on this string here, which is connected to an aboveground bell. (*bell rings*) That'll alert folks to the fact that you may be down, but you sure as heck ain't out.

If we had a competent coroner, I wouldn't be selling so many of these. But that'd suit me fine. I'm not in this business just to make money. I guess I just love handling dead folks. I never met a corpse I didn't like.

So, if y'all give me the honor of becoming your new coroner, I promise you there won't be any more premature burials in Pimento. You can take my word on that. Meantime, my advice is: do not specify cremation. I don't even want to *think* about that. [SHUDDERS]

Y'all take care, now. I'm Harry Chambless, and you bet I approved this message.

CHAPTER 15

Today's news delivers a blow to the solar plexus: Carl Reiner has died.

Why does this feel like a personal loss? He didn't know Carl Reiner. And dying at ninety-eight hardly qualifies as tragic. On the contrary, it's "good innings," as the Brits say. (Why do they say that? Something to do with cricket? He must look it up.)

Not just good innings, either. Fabulous innings. Carl Reiner had a charmed life. He made it through World War II without getting killed. Became a household name in the 1950s as a star on Sid Caesar's *Your Show of Shows* and *Caesar's Hour*. Was part of its fabled Writer's Room, along with Mel Brooks and Neil Simon. (Why are Jews so funny? He must look this up, too.) Was in *The Dick Van Dyke Show*; *The 2,000 Year Old Man*; *It's a Mad, Mad, Mad, Mad World*; *The Russians Are Coming, the Russians Are Coming*. In late life, *Ocean's Eleven* and its sequels. Was married to the same woman for sixty-five years. Son Rob became famous himself for *All in the Family*, *This Is Spinal Tap*, and *The Princess Bride*. Carl Reiner was on his way to a career as a sewing machine repairman when his brother mentioned seeing a notice in the paper for a New Deal works program offering free acting classes. The rest is comedy history. So what's to be sad about? Then it comes to him:

It's 1967, his first term away at boarding school. He's miserable, homesick, scared. On Day Three, he's shooting hoops with another kid. The kid goes up to dunk it, then drops to the ground, turns blue, and gasps like a landed fish. Dies, in front of him. Cerebral hemorrhage. On Day Six, he and another boy are walking back to the dorm in the dark. The boy leaps over what he thinks is a fence but turns out to be the railing of a subterranean stairwell. Plunges fifteen feet, snaps his thigh bone in two. It sticks out his pants leg. So now he's a Jonah. Everyone avoids him, taunts him, or beats him up. In so many words, he is not having a great first term away at boarding school. The only unmiserable time of the week is Saturday night, when they get a movie in the assembly hall. And one Saturday, the movie is *The Russians Are Coming, the Russians Are Coming*, starring Carl Reiner. For two hours, he laughs and is happy. This has to be the reason he feels so sad about Mr. Reiner.

He rents *The Russians Are Coming* from Amazon Prime. Still a great movie fifty-four years later. And can he ever relate to Reiner's character, Walt Whittaker, a playwright who's having act 2 problems with his current project when here comes the hapless crew of a Soviet submarine that's run aground on "Gloucester Island."

After getting into bed, he checks the news on his laptop—never a good idea, really—and finds that Johnny Mandel, who wrote the music for *Russians*, has also died. He sits there in bed next to his darling, who is slumbering peacefully, unperturbed by the day's grim harvest of celebrity death.

In college, he once "sat shiva" (the Irish would say "waked") with a roommate whose father, a survivor of the Nazi death camps, had died. He decides he will sit shiva tonight. Why not? He's awake, despite not having slept at all the night before. He will dedicate tonight's insomnia to Mr. Reiner.

He fires up his iPad. Is it permitted to surf the Web while sitting shiva? Probably not. He'll surf reverently.

Who else from *The Russians Are Coming* has died?

Brian Keith. He played Gloucester Island's police chief, Link Mattocks. Died at seventy-five, of—uh-oh—suicide. Had emphysema *and* lung cancer. And was having financial problems. Crappy trifecta, that. Had given up smoking ten years ago. Was in Camel cigarette ads in the Fifties. Spooky: in his first scene in *Russians*, he's awakened by the fake news—surely—that Russians have landed on Gloucester Island. He listens to the island's busybody switchboard operator prattle on, gropes in an ashtray, finds a half-smoked butt, lights it. Coughs.

"Suicide by gunshot wound."

His close friend Maureen O'Hara—stunning, flame-haired Maureen O'Hara—insisted it couldn't have been suicide. Adamant. Brian was a good Catholic, you see. And had she not visited with him only the week before? And he was in fine spirits. So you see, it had to have been an accident. Brian had a big collection of guns. He loved to show them off. The gun must have gone off accidentally while he was cleaning it.

"Ms. O'Hara did not address the fact that Keith left a suicide note."

Keith's daughter had committed suicide two months before. His Broadway actress stepmother leapt to her death from the *H* in the Hollywood sign in the hills above the city. Suicide by icon.

You'd have to be *really* depressed to shoot yourself if you had Maureen O'Hara for a friend. Keith's life would seem to be another case of good innings. Served with the Marines in World War II as a rear gunner on a Dauntless dive bomber. His first movie role was as a Notre Dame student, standing on a train platform in *Knute Rockne, All American* (starring Ronald

Reagan as the Gipper). Played President Theodore Roosevelt in *The Wind and the Lion.* Roosevelt's biographer Edmund Morris would chuckle as he recited Keith's last line in the movie. Teddy, eager to inspect his stuffed grizzly bear, dismisses his entourage. "I want to be alone with my bear." In his final role, he was President William McKinley. There's a neat trick: playing consecutive presidents, in reverse.

"Keith was fluent in Russian"? He must know more—much more—about this. But it will have to wait. Is *anyone* from *Russians* still alive?

Jonathan Winters died in 2013, age eighty-seven. He played Keith's flustered deputy. Was also in the Marines in World War II. He met him once, in a diner in Montecito, California. He is not the type to accost celebrities, but he had to say a quick thank-you for all the laughter over the years. He did. Took less than ten seconds. Winters followed him back to his booth and launched into riffs, anecdotes, impersonations, improv. *And continued for nearly an hour.* Jonathan Winters, Live at the Diner, a one-man show for an audience of one. It was dazzling. The impersonations ranged from Jimmy Carter to Benito Mussolini. One had Neil Armstrong stepping in dog doo on the moon and furiously trying to scrape it off on the ladder of the lunar landing module, cussing a blue streak, Mission Control frantic, begging him to get a grip. "Neil! *Neil!* Kids are watching! *President Nixon is watching!*" It was unbelievable. You go to the diner for breakfast and get a personal performance by the funniest man in America. Doesn't happen every day.

The strange thing is that the other people in the diner paid no attention to the fact that Jonathan Winters was in their midst, doing stand-up. He later learned why. Winters did this all the time. His dynamo had no off switch. He was always on: at antiques shows, country fairs, gun shops, anywhere, everywhere. He'd go to cash a check at the bank and do a half-hour show for the tellers. His genius came at a price, paid in psychiatric wards and treatments for depression and bipolar disorder. Dear man. Dear soul.

Alan Arkin is still alive, age eighty-six, thank God. It makes the loss of the others more tolerable, somehow. Arkin played Rozanov, the Soviet submarine's *zampolit*, political commissar. *Aha.* Now it makes sense why he could yell at the submarine's captain with impunity. The captain technically outranked him, but as the representative of the party, a *zampolit* effectively out-ranked everyone. In another submarine-themed movie, *The Hunt for Red October*, Sean Connery initiates his defection scheme by killing the *zampolit*, named Putin. (Clancy's novel came out in the mid-1980s, so the name was either eerily pre-scient or just plain Irish lucky.) Now it also makes sense that Rozanov spoke English, which he did hilariously, in a thick ac-cent that baffles the residents of "Glow-Kester Iss-land." Arkin's parents were Ukrainian immigrants. He grew up speaking Rus-sian. Did he and Brian Keith gossip in Russian between takes? Something else to look up tomorrow. It's remorseless, the list.

What time is it? Yikes. Quarter to four. Or *oy*, as one should say while sitting shiva. But there are still a few more cast members to look up.

Theodore Bikel. Died at ninety-one. Played the gruff sub-marine captain who accidentally runs his vessel aground be-cause he wanted to glimpse "Amerr-i-kah." *Russians* wasn't his first time aboard a movie sub. He was "Heinie" Schwaffer in *The Enemy Below*, a crewman on the U-boat trying to sink Robert Mitchum's destroyer. And isn't that him on the German gunship *Louisa* in *The African Queen*?

Bikel was a big deal folk singer. Performed with Pete Seeger, recorded duets with Judy Collins. Cofounded the Newport Folk Festival, where in 1965 Bob Dylan was booed for playing electric guitar. Was the second person after Dylan to perform "Blowing in the Wind." Campaigned for JFK in 1960 while playing Captain von Trapp on Broadway in *The Sound of Music*. That got him in hot water with the producers. In those days, it wasn't kosher for actors to endorse politicians. (*That* was then.) In the 1980s, he got arrested for protesting at the Russian embassy in Washington on behalf of Soviet Jews.

He *must* get to sleep.

But what about Eva Marie Saint? What a beautiful, elegant lady. He clicks. She's alive! Ninety-six and still a knockout. He had such a crush on her in 1966.

More good news: Norman Jewison, who directed *Russians*, is still alive, at ninety-three. He's Canadian. He must know Donald Sutherland! He must immediately send Jewison the screenplay and ask him to pass it along to Sutherland. That is, once he finishes the screenplay. Jewison will totally get that the Baruch role is perfect for his fellow Canadian. Very clever, getting Jewison to give it Sutherland. Canadians have this instinctive bond with one another. Americans aren't in good odor in Canada these days. And no wonder, with Trump constantly insulting their prime minister.

What time is it now—4:30 a.m.? *Fuck.* His eyelids are closing and jerking open, like subway doors with someone's leg between them. Enough. But just as he's putting the iPad to sleep, he sees: "Based on the novel *The Off-Islanders* by Nathaniel Benchley." Hold on.

He met Benchley once, on Nantucket, the model for Gloucester Island. Benchley showed him a book in his shelves: a first edition of a Hemingway novel that had belonged to his father, Robert Benchley, the great wit and Algonquin Round Table member. In those days, publishers didn't allow off-color words. They were expressed with dashes: "———." One night, Hemingway was in his cups and filled in all the dashes, and on the dedication page, wrote: "To Bob 'Garbage Bird' Benchley, from Ernest 'One-Fuck' Hemingway." He inserted an asterisk and footnote: "Sell quick."

In a letter, Edmund Wilson tells the story of Max Perkins, Hemingway's editor, seeking guidance from Charles Scribner as to whether they could publish three particular words: *balls*, *shit*, and *cocksucker*. He couldn't bring himself to say the last word out loud to Scribner, so he wrote it on a memorandum pad. Scribner chided him for his squeamishness. Perkins inadvertently left the pad where everyone saw it. The incident threw the entire office "into a state of acute embarrassment, deep mental and moral distress, and troubling mystification."

He wonders what it was like for Nathaniel Benchley to be generationally sandwiched between a famous father and a famous son. It must have been something of a relief when *The Off-Islanders* was made into a huge movie and he could finally step out from the shadow of his famous father. But the sunshine would be brief, eclipsed when his son Peter created a tsunami-grade splash with his novel about a vengeful shark. Peter had a hard time deciding what to call it. The deadline was looming, the publisher was on the phone, pleading, "We need a title!" Peter's father suggested *Who's That Noshing on My Leg?*

He looks at the time. "———," as One-Fuck would say. The sky's turning orange. Dawn is breaking. The dogs are scratching to go out. And *uh-oh*, herself is stirring. Peaches props herself up on elbows. (The "Bad Moon Rising" pose.) She squints.

"Have you been up *all night*?"

"Um?" he says, trying to sound casual.

"What are you doing?"

"Sitting shiva."

"What?"

"Mourning, darling."

"I know it's morning. I asked why you're still up."

"Mourning with a *U*, darling."

"What are you talking about?"

"The Jewish custom of mourning the dead, sweetheart. I'm sitting shiva for Carl Reiner. And for Johnny Mandel. I don't know if he was Jewish, but probably. I'll look it up."

"Who the hell is Johnny Mandel?" His darling is very sour this morning.

"Sweetheart. He scored the music for *The Russians Are Coming, the Russians Are Coming*. Wonderful movie."

She's about to ask him who's president. But instead says, "I'm making an appointment for you with Dr. Bhong. Today."

CHAPTER 16

Over coffee, he and Peaches have a vigorous discussion on the theme of mental health. Specifically, his. It does not end well. He puts down his foot and stomps off to his study. One advantage to being overweight is that it enhances stomping.

His study is separated from the main house by a short wooden walkway above the garage area. In times of marital stress, he thinks of it as a drawbridge.

He reflects that he is often indignant these days. But why shouldn't he be? There's a lot to be indignant about. He hasn't seen his toes in months, and no one has volunteered to find them. He can't get his morning newspaper without risking snakebite; can't go for a walk without the possibility of being devoured by predators left over from the Oligocene. His iPhone is fat shaming him. Proust can't write a sentence without three dozen subordinate clauses. The feds have put a hold on his passport application in order to draw him into the open. Donald Sutherland's tongue is being ravaged by mouth-eating parasites. Moles lay waste his tomatoes, protected by his own wife. And cast members of *The Russians Are Coming, the Russians Are Coming* are dying off at an appalling rate of two per day. Does anyone care? No. *This* is how civilizations die.

So yes, he's indignant. As they say, "If you're not angry,

you're not paying attention." As they further say, "Some days it just doesn't seem worth the trouble to chew through the leather straps."

By this time of day, his stomach is usually contentedly digesting breakfast. One of the many pleasures of South Carolina is starting the day with a hearty serving of grits, bacon, eggs, sausage, biscuits, and gravy. But today his stomach is growling because breakfast was forfeit to the discussion about his mental state.

Much as he'd like to stomp back to the kitchen, he must not, for that would show weakness, lack of resolve. It would devalue his indignation. Better that Peaches think he is so affronted by her insistence that he see her (absurdly named) Dr. Bhong that he has no thought of food. He must "shelter in place"—as we say in pandemic America—until she recants. But Peaches can be a mighty fortress of resolve herself.

A vision comes to him, of a grilled cheese, bacon, and tomato sandwich. Given a choice between eternal salvation and a grilled cheese, bacon, and tomato, he'd take the sandwich. He swallows another of Dr. Paula's appetite suppressants, but it does not dissipate the vision. He could lower the drawbridge and go back to the kitchen, but the kitchen is where Peaches holds court and conducts business. She has an office upstairs, but she prefers to bivouac here while she goes about her business, running online auctions of federally seized assets. Didn't she mention that she's got a big one today? The belongings of Trump's jailed campaign manager. Odd that seized items that formerly belonged to people of dubious character have such allure. Passengers in your Lamborghini Huracán EVO apparently get a thrill if you tell them, "Know who used to own this car? El Chapo's chief executioner. His nickname was Sierra de

Cadena. Means 'Chainsaw.' He kept one in the trunk, which is about all you can fit in there. Cool, huh?"

Peaches will be at her station, at the far end of the kitchen island, laptop open, two cell phones going. She might not even notice him. He could just ignore her. He holds a black belt in pouting. He's a pro at the stony silence, avoidance of eye contact, opening and shutting cabinets and drawers with just the right amount of excessive force to convey smoldering rage within. But Peaches has her own minxy tricks and devices. She'll wait until the grilled cheese, bacon, and tomato is just coming off the skillet and say, without even looking up from her laptop, "Marianna called. Beau just got a new outboard for his boat. A Yamaha."

How well he knows that ploy! She probably got it from Sun Tzu's *The Art of War*. Break silence by introducing neutral subject matter. If he declines comment, he's the asshole. But if he replies, even minimally, with an "Oh?" it's queen takes king, game over. Loser. No, best wait her out. Meantime, man up, put aside all thought of food; be adamantine, iron willed.

But his stomach is saying, *No. Feed me.*

He rummages in his desk drawers. Surely there's a chocolate and cinnamon granola bar in here. Better still, a packet of those amazing yogurt-covered raisins, from the mail-order place in California. They come in three-pound sacks. He went through an entire one while watching *Lawrence of Arabia*. Mind you, it is a long movie.

He locates a measly three yogurt-covered raisins, hiding at the back of a drawer like scared mice. He must get serious about provisioning. There's room for a small refrigerator. Maybe even a stove top, with two burners. With infrastructure like that, he could hold out for days.

Meanwhile, he comes up with a solution to his present starvation—an "entrance strategy." He composes an email to Peaches, subject heading: "Going Forward, in a Spirit of Mutual Understanding and Harmony." (In diplomatic parlance, a "communiqué.") He proposes a cessation of hostilities, while reserving full moral authority. He stipulates that yes, he did stay up the whole night, sitting shiva for Carl Reiner, a wonderful human being, a national treasure beloved by generations of Americans, a man who brought joy and laughter to millions. For *this* he should be accused of mental instability and handed over for psychiatric evaluation by this Bhong? Bhong. Interesting name. Cambodian? *So, Dr. Bhong, how long were you with the Khmer Rouge?*

Steeled, he lowers the drawbridge and makes his way to the kitchen.

Peaches is at her station, earbuds in ears, Zooming away on her laptop. She does not look up. She's intent, frowning. Doesn't even shoot him the "could you please not make noise?" look when he sets the heavy iron skillet on the burner with an unavoidable clang.

Is no one bidding on the campaign manager's $33,000 blue lizard jacket? Maybe it lacks the éclat of El Chapo's chief executioner's Lamborghini. *"Guess who used to own this tacky blue jacket made from iguana hides? Paul Manafort. Cool, huh?"* Someone's not getting laid tonight.

He goes about his culinary prep.

"Well, what did the mayor say?" Peaches asks.

Doesn't sound like an auction.

"Well, that is just fucking bullshit, is what that is," she says.

Definitely not an auction. His darling has a potty mouth. This has long puzzled him. Her parents raised their eight children according to strict but loving Southern Episcopalian protocol. They insisted on manners. Their children addressed them as "ma'am" and "sir." They got spanked if they said bad words. "Fucking bullshit" would have got them sent to reform school. How is it, then, that his darling talks like someone in a Quentin Tarantino movie? He thinks it must have to do with being the youngest of eight.

He hears references to "the statue" and to "the fucking town council." Also to "those armed fools." Armed fools? That doesn't sound good. He's now more interested in the fucking bullshit than in his grilled cheese.

Peaches reiterates to whomever she's talking with that she "cannot believe this shit" and ends the call. She removes her earbuds and tosses them angrily into a bowl, like earrings angrily discarded at the end of an unsuccessful evening.

"Who was that?" he says casually.

"Tub." Her sister Tituba.

The mayor and town council of Sophia Springs have tabled removing Colonel Ptarmigan Spratt's statue, pending a public hearing. He comments that this sounds like a fairly normal civic procedure. Peaches retorts hotly that the mayor is "a jackass" and "a pussy." He has cravenly caved to the armed fools, a militia group that has set up camp in the town park, complete with lawn chairs, coolers, and their own porta-potty. They are protesting the removal on the grounds that the statue is part of the "fucking town heritage."

He asks, "Is it legal to have weapons in a town park?" Ten years in South Carolina, and he's still learning things every day.

"It is so long as you don't shoot anyone." Reasonable enough.

"So you're only allowed to threaten to shoot people? Interesting. These gentlemen, are they local folks who've come together to express solidarity with the idea that slaves were grateful to your ancestor for trying to keep them in bondage?"

"They're a chapter of the Oath Keepers. These are called Oaf Keepers. Tub says they spelled it wrong when they ordered T-shirts and hats and were too cheap to redo them."

Peaches calls up their website on her laptop. Their mission statement says that they are "committed to the peaceful preservation of Southern heritage by any and all means."

He says, "There was an Argentine political party whose motto was 'Moderation—or death!' Maybe they're affiliated."

"Look at them," Peaches snorts. "With their web gear and guns, pretending to be SEAL Team 6. They're all *fat*."

"I could infiltrate," he says. "My accent might give me away. I could say I'm from the Connecticut Oaf Keepers." He points to one. "I think I recognize that one, the guy with the 'Fuck Nancy Pelosi' sign."

"You *know* that person?"

"No. But he looks a bit like a guy I saw the other day in the Hippo King parking lot. They don't look like SEALs to me. If I were Osama bin Laden and I saw these tubbos coming, I'd tell them to help themselves to the falafel and go back to downloading porn. They look kind of sad, really. But it's nice they've found a cause larger than themselves to be part of. Not much larger. Still."

He offers Peaches half his grilled cheese. She declines, being too exercised to eat, then eats not only her half, but half of his half. It's a small price to pay, for his darling is now focused on the statue, not him.

CHAPTER 17

Each morning in his email, he finds a "Word of the Day," courtesy of a creative lexicographer with the anagrammatical-sounding name Anu Garg. Recent entries seem very much "of the moment," given what's going on.

Kakistocracy: government by the least qualified or worst persons.

Snollygoster: a shrewd and unprincipled person, especially an unprincipled politician.

Chirocracy: government that rules by physical force.

A first glance, today's word sounds somewhat risqué: *cunctation.* It means "delay, procrastination, tardiness." It's an eponym, from the Roman consul Quintus Fabius Maximus Verrucosus (280–203 BCE). His nickname was "Cunctator" (Delayer) after his practice of waging war s-l-o-w-l-y. The Cunctator wasn't one for the old frontal attack. His thing was hit-and-run, like South Carolina's own Francis Marion. He's doubly eponymous, actually. A "Fabian" strategy is one that proceeds by cautious steps; or one that involves a teen idol of the 1950s and '60s.

The word is resonating for him. He's been cunctating a lot

himself, screenplaywise. He *must* get to work on it. But first he must learn more about the Cunctator.

His great adversary was the Carthaginian general Hannibal. In one engagement, Hannibal outfoxed the Cunctator by tying bundles of dry wood to the horns of two thousand cattle, lighting them, and driving the herd over a hill at night. The Cunctator thought the lights were Hannibal's army. Not much fun for the cattle.

The encyclopedia doesn't say if people addressed the Cunctator by that name to his face. Probably not wise unless you were on familiar terms. Romans were very status conscious. They had people called nomenclators, whom you could hire to give you a nice shout-out as you made your way through the Forum. The more you paid, the more effusive the shout-out. Even Julius Caesar, whom you'd think didn't need shouting out, employed them. A Caesar nomenclator might exclaim, "I greet you not as Caesar, but as a god!" That must have turned heads. *Omigod, it's him! He's back from Gaul! Yay! Bread and circuses!*

This tradition of public fawning continues to our present day, in such rituals as the red carpet on Oscar night, where interviewers tell celebrities that they have never looked *this* fabulous. When Trump descended the escalator at the Trump Tower in 2015 to announce his candidacy, an image that still causes many to shudder, even years later, the people cheering him in the lobby were modern-day nomenclators paid to adulate.

Enough cunctation, he rebukes himself. *Why are you rummaging about in the third century BCE? Heimlich's Maneuver takes place during World War II, not the fucking Second Punic War. Get to work, already.* But he can't stop thinking about those two thousand head of cattle with their horns on fire. Dreadful business, war.

Between the flaming longhorns and the thirty-seven African elephants that accompanied him over the Alps, Hannibal was quite the showman, a Carthaginian combination of Wild Bill Hickok and P. T. Barnum. In one campaign, his army annihilated half a million human beings and destroyed four hundred towns. He lost that war, but put such a fright into the Romans that even today, when someone unwelcome shows up at your house—a tax inspector, say, or Silvio Berlusconi wanting to meet your teenage daughter—Italians will exclaim, "*Hannibal ante portas!*" ("Hannibal is at the gates!") When the mere mention of your name is enough to scare the ricotta out of folks two millennia later, you have truly made a lasting impression. According to Pausanias, Hannibal died of an infected cut on his finger that he got from drawing his sword while mounting his horse. To have gone through all that, only to die so prosaically. General Patton died of injuries in a jeep accident after helping us win World War II. Among his last words were: "This is a hell of a way to die."

Hannibal's fire-cattle have him thinking about Bernard Baruch's Hungarian pigs, the ones he imported for his guests at Hobcaw to shoot and copulated like there was no tomorrow. What if Heimlich tied bundles of wood to them and lit them up? It might require some rewording of the usual disclaimer, "No animals were harmed in making this movie." And would present some logistical challenges for Heimlich. But what a spectacular diversion.

Night. Interior, Baruch mansion, Hobcaw Barony.

FDR and his "special friend" Lucy Mercer are playing mah-jongg. Bernard Baruch [think Donald Sutherland] sits in an armchair by the fire reading the Wall Street Journal *and calculating how much money he made today.*

> FDR (*moving a tile with an air of triumph*): Kong. I win.
> MERCER (*moving the same tile FDR has just played, thereby "robbing the kong" and winning*): Oh no you don't. Mah-jongg. I win.
> FDR: Fuck!
> MERCER (*marking her score on a notepad*): Language, Bobo. That's three dollars and seventy-five cents you owe me.
> FDR: How do you want it?
> MERCER: Any way I can get it, big guy.
> FDR: Bernie?
> BARUCH (*looking up from his newspaper*): Um?
> FDR: Got any more gas ration coupons?
> BARUCH: What, you need gas?
> FDR: To pay my gambling debt to this vixen.

Suddenly, in the distance we hear the sound of hundreds of distressed Hungarian hogs. Through the window, we see what appear to be torches approaching the house. The squealing grows louder and louder, building to a hellish din indeed.

> BARUCH: Those pigs. What was I thinking?
> FDR (*concentrating on mah-jongg*): They don't sound very happy.

Highly agitated Army colonel rushes in.

> AGITATED COLONEL: Mr. President! We need to get you out of here, right now!

FDR (*not looking up*): Whatever for?

AGITATED COLONEL: Sir, there are hundreds of flaming pigs approaching the house!

FDR (*rolling dice*): Probably escapees from a barbecue. They're big on that down here. Not very kosher of you, Bernie.

BARUCH: I didn't order barbecue.

Extremely agitated Navy admiral rushes in.

AGITATED ADMIRAL: Mr. President! One of our ships has picked up a sonar signal of a German U-boat!

FDR (*handing the dice to Lucy*): Probably a whale. Your roll, Cupcake.

CHAPTER 18

This word *influencer* sounds like someone who spreads flu. He's certainly being an influencer in the coroner race. He's been so busy churning out material for Harry Chambless he hasn't had much time for the screenplay. That ought to be his priority, but the election is just weeks away.

He's a bit miffed, frankly, that Harry hasn't responded to any of the material he's sent him, including a script for a devastating TV attack ad; talking points for the debate, which, believe it or not, still hasn't been scheduled; and a stem-winder of a victory speech for Harry to deliver on election night. On top of all that, he sent him a thirty-page white paper outlining an ambitious vision for Pimento's coronating future, including a hundred-thousand-square-foot crematoria complex with adjoining twenty-five-acre columbarium, beautifully landscaped, where the bereaved can commune with the ashes of their dear departed. He titled it: "Raging Against the Dying of the Light— A Five-Year Plan for Pimento."

And what has Harry's response been? Nada. Not a peep. Not even a perfunctory "Great, thanks, can't wait to read it." It's possible that Harry is superstitious and doesn't want to jinx himself by announcing a five-year plan until after he's defeated Bobby Babcock. Still. A thanks would be nice.

Wherefore, this silence? Has the glamor and exhilaration of the campaign gone to his head? Has he already forgotten "the little people" who got him where he is today? *Not* a good sign. Politics is a ruthless business, God knows, but is it smart politics to take for granted people who work their hearts out for you? This ingratitude and indifference are troubling. And what happens once Harry gets his hands on the actual levers of power? What happens the day after the election, when Pimento realizes with a collective shudder that it has elected—a monster? As the saying goes, "Power corrupts. Absolute power is kind of neat." And how is he going to feel? He, who—arguably—did more than any other Pimentoan to create this Frankenstein?

It may be too late now to switch horses. Was he too hasty in turning against Babcock because of the fund-raising cold call? But if he defects now, how will Harry react? Not well, most likely. Smart, making an enemy of someone who runs a funeral home. Someone who knows a thing or two about making bodies disappear. What if Harry comes after him, bent on revenge? And he can't flee the country because he has no passport? He feels beads of cold sweat. His forehead is clammy. What has he done? *Damn fine job, Bob.*

"You okay, babe? You look a little pale."

"Fine. Fine. Bit tired."

"Did you take your lisinopril this morning?"

"Yes, darling."

"You know why you're tired, don't you?"

"Yes, darling."

"Because you stayed up two nights in a row. Shooting moles and googling about some submarine movie."

He inwardly groans. How can he explain to Peaches that it is so much more complicated than "some submarine movie"?

How can he tell her that his life—and possibly hers—could be in mortal danger, at the hands of a would-be coroner bent on vengeance?

"You're absolutely right, darling," he says.

He must proceed carefully. First, the passport. Then he must figure some way to keep both Chambless and Babcock happy. It'll have to be convincing.

The State Department website is intimidating. It's obviously designed to scare people off. The photograph of the secretary of state seems larger than necessary. He looks like a hit man in *The Sopranos*. He's smiling, but his expression says, "What are you staring at, asshole?"

A button on the home page says: *para Español, oprime aqui.* (For Spanish, click here.) Uh-huh. How many people have fallen for that? Click and ICE agents will be battering down your door, screaming, "*Muestrame tus manos!*" (Show me your hands!) The secretary now looks like he's saying, "Did you fuck my wife?"

He's completely rattled. He clicks on "Frequently Asked Questions and Suggested Answers."

"*How long does it take to become a U.S. citizen?*"

"*Who's asking?*"

"*José.*"

"*José? What kind of name is José? Relax, José. Just yanking your chain. Now I'm gonna ask you a few questions.*"

"Bueno."

"*No, no. English, José.*"

"Sí. *Yes.*"

"*That wasn't so hard, was it? So, José, are you in a position to make a donation?*"

"*Donation?*"

"If you're gonna repeat everything I say, we're gonna be here all day."

"Donation for . . ."

"The secretary's PAC. You see, José, the secretary is thinking of running for president. He would make a very good president. Don't you agree?"

"Oh, yes. Very good."

"You're a smart guy, José. I like you."

"Gracias. Thank you."

"I could even get to like you so much I might give you a green card. But that would depend on your donation."

This is not helpful. He's already a citizen. He just needs his replacement passport. And frankly, it seems a *bit* much that the secretary of state is hawking citizenship in exchange for campaign contributions.

"Iniquitous," he mutters. He uses archaic language when expressing indignation. He feels it gives it more oomph. "This is intolerable" or "This is beyond the limit of human endurance" are more attention getting than "This is unsatisfactory." Of course, the indignation has to be calibrated to the situation. Last week he told the pool guy that his failure to remove the dead frogs clogging the intake pump was "of a negligence unequaled in the annals of human history." The guy just stared. And nothing was accomplished by telling the so-called customer care representative in Mumbai who kept him on hold for twenty-seven minutes: "This is a monstrous villainy!" All it did was initiate an interminable spelling bee. "No, no, no. Not billany. *Villainy.* With a *V.* As in viceroy. Like Mountbatten. Your last English ruler. Hello? Hello?"

CHAPTER 19

He's very pleased with his Hungarian pig plot device. If you're looking to sow confusion and panic, there's nothing like a horde of squealing, flaming pigs. But he still has to get Roosevelt onto the U-boat. Spooked as they might be by the pigs, presidential bodyguards don't just abandon their principal because a herd of fiery swine is headed their way. While the Secret Service is trained to handle every eventuality, this particular scenario might not be in the manual. So far, no presidential assassination has involved flaming pigs, though the way things are going, the day may not be far off.

They'll want to get the president out of there. The road will be on fire, owing to the pigs. Helicopters haven't been invented yet. They'll have to evacuate him . . . by sea. Baruch's house is right on the water. And there's a dock. On the other hand, the Secret Service aren't likely to say, "Great, here's a Nazi U-boat. Let's put him on that."

The solution comes to him. A thing of beauty.

Exterior. Day. Naval shipyard, Kiel, Germany.

In the background, we see workers, ships, cranes, shipyardy-type things, cascades of sparks from welding torches, etc.

In the foreground are Heimlich; Grossadmiral Karl Dönitz, su-
preme commander of the Kriegsmarine (German Navy); and
naval architect Fritz Schmidt. They're studying a large blueprint.
Dönitz looks sour, as does architect Schmidt.

[*English subtitles*]

> HEIMLICH: It's not rocket science. I just need you to make
> the U-boat look like an American Coast Guard cutter.
>
> SCHMIDT (*exasperated*): It would be easier to make a Coast
> Guard cutter look like a U-boat.
>
> HEIMLICH: There's no need to get Hegelian.
>
> SCHMIDT (*angrily*): A cutter is a surface vessel. A U-boat
> is a submarine.
>
> HEIMLICH: Well, check out the big brain on Fritz.
>
> SCHMIDT: It's madness. It cannot be done.
>
> HEIMLICH: If you say so. But I don't think the führer is
> going to be pleased. As he says, there is no *jawohl* in
> N-E-I-N.
>
> SCHMIDT (*pleading*): I cannot overrule the laws of physics!
>
> HEIMLICH (*mimicking Alfonso Bedoya in* Treasure of the
> Sierra Madre): Physics? We don' need no stinkin' *phys-*
> *ics*. Schmitty. Chill. All you have to do is weld a few steel
> plates onto the U-boat. It doesn't have to be perfect. Do
> you think the Trojan horse actually looked like a horse?
> I don't think so.
>
> SCHMIDT: It will sink!
>
> HEIMLICH: It's supposed to sink. It's an *untersee*-boat. Not
> an *übersee*-boat. (*To Dönitz*) Admiral, am I right?

Dönitz sighs and gestures "Whatever."

SCHMIDT (*grumbling*): Perhaps an alloy of aluminum und molybdenum . . .

HEIMLICH (*grinning and slapping him on the back*): That's my *übermensch*. If more Germans had your attitude, this Reich might just last two thousand years. Now we're going to need a wheelchair ramp, and an elevator. I assume that's not a problem.

SCHMIDT: Why do you need those?

HEIMLICH: Well, it's kind of top secret, but I suppose there's no harm in telling you. Okay by you, Admiral?

Dönitz, past caring, gestures "Go ahead."

HEIMLICH (*continues*): See, we'll be transporting President Roosevelt. You didn't hear that from me. He can't walk. Polio. But look at what he's managed to accomplish. Pretty impressive, huh? Anyway, South Carolina to Bremerhaven is a schlep. So he'll need some space on deck get some sun and fresh air. Enemy ships permitting, of course.

SCHMIDT: A sundeck? On a U-boat?

HEIMLICH: It doesn't have to be fancy. Enough to accommodate a chaise longue, a card table, sun umbrella. A wet bar would be nice, but it's not a deal breaker. Oh, and space for a massage table. Before you go ballistic, it's not a luxury. He needs daily massage, for the circulation in the legs.

SCHMIDT (*snapping his pencil in two*): You want a cruise ship, not a U-boat!

HEIMLICH: Schmitty. We're talking basic amenities. He's an old guy and not in the best of health. We may be

Nazis, but we're not inhuman. (*To Dönitz*) Admiral? Am I right? (*Dönitz is rolling his eyes.*). Look, Schmitty, Roosevelt's no good to the führer dead. And do you think that would make the Americans happy? I don't think so. God forbid we should lose the war. We won't because the führer is the greatest leader who has ever lived. But *if* we did, do you think the American prosecutors at the war crimes tribunal will be impressed when you tell them (*imitating feeble voice*) "But there wasn't room for a massage table"?

DÖNITZ (*shaking his head*): Do as he asks.

HEIMLICH: Now, we're going to have to convert the officers mess into the presidential cabin, with en suite bath.

SCHMIDT: Where will the officers eat?

HEIMLICH: Standing up. Upside down. In the torpedo tubes. Do I look like I give a shit where the officers eat?

It's coming together beautifully. It's so satisfying when the individual pieces snap together with a click, like a jigsaw puzzle.

He takes a break and goes out to get the mail. No snake, and inside the mailbox is a hard, flat envelope. His passport. The gods are smiling today.

CHAPTER 20

He goes to the kitchen to make lunch. Jubal's wife, Angie, is there with Peaches. He loves Angie. He calls her Angina because when she and Jubal were courting, Jubal told her he loved her so much it made his heart hurt.

Angina is a boon companion in overweightness. They find mirth in their girth. She does hilarious impersonations of a fat shamer barking through a megaphone at passengers on a cruise ship. (She uses an actual megaphone.) *"Attention, fat family at the buffet! That's your third helping of shrimp! Leave some for the rest of us!"* Angina reminds him of the retro refrigerator magnets of 1950s housewives with captions like "If that's how babies are made, I'll adopt!" and "Honey, these *are* my big-girl panties."

Her complexion is florid, from either laughing or her noontime vodka and soda, or both. As she says, "If you don't start drinking before noon, you can't drink all day."

Peaches looks a bit grim about the mouth.

Angina greets him with a socially distanced air kiss. "And speak *of* the devil."

Peaches says, "Angie tells me everyone's talking about you." She adds an edgy "darling."

He senses this is not the time to trot out the Oscar Wilde chestnut about how the only thing worse than being talked about is not being talked about.

"Oh?" he says.

"Jubal was golfing the other day with Harry Chambless," Angina says. "Harry knows we're friends with y'all. He said to Jubal, 'That Yankee writer who wrote the titty movie they filmed on your plantation . . .'"

He groans. He has come to the kitchen to make lunch, not to listen to outdated, secondhand abuse about *Swamp Foxes*. Peaches says, "Go *on*, Angie."

"Harry said to Jubal, 'This fellow, is he all right in the head?' Jubal told him of course. And emphasized what a dear friend you are. Harry told him that you sent him a fifty-dollar donation for his coroner campaign. Which was nice, but was accompanied by a ten-page letter—"

"Eight pages," he says.

Angina is having a hard time containing herself. She's trying not to giggle, which only makes her jiggle like a Jell-O mold during a seismic event. "He said . . . he said . . . sorry . . . it's just . . ."

"Would you like a glass of water?" he says.

She takes a slug of vodka and soda. "Harry said, 'This *letter* he wrote me. It was *most* peculiar. It went on and on about his . . . his . . . *mole* problem. What does a coroner have to do with garden pests?'"

Angina, convulsing anew, dabs at her eyes with a tissue.

"Then he told Jubal, 'I don't want to say it was crazy, him being your friend, but this letter . . . it went on about how he'd discovered some flaw in his iPhone that was going to bring about another 9/11. He said I wasn't to worry about that. He would inform the Department of Homeland Security about it himself. He just wanted to put me quote-unquote in the picture. You can imagine that was a load offa my mind. He said the main reason he was writing me was to inform me that Bobby Babcock is violating the law. Shaking down taxpayers for campaign contributions. He told me Bobby ought to spend the next four years in prison, not the county coroner's office.'"

Angina is now in the throes of a full-blown bronchospasm and turning blue.

"Is this true?" Peaches asks him.

"Sweetheart. If you'll recall, you were the one who suggested I send Harry Chambless a donation."

Peaches sighs. Angina is eager to continue her narrative, despite her difficulty breathing.

"So then . . . Harry told Jubal . . . he got a phone call from you. Informing him . . . informing him . . . that Bobby . . . was running . . . television ads accusing Harry of being . . . a . . . third-generation . . . *war* profiteer."

Peaches says, "Please tell me she's exaggerating."

Angina wipes her eyes. "Well. By this point, Jubal didn't know *what* to say. He kept trying to change the subject. But Harry wasn't having any of that. 'There's more,' he told Jubal. 'He sent me this forty-page-long proposal for a giant *crematorium*. And then sent me a script for a television ad attacking Bobby. Claiming . . . Bobby was responsible for premature *burials*. In Pimento. Premature burials! And that Bobby drinks embalming fluid . . . and goes around tying morgue tags on people's . . . toes . . . while they're napping in hammocks. And the next thing they know . . . they're in a coffin . . . being lowered into the grave, banging on the coffin and shouting, "Let me out! I ain't dead! Let me out!"'"

Angina wheezes. "I said to Jubal, 'Well what did you *say* to Harry?' And he said, 'I didn't know what to say, so I said, 'You're up.'"

CHAPTER 21

Would you like to hear my side of it?" he asks after Angina has left.

"Not particularly," Peaches says, scrubbing a pot with unwonted vehemence.

"Are you saying I shouldn't have informed Chambless about the Babcock ads?"

Peaches pauses in midscrub. "You *saw* the ad? With your own eyes?"

"Of course. Do you think I'd make something like that up?"

"At this point, sweetheart, I'm not sure what I think. No one else has seen it. And what the fuck was that about the forty-page proposal for a crematorium? This is Pimento, not Auschwitz." Peaches resumes scrubbing so violently the Teflon may come off.

"If you'd stop yelling, darling, I'd be happy to discuss it. First of all, it was thirty pages, not forty."

"Oh, well, then never mind. That changes everything."

"Secondly, as you seem to be unaware, Pimento County is experiencing unprecedented growth as a retirement community. And retirees tend to die. We're looking at a 17 percent uptick in mortality over the next twenty years. I don't have the exact figures in front of me, but—"

"Stop. Or there's going to be an uptick in mortality in this house!"

"Hear me out, sweetheart. The aggregate funereal acreage in Pimento, comprising all three cemeteries, is 276 acres. Now that may sound like a lot, but I've done the math, and by my calculations, our cemeteries will be at capacity by 2046. If not sooner. So unless we start burying people vertically—feet down, head up—we're going to run out of space. What's the solution? More cemeteries? A lovely idea. I like cemeteries as much, if not more, than the next person. But retirees don't want cemeteries. They want golf courses. So, you tell me—what's Pimento going to do with all the bodies? Send them out to sea? Viking funerals? That's not going to work. Nasty leftover bits will be washing up on our beaches. Try selling that to the C of C. Darling, have you heard one word of what I've been saying?"

"No!" Peaches snarls, flinging the dish towel at the sink and opening her laptop. Her fingers go *rat-a-tat-tat* on the keys like the heels of a methedrine Flamenco dancer.

"Now," he continues, "any coroner worth his salt would have a plan on how to deal with this surge in human remains. But neither candidate has seen fit to address it, much less come up with a proposal. So I thought I'd have a crack at it. And whichever way I sliced and diced it, I kept returning to the same conclusion—enhanced crematory capacity."

"So, *you're* running for coroner? Is that it?"

"No. Frankly—and sad to say—I'm not sure a Yankee could get elected coroner down here. By the way, in the course of her Homeric recitation, Angina left out mention of the landscaped columbarium adjoining the crematoria complex. And if I may say, darling, I think it's in dubious taste to compare my white paper to the agenda at the Wannsee Conference. In fact, I think an apology is in order."

No apology is forthcoming, so he stomps off to his study, and again, a meal is sacrificed on the altar of his indignation. He puts aside hunger and sets about collecting evidence for his defense.

First he will listen to the rest of Bobby Babcock's phone call and transcribe it. He only got as far as Babcock saying he was "returning" his call.

He listens to it. Babcock's tone is not at all craven, the way people are when they're scraping for donations. He sounds rather agitated, in fact:

"Y'all called me a couple days ago and said Harry Chambless is running nasty TV ads against me. I have checked with every TV outlet between Charleston and the North Pole, and not one of 'em—not a *one*—has run any Harry ads. This being the case, I would very much appreciate an explanation from you. Running for public office is hard enough without this kind of harassment. And now I will say good day to you, sir."

Well, listen to Mr. Huffy. The gall of this man. That does it. Bobby Babcock will not be getting his vote. And what on earth is he talking about? He's never spoken to Babcock. Is the man demented? Who's harassing whom?

He googles to find the articles he's read in the local press about Harry and Bobby going at each other.

Nothing. How can this be? Weirder still, the only articles he can find make the coroner race sound like a pillow fight during a slumber party. In one, Harry calls Bobby "salt of the earth. A great Pimentoan. He's done a great job as coroner. I'm only running so he can get some rest."

Something is very, very wrong here. Babcock's voice mail is clear evidence that the man is a psychopath who should be caged.

Another article has Babcock gushing, "I've known Harry since high school. A finer man does not walk this earth. He'd give you the shirt off his back. The Chambless family has been handling our dear departed since the 1920s. Harry would make a terrific coroner. I'm just not quite ready yet to call it a day. I guess I just love handling dead folks."

What is going on? They're lobbing Hershey's Kisses at each other.

He googles again, this time using more precise search terms: "bitter contest," "ad hominem," "personal insults," "mano a mano," "repugnant," "undignified," "wife beater," "drunk," "tax cheat," "embalming fluid drinker."

Nothing! He stares at his laptop, as if it's going to say, "Kidding!" and show thousands of hits revealing the Pimento coroner race to be the nastiest in history, going all the way back to that earliest—"it's said"—European settlement. But it does not. He feels like Shelley Duvall in *The Shining*, flipping through page after page of Jack Nicholson's manuscript and finding a Proustian number of sentences saying, "All work and no play makes Jack a dull boy."

Then he realizes what's going on. Well, well, well.

He goes back to the kitchen. Peaches says without looking up, "You have a four o'clock appointment with Dr. Bhong in Charleston. Tomorrow."

"I'm afraid I've got some unsettling news, darling."

"What?" she says, still not looking up.

"Looks like the Russians are involved."

Peaches glares at him furiously. Then her expression softens, tone that of a mother speaking to a six-year-old who has just told her he's seen the bogeyman.

"What Russians, sweetheart? The ones in the submarine?"

"No, sweetheart. And could we forget about the fucking submarine? I'm talking about Russian intelligence. I'm talking about Vladimir Putin. He swung the election to Trump in 2016. Appears he's at it again."

"Okay. And *why* do you think this?"

Her iPhone rings.

"Fuck, it's Tub. I've got to . . . Tub? Call you back in three minutes. . . . Sweetheart, I'm not sure I follow. Are you saying Putin is . . . interfering in a coroner race? In South Carolina?"

"Walk with me," he says. He lays it out for her, in all its dreadful clarity. "Pimento is within fifty miles of not one but two U.S. military bases. God knows what Russian cloak-and-dagger stuff goes on, but Moscow would certainly want to have the local coroner or funeral home director in its pocket. They'd come in very handy when it comes time to dispose of the bodies. I've just discovered that they scrubbed the Internet of all the news stories about how Harry and Bobby hate each other, and substituted fake news stories depicting the race as a lovefest. How insidious is *that*?"

Peaches listens impassively. She says, "Well, it certainly sounds complicated. We need to tell Dr. Bhong all of this."

"Believe me, I plan to. What do you mean, we?"

"Together. I'm coming with you to Charleston."

"No, you're not. I'm not ten years old. I don't need Mommy to take me to the doctor, for heaven's sake."

"Sweetheart, I'm going with you."

"Then *I'm* not going."

Peaches finally relents—a rare occurrence. He congratulates himself, but suspects that this victory is due to the auction she has tomorrow. Personal effects of dead celebrities: an inflatable *Titanic* pool toy owned by Clive Cussler; Kirk Douglas's loincloth from *Spartacus*, and Honor Blackman's brassiere in *Goldfinger*. He'd bid on that.

Peaches is also stressed about what Tub has reported. Their brothers, Atticus and Dill, have conceived a plan to distract the Oaf Keepers "protecting" the statue of great-great-great-grandfather Ptarmigan. Atticus will pose as a brother Oaf Keeper from another chapter. He'll drive up to the town park in his pickup, announce that all Oafs are urgently needed in Blastonia, where Black Lives Matter protesters are trying to pull down the statue of segregationist hero Strom Thurmond. Atticus will lead the Oaf motorcade to Blastonia, while Dill removes the statue and replaces it with an identical-looking one of civil rights icon John L. Lewis. Atticus was a NASCAR racer. He'll lead the Oafs on a merry-goose chase, then leave them in the dust. They can then return to Sophia Springs and protect John L. Lewis.

He thinks it's a nifty plan, but Peaches is worried. "Lot of moving parts."

CHAPTER 22

He phones Dr. Paula in the morning to refill his Lysolo-quine. He tells her about his upcoming forced march to Charleston for psychiatric evaluation.

"My wife thinks I'm nuts."

Dr. Paula laughs. "Most wives think their husbands are. Not to pry, but why?"

He'll be getting down into these weeds later today with Dr. Bhong and doesn't feel like going into it all now.

"She seems to regard my interest in local politics as an indication of mental derangement."

"Well, politics these days do seem to be a cause of general derangement. Can you believe people are blaming the president for the pandemic? But don't get me started. How's our weight? Any sign of our ten little piggies?"

"I caught a fleeting glimpse yesterday of a toenail, but I had to hold in my stomach so hard I almost herniated myself."

"How's our appetite?"

"I would describe our appetite as robust."

"I cannot figure you out." Not an encouraging thing to hear from one's doctor. "You're on fifty milligrams a day. Okay, let's notch that up to sixty. I don't want to go too high while you're on the Lysoloquine."

"Did I see on TV that's the drug Trump is taking?"

"Uh-huh."

"Oh. The media made kind of a thing about it."

"The media. Don't get me started about them. They make a thing out of everything the president does. Jiminy Cricket, do they really think his fourteen physicians would let him take a drug that isn't safe? They really are enemies of the people."

"The president's doctors?"

"No, the media. Last night driving home I accidentally tuned into CNN. Within three minutes I was screaming at the car radio. Any unusual symptoms? Vertigo, hallucinations? Mental impairment?"

"Aside from caring about local elections, no."

"I'll call in the refill. Now, no stopping at the Hippo King on the way to Charleston. Or the way back. Promise?"

"Um . . . could be a problem. They're bringing out a new lunch sandwich. They're calling it the Tower of Babel Burger. *Seven* patties. I'm very excited."

Dr. Paula groans. "How do they serve it? On a gurney? Give my best to your toes. In the unlikely event you see them."

He packs an overnight bag for Charleston. It's a two-hour drive. His appointment is at four. He's not up to driving back to Pimento, so he'll stay over and return in the morning. Assuming Dr. Bhong doesn't commit him to the loony bin. A night in Charleston would be pleasant. There's very good eating there.

The prospect of a meal that isn't home cooked or from Hippo King is appealing after all these months.

Packing seems to have activated Peaches's maternal instincts. She hovers and fusses, as if he's headed off to his first time at sleepaway camp.

"Toothbrush?"

"Yes, darling."

"Meds?"

"Yes, darling."

"Shaving things?"

"*Yes*, darling." Is she going to ask if he packed calamine lotion for poison ivy?

"You're not wearing those pants, I hope."

"Why not?"

"Sweetheart. They look like you sleep in them. You can't go to Dr. Bhong looking like a homeless person. He's a smart dresser."

"Is the purpose of my visit a wardrobe consultation?"

"No, but you don't have to look slovenly. Don't you want to make a good impression?"

"You're kidding, right?"

"Suit yourself." She adds tenderly, "I'll miss you."

"It's one night, darling. But I'll miss you, too."

"Will you call me after and tell me how it went?"

"Certainly not."

"Why?"

"Darling, he's a shrink, not a dentist."

"So?"

"Okay. I'll call. *'Darling, you were so right. Dr. Bhong is a genius. He figured it all out right away. It all goes back to when I blinded Dad's horses and set fire to the barn.'*"

Peaches stares. "Whoa. Where did *that* come from?"

"*Equus*. Movie."

"That is just sick."

"A bit judgmental, but stipulated, the lad did seem to have some issues."

"I'm not sure you're going into this with the right attitude."

"Darling, the only reason I am 'going into this' is to keep you from staging an intervention. Every morning, I hold my breath when I enter the kitchen, expecting to find everyone I've known since childhood, including Miss Mahar, waiting to tell me, 'We're here because we love you.'"

Where did that come from? He hasn't thought of Miss Mahar in ages. Ah, Miss Mahar, of the tight black sweaters and always a bit of white bra strap showing at the collarbone.

"Who's Miss Mahar?" Peaches says.

"She taught ninth-grade English. But I remember her for other reasons."

"Like what?"

"I'll leave it at that."

"Are you telling me you had sex with your ninth-grade teacher?"

"Darling, are you jealous of something that happened forty years before we met?"

"I'm not jealous. I'm appalled."

"I'll be sure to mention your umbrage to Dr. Bhong."

"Please do. Along with your loony—"

"Should I tell him about blinding Dad's horses?"

"Stop. I'm suggesting you tell him about accusing Bobby Babcock of burying people alive. We're lucky he's not suing us. And about your proposal for a Nazi crematorium in Pimento. And about Putin interfering in the fucking coroner race."

"Seems rather a lot to hit the poor man with on the first date."

"If you don't tell him, I will."

"Kibitzing with your spouse's psychiatrist? Is that ethical?"

"Sweetheart. Just be honest with him. That's all I'm asking. I'm worried about you. And I'm not the only one."

"Okay. Will do."

"Thank you. Are you sure you're okay to drive?"

He sighs. "What can you possibly mean?"

"You haven't driven anywhere other than the HK since March."

"Are you worried I've forgotten which side of the road Americans drive on? Remind me—which pedal is the gas? The one on the left?"

"I'm just saying you haven't driven any distance since your seventy-five-thousand-dollar-a-year concierge doctor put you on God knows what pills." Peaches sighs. "Sorry. I'm in knots about the fucking statue. I wish it would just sink into the earth and disappear."

"When is Operation Bait and Switch taking place?"

"Tonight."

"Well, I'm sure it'll go fine. It's a good plan."

His darling looks worried. He gives her a hug.

"Tell you what. I'll call you after I see Dr. Bhong. But only to hear how it went with the statue. What I tell Dr. Bhong about my initiation into bliss in the arms of Miss Mahar stays between him and me."

"You're such an asshole."

"I love you, too." And he does.

CHAPTER 23

He has not forgotten how to drive. Hooray. He feels like Lewis and Clark, setting out to cross a continent. Nothing like the open road to clear the head. (Technically Dr. Bhong's job.)

Hobcaw looms on his left as he drives across the bridge. He can make out the dock where Heimlich's ersatz Coast Guard cutter will take Roosevelt aboard. What a scene that's going to be. Hundreds of flaming pigs, driving the presidential party into the waiting arms of Heimlich and his elite commandos. There remains the problem of how to separate the president from his elite protectors. Maybe Dr. Bhong will have an idea. For $350 an hour, he should.

He's thinking it might be prudent to get the animal rights folks on board before the start of principal photography. To establish bona fides and gin up some "pay it forward" goodwill.

Is there a separate organization for the ethical treatment of swine? He asks Siri to dial up whatever she can find. Very helpful, Siri. Never complains and knows the location of every Hippo King in North America.

He explains the nature of his call to a series of increasingly huffy staffers and is finally put through to the person in charge of "motion picture and television humanitarian compliance," a Ms. Horrocks. He explains why he's calling and mentions that the inspiration for the flaming pigs came from Hannibal.

"Hannibal Lecter?" Ms. Horrocks says.

"Hannibal Barca. The great Carthaginian general. Second Punic War. Ring a bell?"

"No."

"Alas, the demise of the core curriculum. Being a classically educated German, Heimlich—the hero, or antihero, whatever— would know all about Hannibal. He probably even read about him in Latin, though my script doesn't go into that."

"I don't care who came up with the idea of setting animals on fire. It's barbaric."

"No argument there, ma'am. *Res ipsa loquitur*. Those Carthaginians played rough. And not just with cattle. It can't have been a picnic for Hannibal's elephants, crossing the Alps."

"I don't understand what you're getting at. I assume this despicable scene will be done with computer-generated imaging."

"Ah. That's kind of why I'm calling, ma'am."

"Would you please stop calling me 'ma'am'? What do you mean?"

"If it were up to me, I would absolutely prefer to do it with CGI."

"What's *that* supposed to mean?"

"I'm only the writer. The writer is the least important person involved. Do you know the one about the Polish actress who went to Hollywood and slept with the writer?"

"What?"

"She slept with the writer. Get it?"

"No."

"A smart actress would sleep with the producer or director. Old industry joke."

"I don't find it funny. I find it highly offensive. Along with everything else you're telling me."

"Are you Polish? I certainly didn't intend any offense. The Polish people have no apologies to make in the brains department. Copernicus was Polish. Chopin. Madame Curie. Pope John Paul II—"

"I am not Polish! That has nothing to do with it. As regards your twisted, disgusting, sadistic movie, I will insist on written assurance that real animals will not be used."

Listen to Miss Bossyboots.

"Believe me, *Ms.* Horrocks, I'm on your side. But it's the director's call. Thing is, the director that the studio has in mind is—I guess you'd call him 'old school.'"

"I have no idea what you're talking about."

"He's big on naturalism. Did you see his remake of *The Charge of the Light Brigade*?"

"No."

"Probably not your cup of tea. He got a bit of flak for it. Actually, quite a lot of flak. But what can you expect, with six hundred horses and live artillery? It wasn't pretty, but it's a hell of a movie. Anyway, I just wanted to reach out and put you in the picture. So to speak. So if we end up across a conference table from each other in a lawyer's office, we won't have to scream quite so loudly."

Ms. Horrocks does not end the call on a note of reciprocal courtesy. But she won't be able to claim she was blindsided. A worthwhile call. He mentally crosses "Mollify Animal Rights People" off his to-do list. And what do you know, the whole time he was talking to Ms. That's Not Funny, he drove right past the HK. He feels as virtuous as a Trappist monk.

Less virtuous as he executes a deft, even daring, U-turn. But it's lunchtime, and it's two hours to Charleston, most of it through swamp, on roads with names like Dead Horse Lane and Dismal Way. Break down out there, and you could die of starvation. After being sodomized by banjo-strumming, toothless hillbillies.

He expected greatness in HK's new Tower of Babel Burger, and he is not disappointed. Hippo King just keeps taking the burger concept to the next level. The Tower of Babel is more than a lunch sandwich. It's nothing less than a paradigm shift. Its only drawback is that his stomach is now pressing so tightly against the steering wheel that it's hard to steer. He has to use both hands. But it's good upper-arm exercise, and fortunately the roads are mostly straight.

He crosses the Wandoodree River. There on the far side is the familiar sign, Itchfield Plantation. Driving past it never fails to stir a jambalaya of mixed emotions. But there's no other road between Pimento and Charleston, unless you go through Mingo's Corner, which adds thirty miles and takes you past a depressing federal prison and an Air Force bombing range with signs every ten feet saying that you *really* don't want to trespass here.

He arrives in Charleston and checks into the Congaree Inn. It's a bit off the grid. He chose it because he'd rather not bump into someone he knows, which would mean having to lie about why he's in town. The Congaree is more or less as advertised on Travelocity: courtyard and fountain in front; courtyard and fountain out back; lobby ceiling embedded with twinkly lights to simulate the Milky Way; dimly lit bar from which waft saxo-phone notes of mellow jazz and the decadent *ch-ch-ch-ch-ch-ch* of cocktails being shaken in the middle of a weekday afternoon. He remembers someone telling him that the Congaree is a popular trysting spot. But like the Marquis de Lafayette, he has not come to get laid.

CHAPTER 24

Dr. Bhong is less fearsome in the flesh than in the imagination: mustard-colored, fifty-something, soft-faced, shiny bald pate, rimless specs, and gratifyingly plump. He, too, may not have seen his ten little piggies lately. And what a lovely touch, the plate of oven-warm chocolate chip cookies next to the box of pastel-colored tissues for his patients to sob into as he leads them gently by the hand from one repressed memory to the next.

"Do you mind if I ask where you're from? Your surname is sort of exotic."

"Not at all. Pakistan. But I have been here ages."

"Pakistan? No kidding. Fascinating place."

"You've been?"

"I almost went, once."

Wow, fascinating. No doubt Dr. Bhong is dying to hear more about how you almost *went to Pakistan. Or is it too good a story to waste? Better to save it for the memoir. "And then there was the time I almost went to Pakistan. I remember as if it were yesterday . . ."*

"Sorry. You were saying?"

"You were telling me that you almost went to Pakistan."

"The financing fell through at the last minute, so we shot it in Mexico instead."

Dr. Bhong has that look Peaches gets when she's about to

ask him who's president. "Did you have to change the villain's name to Osama bin Gonzalez?"

"Sorry? Ah. Very good. Sorry, bit slow on the uptake. I'm a little frazzled these days. Lot going on."

"Would you like to tell me about it?"

"Okay, but I'm not sure it's as fascinating as the time I almost went to Pakistan. Let's see. There's the screenplay."

"What an interesting business you're in. Is it going well, your screenplay?"

"It's going slowly. It was going gangbusters until I got caught up in this fucking—sorry . . ."

Dr. Bhong smiles benevolently. "You'll have to work much harder than that to offend me. What is the fucking thing that's got you caught up?"

"Local politics. Coroner race."

Dr. Bhong frowns nonjudgmentally. "Coroner as in the person who determines cause of death and issues the certificate and such?"

"Uh-huh. Believe me, Doc, it was never my intention to get involved. But I am now. Am I ever."

"Interesting. How did this come about?"

"I didn't even know they had elections for coroner. One morning I'm dealing with a poisonous snake when I see this lawn sign. Anyway, that's how it started."

Dr. Bhong nods. "I'm glad you escaped snakebite."

"I imagine you've got some pretty hairy snakes in Pakistan. I thought coroners were appointed. But one of the many things I've learned in the course of this saga is that people campaign to be coroner. And it's every bit as nasty as any other campaign. Politics red in tooth and claw, you might say."

"Tell me more. I'm interested."

"Lordy. Where to begin?"

"Wherever you begin is the beginning."

"Well, I don't want to sound paranoid. I imagine you get enough of that in this line of work."

"What is it that would make me think you're paranoid?"

"I feel like I'm in an Alfred Hitchcock movie. Are you familiar with his work?"

"I've seen many of his movies." Dr. Bhong smiles. "I hope we're not talking about *Psycho*."

"Nah. I had Mother cremated, not stuffed. And I haven't stabbed anyone in the shower. Not my thing."

"As they say down here, that is a load offa my mind."

"I feel like I'm . . . running from biplanes, dangling from a window ledge, being thrown off Mount Rushmore. I wouldn't complain if Grace Kelly or Ingrid Bergman were in love with me. But the rest pretty much sucks. Anxiety making."

"I shouldn't want to be thrown off Mount Rushmore myself. Why do you think someone is intending you harm?"

"Russians don't typically intend you *well*."

"Russians?"

"Uh-huh. Turns out they're involved. I only just found out."

"Involved in . . . ?"

"The election."

"The presidential election?"

"Oh, I'm sure they're up to their Slavic armpits in that, too. Making America even greater. But no, I'm talking about the local election."

"I'm still not sure I understand. I apologize for being obtuse."

"You're in good company, Doc. No one understands. Frankly? I'm not sure they want to."

"Understand what, exactly?"

"That the Russians are trying to install Harry Chambless as coroner."

"Ah. I see. And why do they want Mr. Chambless to be coroner?"

"To dispose of the bodies. We've got two military bases in Pimento County. You know what goes on in those places. Who better to help you get rid of the bodies than the guy who owns the biggest funeral home in the county? The Arthur T. Chambless Funeral Home. Founded in 1927, by Harry's grandfather. I bet Grampa's rotating in his grave."

"Are you saying that Russians are killing American military personnel?"

"Maybe not yet. But when it comes to that, which it always does, they'll want to have their man in place, so he can say, 'Never mind the bullet hole in the middle of his forehead. He died of natural causes.'"

"I see. The plot thickens, as they say."

"Mind you, Doc, I'm not saying that Harry Chambless wouldn't be an improvement over the current coroner, Bobby Babcock. The man's a mass murderer."

"He is?"

"See? *You* don't even know about it. That's not a criticism. No one knows. Why? Because the Pimento media is ignoring it. It's like in *Jaws*. The mayor who's terrified tourists will stay away if they admit that a huge shark is eating everyone. The Pimento economy depends a lot on Yankee retirees. If it gets out that the coroner is burying them alive . . . Think that might put a damper on immigration? 'Welcome to Pimento. Proudly burying people alive since 2016.'"

"Yes," Dr. Bhong says. "I imagine that would have a dampening effect."

"There's been a huge spike in premature burials thanks to Bobby. People are afraid to take a nap in their hammock, for fear they'll wake up on a slab in the morgue with a toe tag. Or worse, as their coffin's being lowered into the earth. *And no one wants to talk about it.* You bring it up and they go, 'Oh? Really? Fascinating. Can I freshen your drink?' It's very frustrating, Doc."

"It must be, yes."

"I'm not looking for medals. I'm just trying to be a good citizen. I love it here."

He leaves Dr. Bhong's office feeling ten pounds lighter, even after eating the entire plate of his excellent chocolate chip cookies. His darling was right. Dr. Bhong is wonderful. He *listens.* And doesn't ask you who's president. The fifty minutes flew by. And he is very much looking forward to their next session. Dr. Bhong wants to see him three times a week. He feels validated. Dr. Bhong gets that Pimento is in denial about the Russians. And about the premature burial crisis. He also clearly understands about the urgent need to expand crematorium capacity. And he loves the premise of *Heimlich's Maneuver.* What a find, this guy.

He celebrates at the Congaree's bar with a Negroni, the delicious, if somewhat lethal, cocktail of vodka (or gin), Campari, vermouth, and slice of orange. Ambrosia, or whatchamacallit, ichor, the stuff that flowed in the veins of the Olympian gods, never tasted this good. Peaches doesn't allow him to have them at home ever since he went to sleep on the billiard table during their fund-raiser for turtle rescue.

He calls her from the bar, all chirpy about how right she was about Dr. Bhong. She sounds down.

"Everything okay, sweetheart? How'd the auction go?"

"Pussy Galore's brassiere was the high lot. Kirk Douglas's

loincloth didn't meet the reserve price. And no one bid on Clive Cussler's squeezy *Titanic* toy."

"Bummer. No surprise about the brassiere. I had such a jones for Honor Blackman when I was fourteen."

"Did it make your cougar English teacher jealous?"

"Me-ow. Darling, I think you're the one who's jealous."

"It's been a for-shit day. The statue thing went south. Big time."

He'd forgotten about the statue.

"The Oaf Keepers aren't quite as dumb as they look. Somewhere between Sophia Springs and Blastonia, they figured out they were being taken for a ride and that Black Lives Matter wasn't toppling the Strom Thurmond statue. They weren't happy about it."

"How did they figure it out?"

"Maybe they googled on the way to Blastonia. There were six carloads of them: guns, bellies, beards. They looked like a delegation of fucking Taliban. They kept trying to run Atticus off the road and box him in. Thank God he used to race NAS-CAR. Fuckers chased him all the way to Spartanburg."

"Spartanburg? Holy camoly."

"Atticus figured it best to keep going, instead of pulling over and getting beaten to death. It became a regular highway sensation. By the time they got to Spartanburg, half a dozen South Carolina state troopers had joined in, plus a helicopter. It's all over the news."

"Well," he says, "as Clausewitz said, no battle plan survives first contact with the enemy."

"Dill swapped out the colonel's statue with the John L. Lewis one. For God's sake, don't mention that to anyone. The Oaf Keepers Facebook and Instagram feeds are full of death threats. Atticus ain't coming home anytime soon. He's thinking this might be a good time to visit Easter Island. I'm glad it went well with Dr. Bhong. I knew you'd like him. He's really perceptive. Were you honest with him?"

"Yes, darling."

"About the Russians and the premature burials?"

"Yes, darling. And he's appalled at what's going on. He was particularly horrified about the premature burials."

"I'm sure he was."

"He wants to see me three times a week."

"Really? Well, uh, great. Where are you? I hope you're not in some crowded restaurant."

"I'm at the hotel bar, which is practically empty. And speaking of being honest, guess what I'm having? A Negroni."

Peaches laughs. "You earned it."

"I wish you were here. We could order room service and watch *Swamp Foxes*."

"I wish I were there, too. If you're drinking Negronis, don't drive. Order room service."

"Yes, darling."

"I love you."

"Love you, too. I'll be home well before lunch."

CHAPTER 25

Back in Charleston a few days later, he tells Dr. Bhong, "My wife sends her best. She thinks you walk on water."

Dr. Bhong pats his tummy.

"She is far too kind, but with my belly I wouldn't dare walk on anything less solid than reinforced concrete. How is your appetite? Has this pandemic affected your eating habits?"

He chuckles. "I don't seem to have lost my sense of taste."

"What about blood pressure? Are you having regular checkups? Cholesterol, PSA levels, and the rest? The dreaded colonoscopy?"

"I've got a new doctor. The last one dropped dead of a heart attack. Training for a marathon."

"You seem amused."

"May he rest in peace, the man was a Nazi. If I gained three pounds, he'd go, '*We better have a discussion about diabetic blindness and amputation.*' He was a lot of fun. Best he's no longer here, to see me now. He'd have another heart attack."

"Your new doctor, has he done a thorough workup?"

"She. Dr. Paula. No, but we're definitely going to do that soon as things calm down."

"It's none of my business, but it does seem a bit unusual that she hasn't done one. Given your . . . physical situation."

"Physical situation, Doc?"

Dr. Bhong laughs. "I think we both know what I mean."

"Have you been talking to Peaches?"

"No. Nor would I. Why do you ask?"

"She doesn't approve of my new doctor, either."

"I didn't say I don't approve of her. Why does your wife not?"

"She's a concierge doctor."

"Ah. Yes, some people have difficulty with the concept."

"She thinks they're mercenaries in white gowns. Between you and me—"

"Not to interrupt, but I want to be clear: everything you and I discuss is 'between you and me.'"

"Roger that. Thank you. Not to sound catty, but I suspect my darling also doesn't like the fact that Dr. Paula is easy on the eyes. But she's highly qualified. Believe me, I'm not paying her seventy-five hundred dollars a year to stare at her tits. Sorry, that came out coarsely."

"Do you think your wife is jealous of Dr. Paula?"

"No. It's just . . . in my previous marriage, I wasn't what you'd call a model of fidelity. And I regret that. I really do. I was an asshole. But that was then. Peaches is the only girl for me now. I barely notice when a babe walks by. And anyway, what babe on this planet would be remotely attracted to a fat, old blob like me?"

"If you say."

"I do say. The only wet dreams I have these days are about HK's latest menu addition. Sad, I stipulate. Pathetic, even. But it does make life *so* much simpler."

"Have you and Dr. Paula discussed your weight?"

"Oh yeah. She'd have me on a diet of kale smoothies if she

had her way. But that's the advantage of having a concierge doctor. For seventy-five hundred a year, you've got leverage. She put me on these appetite"—he makes air quotes—"suppressants."

"Why the . . . ?" Dr. Bhong mimics his hand gesture.

"They don't seem to suppress much. But they do give you an energy boost. She says it sometimes takes a while for them to seep into the bloodstream."

"What's the name of the medication?"

"Nal-trex-o-something."

"Naltrexone. Contrave."

"That's it. Do you take it?"

"Heavens, no. I'm not a fan of those drugs. Are you on any other medications?"

"The usual. Antihypertensive pills. Anticholesterol pills. Anti-Covid pills . . ."

"Anti-Covid?"

"It's got this endless name, like one of those German compound nouns. Do you know the word 'Schlimmbesserung'?"

"No."

"Fabulous word. A solution that makes the problem worse."

"That is a good word."

"Lysolo-something."

Dr. Bhong's eyes widen. "Lysoloquine?"

"There you go."

Dr. Bhong frowns. "It's not my place to second-guess your doctor, but that's an antimalarial drug."

"What happened is, some weeks ago, I was in the drive-through at the HK and the guy handing me my food sneezed. We're not talking a normal, human, achoo-type sneeze. I was drenched. It's a miracle I'm here to tell the tale. So, she put me on it. Then one night on the news Trump says he's taking it.

I called Dr. Paula and said, 'Look, this isn't about politics, but frankly this is not confidence inspiring.' She said stop worrying. I said okay, but I draw the line at injecting Clorox or shoving a lightstick up my ass."

"Well," Dr. Bhong says. "I hope you and Dr. Paula don't wait too long on the physical. So, I've been thinking about our talk last week, particularly the coroner election. And I wanted to run something by you. Do you think your interest in it might be connected to your own feelings about death? You are at an age when a person quite naturally thinks about mortality. And on top of that, this dreadful pandemic has us all thinking about end-of-life issues."

"Could be. Wouldn't rule it out. You're very perceptive, Doc. But that doesn't change the fact that the Russians are trying to install Harry Chambless as coroner. And that Babcock's been burying people alive."

Dr. Bhong stares.

"The way I see it, Doc, I'm doubly fucked."

"How so?"

"I've managed to make enemies of both Chambless *and* Babcock. Damn fine, job, Bob.

"Who's Bob?"

"Not important. I'm the guy who called bullshit on the premature burials. I'm the guy who figured out about Harry's cozy little arrangement with Putin. You don't think Babcock's itching to sign my death certificate? That the Chambless funeral home wouldn't love to get their mitts on my corpse? I told all this to Peaches. Which I regret, because now *she's* in danger."

"What did she say?"

"What she always says. 'Who's president?'"

"That must be frustrating for you."

"Actually, she no longer asks me that. Now she says, 'Be sure to mention that to Dr. Bhong.' So here I am, mentioning it. By the way, Doc, these cookies are out of this world. Do you make them yourself?"

"Can't you tell from my waistline? I add a pinch of cardamom."

"Cardamom. I *knew* it! Stunning. You missed your true calling."

Dr. Bhong asks if he'll answer a few "general questions," to establish a "baseline."

"Fire away," he says, reaching for another cookie.

"What do you think is meant by the saying, 'One swallow doesn't make a summer?'"

"Sounds borderline pervy, if you don't mind my saying."

"How about this one: People who live in glass houses shouldn't throw stones."

"I'd say that people who live in glass houses should plan on spending a lot of time wiping bird brains off the walls."

"Ah?"

"Birds are always flying into our glass. I put Post-it notes on the glass doors and windows. But they still fly into them. They're kamikazes. It's awful, but what can you do? You can try to intercept them with stones, but that's a full-time proposition. And you have to live your life, right? It's off-putting for your guests. They like to be welcomed in, made comfortable, handed a drink, not stones, and told, 'Incoming! Starling, two o'clock!' You won't have guests after a while. And no wonder."

Dr. Bhong seems pleased with the answer and asks him to count backward from one hundred in increments of seven.

"Why seven? Why not four?"

Dr. Bhong likes that, too. He says he's going to name five

objects. They'll continue to chat, then he'll ask him to repeat the five objects, in order. He names five. They talk about how Philip Johnson the architect must have hated birds.

Dr. Bhong asks him to name the objects. Without hesitating, he says, "Adolf, Hitler, is, the, führer." Dr. Bhong looks blown away. Psychiatrists try not to reveal what they're thinking, but it's obvious that Dr. Bhong is impressed by his power of recall.

Later, at the Congaree's bar, sometime between the second and third Negroni, he realizes that the five words he told Dr. Bhong were from his screenplay. *Fuck!* No wonder he looked blown away.

He phones him, gets his voice mail.

"Doc," he says. "It's me, Adolf-Hitler-is-the-führer. Don't worry. I'll explain when I see you."

He hangs up and reaches for his Negroni. The bartender is staring, and he, too, looks blown away.

CHAPTER 26

Thank you for your call the other night," Dr. Bhong says at the start of their next session. "I confess I had been wondering how 'apple, biscuit, oven, teapot, pencil' turned into 'Adolf, Hitler, is, the, führer.'"

"I understand that may have set off a few alarm bells." He explains about the screenplay.

"There's this great scene at the Eagle's Nest, Hitler's place in the Bavarian Alps. The gang's all there. The war's not going well, so on top of the Sturm und Drang, he wants to project some mental health, to buck up the boys. So he tells them that his concierge doctor, Theodor Morell, gave him the same kind of mental test you gave me. And tells them that he aced it by remembering the five words 'Adolf, Hitler, is, the, führer.' His toadies go, 'Ooh, that is *so* impressive!' But what they're really thinking is, '*This Reich isn't going to last until Tuesday, never mind a thousand years.*' I guess my wires got a bit crossed. Anyway, sorry. Didn't mean to give you a start."

Dr. Bhong smiles. "What a complex process it must be, writing a movie script."

"It's not rocket science. You throw balls up in the air and try not to let them hit you on the head on the way down."

"It interests me that you referred to Hitler's physician as his concierge doctor."

"I did?"

"Yes."

"Interesting. Would that be a Freudian slip?"

Dr. Bhong smiles. "You tell me."

"I'll take a mulligan. I certainly didn't mean to equate Hitler's quack with Dr. Paula. Whatever her politics. Meanwhile, scriptwise, I'm having a hard time figuring out how to get President Roosevelt onto my guy Heimlich's U-boat."

"You certainly do have many balls in the air. You said just now 'my guy, Heimlich.' I take it he's the German commando who is kidnapping President Roosevelt?"

"A good man in a bad cause. I go to considerable length in act 1 to establish his fundamental moral and ethical decency."

Dr. Bhong smiles. "There's another load offa of my mind. It's not easy to make a hero out of a Nazi."

"Did you know that Nazi was a derogatory term?"

"Well, yes. I think that's pretty well established."

"No, I mean it was a derogatory term in Germany. Back then. Nazis didn't call each other Nazis. It meant 'idiot' or 'dolt.' It actually predates Hitler. It's a hypocorism—a pet name—from *Ignatz*. Bavaria, southern Germany, was very Catholic. Ignatius was a common name. Northern Germans looked down on Bavarians as bumpkins. An *Ignatz* was a dumb peasant. So, when the National Socialist German Workers' Party movement started up in Bavaria, their opponents called them Nazis. It's also a phonetic abbreviation of *Nationalsozialistische Deutsche Arbeiterpartei*. How's that for a mouthful? You might even say it was the N-word of its day. Sorry. Didn't mean to prattle. Peaches hates it when I do that. Where were we?"

"Heimlich."

"Right. I've become kind of fond of the guy. I'm thinking he should have a road-to-Damascus moment. On the U-boat, on the way back to Germany with FDR. A *what-the-fuck-am-I-doing?* moment of clarity. The action takes place in the spring of 1944, so theoretically, he could then hook up with Stauffenberg and his crew, in the plot to blow up Hitler."

"That would certainly make him more likable. You can't do better, redemptionwise, than assassinating the führer."

"You like the idea?"

Dr. Bhong laughs. "Yes. But I've no qualifications as a film scenarist. I like the road-to-Damascus moment, but if it takes place in the middle of the Atlantic, the road's going to be rather wet, won't it? What will he do after he sees the light? I suppose he could escape on a life raft with President Roosevelt, but wouldn't that make the U-boat crew wonder?"

"I haven't worked that out. First, I need Heimlich and FDR to do some male bonding."

"Ah. A buddy movie."

"The pitch to the studio would be: 'He set out to kidnap a president. Instead, he found a friend.'"

"I like that. I must say, you make me grateful I don't depend for my livelihood on writing movies. I'd weigh a lot less than I do now."

"That's not the hard part."

"Oh?"

"The hard part is not strangling the producer who says he loves your idea but adds, 'Does it have to be Roosevelt?'"

"Does that happen often?"

He chortles bitterly. "'Does it have to be World War II? Why not the War of the Spanish Succession? Brad Pitt's dying to play the duke of Alba.'"

"That must be frustrating."

"I should have listened to my dad and gone into the business."

"What did he do?"

"Insulation. Roofing. My brother took it over. He's done very well."

"Beneath your frustration, I sense satisfaction, even passion, when you talk about your work. I think you like to tell stories."

"Oh, it has its moments, sure. Sitting there for the first time, looking up at the screen and hearing words you wrote come out of an actor's mouth—that's something you don't forget. Even after forty years of 'Does it have to be Roosevelt?' Remember what Hitler's original title was for *Mein Kampf*?"

"No."

"*My Four-and-a-Half-Year Struggle Against Lies, Stupidity, and Cowardice.* Everyone needs an editor. Even Hitler."

"Well, there's your next movie. Hitler's editor. So, our time is up. With your permission, I'd like to touch base with Dr. Morell."

"He's, uh, kind of dead, Doc."

Dr. Bhong blushes a deeper shade of Dijon.

"I can't believe I said that. Profound apologies. I meant Dr. Paula."

He grins. "Guess we're one-up on Freudian slips. What do you want to talk to her about?"

"The meds she's got you on. Your general health. Would you be okay with that? I promise not to call her Dr. Morell."

"Sure. I mentioned to her that Peaches was shipping me off to have my head examined."

"Also, with your consent, I'd like to have a few tests done. Have you ever had an MRI or CAT scan or PET scan?"

"Sounds like more than a few."

"Sorry. Didn't mean to hurl the entire alphabet at you. Each test measures different things. I just want to cover all the bases."

"We on a tumor hunt, Doc?"

"No. That is, not necessarily. Just a thorough neuropsychological evaluation. You've got an interesting engine. I want to have a look under the hood."

"Well, if you think it . . ."

"Thank you. I'll pull together some dates, and we can discuss it next time."

"Great," he says, but he's thinking, *Fuck, fuck, fuck, fuck, fuck.* Five words he'll remember, in order.

CHAPTER 27

'N other?"

"Why not?"

His plan had been to drive home to Pimento after today's session with Dr. Bhong. But he's so staggered by all this testing, he found himself in urgent need of Dutch courage. It's obvious what Dr. Bhong thinks is going on. The D-word. Dementia. And now that he's on his second—or is it his third?—Negroni, he's thinking that driving back to Pimento tonight might not be the smart move. He calls his darling.

"Hey, babe."

"Hey, sweetheart. How did it go with Dr. Bhong?"

"Great. Listen, my stomach's having some kind of issue. I had oysters for lunch, and they may be planning an uprising. I'd rather not be in a car in the dark on Dead Horse Road in the Francis Marion national swamp. Think I'll spend the night here."

"Oh, sweetheart. I'm so sorry. Want me to drive down?"

"Thanks, but this kind of misery doesn't really want company."

"Is everything else okay? You sound down."

"I'm good. Except for the uppity oysters. That would make a good name for a raw bar. The Uppity Oyster."

"Sweetheart, 'uppity' doesn't have a real good resonance down here."

"Good point. A raw bar in Connecticut, then."

"Eat some crackers, drink fizzy water, and get into bed."

"Will do."

"Remember, Angie and Jubal are coming for dinner tomorrow."

He groans. "Is that wise, babe?"

"Angie swears she's been sheltering in place."

He snorts. "You know I love Angina. But the last time that girl sheltered in place was in her mother's womb. She's more social than socialism."

"I made her swear to get tested. And to get Jubal tested."

"Fat chance. The only sheltering Jube's done is at the Tuna, with his two hundred closest friends. And not a one of them masked."

"Angie promised."

"Okay. But if it turns out to be the Last Supper, it's on you "

"If I put on my hazmat suit and do the shopping, will you make your spaghetti carbonara? Angie specifically asked for it."

"Babe, please can we not talk about food right now?"

But it's not food, or Covid. It's the thought of dinner with his wife and their two best friends after learning he's got dementia.

"Go to bed, sweetheart. Call me if you need me. Love you."

"Love you, too."

Dewey, the bartender, brings his third—or is it fourth?—Negroni. He's been tipping Dewey lavishly since the night he overheard him telling Dr. Bhong's voice mail that Adolf Hitler is the führer. The tips seem to have reassured Dewey that his new regular customer isn't going to pull out a Luger and demand he join him in a toast to the Third Reich.

"Ready for some devils on horseback?"

Dewey's a good barkeep, attentive, proactive. His new regular can't get enough of the Congaree's grilled bacon-wrapped prunes. He also likes their jalapeño poppers. He had two orders last time. He likes the Cajun shrimp popcorn, too. And the Wagyu sliders with onion and pear chutney. Really, there's not much on the Congaree bar food menu the gentleman doesn't like.

"Why not?" he tells Dewey.

"Double order?"

"Why not?"

"Coming up."

It's a slow night, like most these days. Covid must have a dampening effect on adulterous libidos. But one couple is clearly enjoying itself, illicitly or otherwise, in a booth.

Dewey senses he's feeling down tonight. He stations himself nearby and polishes the already-polished glasses.

"So, what's bringing you to Charleston these days?"

"Hmm? Oh. Work."

"What line are you in?"

Dewey seems like a nice lad, but he's not in the mood for a chat. But he doesn't want to seem rude.

"IRS." *Been reporting those big tips I've been leaving you, Dewey?*

"Yeah? Cool. Let me go check on your devils."

Solitude. *Ahh.* He's musing about mortality. He's sixty-eight, his predicted life expectancy when he was born in 1952. Someone told him an interesting thing. It goes like this: Of all Americans, going back to the Revolution, who have lived to the age of sixty-five, half of them are alive today. Now we live to be old enough for our brains to turn into cream of wheat. We used to call it senility. *"Okay, kids, listen up. Gramps is senile. It's not his fault. If he says something weird like 'Adolf Hitler is the führer,' just ignore it."*

It occurs to him that he's a cliché: the sad guy alone at the bar, staring into his drink. The huge TV over the bar is on, sound muted, closed-captioning on. Football. He is not a sports person. He finds organized games boring. Unorganized ones, too, for that matter. He realizes that this is a social debility, which does not make sports any more interesting to him. He'd sooner watch the Weather Channel than the Super Bowl. An impediment to male bonding, to be sure. He imagines friendships that might have been. But when someone he's just met says, "How about that fourth-quarter interception by Grabinarksi? Was that amazing or what?" All he can say by way of reply is, "It was. Truly." That only encourages the person to drill deeper so that together they can thoroughly analyze the superbness of Grabinarksi. And it will quickly become apparent that he *has* no insight into Grabinarski's superbness. Which will leave the friend-who-might-have-been feeling somehow deceived. And yet another relationship that—who knows?—might have developed into a fine, even beautiful one, is stillborn. He once forced himself to read an entire issue of *Sports Illustrated*, but all it illustrated was his aversion to sports.

Musing on this gets him thinking about his stepdaughter Atalanta in Atlanta. She's not yet thirty and is already in demand as an interior designer among a niche clientele: pro athletes. It's lucrative, plus she gets free tickets to games that people pay fortunes to attend. She spends a lot of time trying to convince her clients, and their wives and lady friends, that not everything

needs to be finished in gold and that larger-than-life-sized por-
traits of themselves over the mantel are fine but will look more
"dignified"—her word—if their extravagantly tattooed body
parts aren't all on display.

Cometh Dewey, bearing a plate of sizzling devils on horseback. He sets them down with an unnecessary warning that they
are hot. He folds his arms across his chest and looks up at the
TV. He shakes his head.

"Cam can't catch a break tonight, can he?" Dewey asks.

How is he supposed to unpack that sentence, with its "Cam"
and "can't" and "can"? Is Cam a person? One of the football
players? Presumably. Dewey looks at him eagerly, like a puppy,
seeking affirmation.

"No," he says. "He can't. It's sad. Very sad."

"But that Philly defense. Jeez Louise. It's not all his fault."

He prongs a devil on horseback into his mouth.

"Hah-hah-*hot*." The devil is not unendurably hot, but he
pretends so, in order to spare himself having to comment on
this "Philly defense."

Dewey's companionability is implacable. "You know who
they remind me of?"

He quickly prongs another diversionary devil into his
mouth.

"Whaoh?"

"Seattle, 2011."

He nods and makes an affirmative sound, "Uh-*huh*," to convey that he well remembers "Seattle, 2011." Who could forget?

"Hykenmuhler, Tuback, Kwanz, Fumerelli, Kuputnik,"
Dewey says, as if naming Olympian gods. "No *one* got past
them. 'The Blue Wall.' Remember?"

"Um-*hmm*," he says.

"'Nother Negroni?"

"Please."

He doesn't want another Negroni, but anything to forestall continued man-chat. He swivels on his bar stool to face away from the TV, as if taking in a *tour d'horizon* of the Congaree bar. He's mindful that some here may have come to be partners in extramarital lust, so he doesn't let his gaze linger impolitely in any one direction. The booths are partially concealed by beaded curtains, à la casbah. The pair in one booth are having a smoochy time. This makes him feel even more down and lonely. It reminds him of the smooching he and Peaches did in public places. He even feels a stirring in the old groin. They used to go at it like . . . He smiles, remembering the time at the three-star Michelin restaurant in Paris—ah, Paris—when she crawled under the table, and he was hissing at her to stop or they'd be arrested. One for the memory books. How much longer will he be able to remember it, with dementia?

What is he doing here, crying into his Negroni, when he could be with his darling, rogering her senseless? He's outta here.

His inner John Wayne warns, *Steady, pilgrim. How many Negronis have you had?* More than one, anyway. But he doesn't feel drunk. Dr. Paula's pills may not suppress the appetite, but they do keep you alert, even with a pint or two of Negronis in your belly. He can do this. Piece of cake.

He pulls a Benjamin from his wallet and tucks it under the plate of devils, for Dewey. He smiles, wondering if he'll report it on his taxes.

He retrieves his overnight bag from behind the front desk and gives his parking stub to the college kid valet, who sprints off, sneakers on cobblestones. Ah, youth. As George Bernard Shaw said on turning eighty, "Oh, to be sixty again."

Should he call Peaches to tell her that the uppity oysters were turned back by Pepto Bismol and that he's on his way home? No oyster, however uppity, could get past "The Pink Wall." Like Seattle, 2011, only pink. He's made a sports metaphor! He feels manly.

He decides not to call Peaches. He'll surprise her. He thinks of the night in Lucerne when they bought her that Oktoberfest beer-waitress outfit—one of those dirndl jobs with the push-up front that make your boobs look like Stormy Daniels's. *Yodel-ay-hee-hoooo!* That was a night. Fuck it. If he's losing his marbles, then he's going to spend every remaining conscious minute bonking Peaches—until *she* goes crazy.

The valet brings his car around. He gives him a Benjamin. The kid's eyes bug. The Congaree staff will be buzzing. "*That IRS dude tips big for someone on a government salary. We sure he's really with the IRS?*" He's created an aura of mystery. On his next visit here, they'll all stare. *Who* is *that man?*

He gets into the car, fastens the seat belt, adjusts the rearview mirror, puts his cell phone on the console, turns on Bluetooth, and does the other checklisty things before a long drive. Should he take a pee? Nah. Good to go.

Another valet pulls up and parks in front of him. The car is a gleaming, late-model Mercedes with a Keep America Great bumper sticker, just like Dr. Paula's.

A couple emerges from the hotel front door, arm in arm. He recognizes the fuchsia dress as the one on the woman in the booth.

It *is* Dr. Paula. And—holy shit—Jubal.

Well, well, well.

He slumps down in his seat as they walk to her car. He peers over the dash, the way he does on the bathroom scale trying to see the toes. Dr. Paula—the Jezebel!—is on Manolo Blahnik heels, which don't make for smooth walking on cobblestones. Jube—horn dog!—tips the valet, probably not a Benjamin. Dr. Paula gets in the driver's side.

Now what? What does one do in this situation? His best friend here, who's married to his wife's best friend, has just been revealed to be fucking *their* concierge doctor. The concierge doc he recommended. He was drumming up business for his squeeze. It feels like he's been smacked across the face with a frozen haddock.

Abelard and Héloïse are pulling out of the driveway. Without understanding why, he shifts into drive and follows.

He goes up on the curb. *Oopsie. Easy does it. Is this a good idea?* He sits upright in ramrod posture. He veers into an on-coming car. It honks. (Quite rightly.) *Look, if you're going to do this, we need to focus.*

It occurs to him that this is the first time he's tailed another car. Just like in the movies.

Look out. Jesus, slow down. Shall we try not to kill anyone?

Good idea.

Remind me why we're we doing this?

No idea. None.

Okay, so what's the plan?

There is no plan. We're just going to follow them. Could you shut up so I can concentrate?

But why are we doing this?

I told you. I don't know. Now will you please shut up? I need to concentrate here.

He's hoping they'll head back to Pimento or Purrell's Inlet, where Dr. Paula lives—presumably on Wisteria Lane, with the other desperate female concierge doctors. He'd much rather follow them on a highway than into downtown Charleston.

They're approaching East Bay Street. *Please turn left, toward the Ravenel Bridge and US-17.*

Fuck.

The strumpet is turning right, toward downtown.

It's okay. You can do this.

No, you can't.

Yes, I can.

Okay, but let's not run over the pedestrians.

I can do this. It's not rocket science.

No, it's called driving under the influence. Know what they do to people who do it?

Would you just please shut up.

Why are you doing this?

I don't know. Just shut up.

No, I won't.

SHUT UP!

I'll make a deal with you. Give me one good reason why you're following them, and I'll shut up.

I'll explain later.

No, explain now.

"Police! Freeze! Show me your hands, motherfucker!"

Jesus! He raises his hands and for some reason steps on the gas. The car hurtles forward and—*bam*, his head is violently knocked backward. Everything goes dark.

Voices: "Call 911!" "Is he all right?"

His stomach is pressed against the wheel even more tightly than after lunch at the Hippo King. Why is there a balloon on his lap? Aha. The air bag. He gropes for the door handle with his left hand and with the other tries to locate the seat belt hasp. After Houdini-like contortions, he manages to jimmy himself out—no small feat, given the inflated air bag and his general rotundity.

He stands by the car, wobbling. Dr. Paula's car has merged with his. Her door swings open violently. She emerges and turns on her assailant with ferocity.

"You fucking *asshole!*"

Well, fair enough.

Jubal's door opens and out he lurches, flush faced, ready to inject testosterone.

They stop and stare as they realize who has rear-ended their love wagon.

Dr. Paula's medical instincts kick in. She strides toward him on her Manolos like a determined heron. Jube hangs back and assesses the damage. The point of maximum impact is the Keep America Great bumper sticker. (You can't make this stuff up.) The former sleek contour of the Mercedes's rear is now a mashed concavity.

Dr. Paula pushes him up upright against his car and pries open his eyes, peering into them. She smells terrific, but this is probably not the time to ask what perfume she's wearing. (*Asperge* by Proust?) She sniffs his breath and whispers—for bystanders have gathered—"How many drinks have you had?"

"No more than three. Possibly four."

"*Smart,*" she mutters.

Hold on, he thinks. *People who live in summer houses shouldn't throw swallows.*

She holds up a manicured finger. The nail color is just the right shade to complement her fuchsia dress.

"Follow my finger with your eyes."

She tells Jubal to fetch her flashlight from her purse. Jubal brings it.

"How y'all doing, old buddy?" he asks.

"Fine. Funny running into you like this."

Dr. Paula pries open his eyelids, aiming her penlight into his pupils.

Now comes an annunciatory whoop of siren and flashing lights. Two officers of the peace emerge. One hangs back by their car. The other approaches.

"Let me do the talking," Dr. Paula whispers. Very take-charge. Kind of a turn-on.

"Anyone injured?" asks the approaching officer.

"No," Dr. Paula says. "I'm a physician. His pupils are three centimeters and reactive. No indication of head injury."

"What happened?"

"It was my fault," she says. "That's my car." She points at her outraged Mercedes. "This gentleman's our friend. He was following us to the restaurant when this *dog* ran out in front of me. I slammed on the brakes." She raises her voice in the direction of the half dozen people looking on. "Someone needs to buy a *leash*! For their *dog*!"

"Sir, how fast were you driving?"

"Officer," Dr. Paula interjects. "I need to get him to the hospital."

"I thought you said he wasn't injured."

"I'd like to make sure. Assuming that's all right by you."

"I'm going to have to Breathalyze him. Standard procedure, ma'am."

Dr. Paula unleashes her inner dominatrix.

"First of all, it's 'Doctor.' Second, he's not intoxicated. Third, it was *my* fault. Okay?"

"Standard procedure. *Doctor.*"

Things are getting edgy.

"Okay, then. You can follow us to the hospital and do your standard procedure there "

"No, ma'am. Doctor. Not how it works."

And everyone was getting along so well, too.

Jubal is peering at the officer standing by the police car.

"*Rusty*? That you?"

"Mr. Puckett?"

"Well, I'll be a monkey's great-uncle," Jubal joyously declares, as if he has just been reunited with the twin brother from whom he was separated at birth, and for whom he has been relentlessly searching ever since. It transpires that Officer Rusty, when not preserving the peace of Charleston, moonlights doing security at Itchfield during weddings and other fêtes.

Jubal pivots and addresses Officer Not-Rusty.

"Officer. What did you do to make Chief Tom"—of course Jube would be on a first-name basis with Charleston's chief of police—"so mad as to partner you with this *blot* on the good name of the Charleston police force?" he says, pointing at Officer Rusty.

Officer Not-Rusty is grinning. *Go, Jube.* His good-old-boy centrifuge is spinning fast enough to enrich Iranian plutonium. Jube is telling the cops that he's got a ton of "e-vents" coming up at Itchfield that will be requiring security of the finest kind.

"Y'all are doing e-vents? During the pandemic?" says Officer Not-Rusty.

"Many as Governor Henry tells me I can." Jube is of course on first-name terms with the governor. "I'll give y'all a shout on Monday, tell you what we got on the schedule."

Dr. Paula says in a tone of *look, fellas, I'd love to give you both blow jobs that would make your eyeballs spin like reels in a slot machine,* "I don't mean to interrupt this lovefest, but I'd like to get our friend here to the hospital."

"That'll be fine, ma'am. Doctor. Y'all go on." Officer Not-Rusty adds, "You can't drive this car. One headlight is shot and the air bag's deployed."

"I'll drive it," Jube says. "It's only five blocks. I'll call Triple-A from the restaurant, get it towed."

"How're you going to steer with that bag in your face?"

Jube grins. "Anyone got a knife?"

Naturally, Officers Rusty and Not-Rusty both have knives. They go at the air bag like kids at a piñata. When they're finished, the interior is awash in shreds. It looks like a hamster cage.

"It ain't pretty, but y'oughta be able to drive," says Officer Rusty. He and his partner leave.

"You guys were *great,*" he tells Jubal and Dr. Paula. Her expression instantly defaults to her *You fucking asshole!* mode.

"You should go to the hospital and get checked out," she says.

"Sorry about your car."

"Where you headed, old buddy?" Jube asks.

"The Congaree Inn. On Calhoun? Off Magnolia?"

Jube and Dr. Paula exchange looks. Jube says, "I'll drive him. You follow."

On the way to the hotel, Jubal says, "Her and me happened to bump into each other."

"Jube. Stop."

Jube abandons protestation of innocence and pivots to indignation. "Okay, but if you don't mind me asking: What the *fuck,* old buddy? My neck feels like it's broke."

He examines his cell phone. Sure enough, there it is: missed call: Themistocles. He explains to Jube about Them's ringtone retaliations. This one must be for hiding his surfboard after Peaches, worrying about sharks, asked Them not to go surfing.

"You have to hand it to him," he says. "He keeps taking it to the next level."

Jubal rubs his neck. "Y'all need to have a *serious* talk with that boy."

"What do you suggest I tell him? '*Now, Them, getting me arrested by TSA is one thing. But making me smash into Uncle Jube's girlfriend is going too far.*'"

"She's not my girlfriend "

"Sorry. Squeeze."

At the Congaree, the valet parker stares at the smashed front and the hamster cage interior and remarks, "*That* doesn't look good."

Dr. Paula pulls up with an expressive screech of tires. She does not get out to exchange good night pleasantries.

"Well," Jube says. "Let's do this again, real soon. Damn, my neck . . ."

"Why don't you ask *our* concierge doctor to give you an opioid? See you tomorrow."

"Tomorrow?"

"You and your wife are coming to dinner. Remember?"

Jube deflates like a knifed air bag. "Aw, *shit.*"

"Cheer up. I'm making carbonara. Maybe Dr. Paula would like to join us."

CHAPTER 28

Next morning on the drive home, he passes not one but three Hippo Kings and doesn't even slow down. As he whooshes by the third, he wonders if it's PTSD from the car wreck. Or could his lack of hunger be related to the unpleasant smell from the burst air bag?

He asks Siri what goes into air bags. Siri reports that air bags inflate in forty milliseconds and names a dozen chemicals that make possible this miracle of instantaneity. Could it be the sodium azide and nitrogen that's suppressed his appetite? Maybe he should tell Dr. Paula to prescribe air bag propellant instead of Contrave. He could suggest it to her at dinner tonight. He's looking forward to dinner. Where better than a cozy meal with good friends—and your friend's mistress—to *ding-ding* your knife on the wineglass and announce, "So, guess who's got dementia?"

Should he do it when they sit down at the table or with dessert? Better with dessert. Carbonara needs to be eaten right away, hot. If he announces that he's bonkers, the girls might be too upset to eat. Peaches, anyway. Angina, maybe. It's not that she doesn't love him, but it's possible she loves his carbonara as much, if not a tad more.

Hold on, he interrupts himself. *Why do you have to bring it up at dinner?* He doesn't, in fact. Then he thinks: *If I have dementia, I might blurt it out while everyone's digging into the carbonara. It's just the sort of thing a person with dementia might do.*

This is becoming problematic. A solution comes to him. He phones Jubal.

"Hey."

"Hey." Jube sounds hungover, or miserable for some other reason.

"Good time to talk?"

"All right. I guess." Not very enthusiastic. Clearly, having a chat with his "old buddy" is not at the top of Jube's things-I'm-looking-forward-to-today list. Along with dinner.

"How's your neck?"

"It hurts. Significantly. I'm wearing one of those collars. And I've got a stomachache from all the damn ibuprofen."

"Ouch. Sorry."

"What was it you wanted to talk about?"

"I need to fill you in on a recent development."

"Go on, then."

"But first, I feel terrible about last night."

"Not half as terrible as me. But we don't need to talk about that."

"You must be wondering why I was following you."

"It don't matter. Okay? Water under the bridge."

"What I'm driving at . . . oops, pun alert. In the event you and Dr. Paula were thinking 'He's nuts,' you would be technically correct. By the way, she looked great. She *is* a hot one, our concierge doctor."

"What are you talking about, 'technically correct'?"

"Tailing people in a car isn't something I normally do, Jube."

"We figured you'd had a few belts. She said your breath

smelled like a distillery. As to being nuts, it *was* nuts, you driving in that condition. But I understand how that little fucker Themistocles about gave you a heart attack."

"An accurate description of events, stipulated. But there's a missing piece."

"I'm listening."

"Might as well give it to you straight. I'm losing it, Jube. My marbles, that is."

Jube snorts. "Well, I don't call that news. I've known that for about ten years."

"I have dementia, Jube. Alzheimer's or some version of it. I learned yesterday afternoon. That's why I was in the bar, knocking back Negronis."

"You messing with me?"

"I wish. The shrink Peaches sent me to—by the way, wonderful guy. If you ever . . . He's from Pakistan, of all places. Anyway, he's ordering a bunch of tests on me. Brain scans and such. But I can read handwriting on a wall, especially when it's in block capital letters. This ship is going down, with all neurons aboard. I realize I'm mixing my metaphors, but you get the drift."

Silence. "Well, damn, old buddy."

"I've had a good run. These past ten years with Peaches have been the happiest of my life. Anyway, the *reason* I'm telling you this now, before dinner tonight, is this being the case, I might not be in control of what comes out of my mouth."

"Meaning what?" Jube sounds like he just sat up straight.

"I don't know. Like if I start yapping about last night."

"Hold on, now. Hold on. I'm not receiving you. Why in God's name would you do such a thing?"

"Because I'm nuts, Jube."

"Are you shitting me?"

"Jube, I have no intention of talking about it. I'm just warning you that I can't guarantee that I won't."

"Is this like that Tourette's deal, where people spout crazy shit in church during the Christmas pageant about wanting to fuck the minister's wife?"

"I'm not up to speed on the neurochemistry. I suppose there could be some overlap. Tourette's is a neural inhibitor disorder. I think this is different. But it is what it is. You heard yourself from your pal Harry Chambless the kind of stuff I've been saying."

"About him being in some cahoots with the Russians? That stuff?"

"Yes. Now, mind you, that doesn't mean Harry *isn't* in bed with Putin."

"Aw, hell . . ."

"Hear me out. Hear me out. I stipulate he might *not* be working for Putin. I hope he isn't. One of the challenges for me, going forward, will be to separate the wheat from the chaff. If you see what I mean."

"No, I do not."

"Then let me spell it out for you. I'm talking about being able to distinguish between what's real and what my wacko neurons have me thinking is real. Meanwhile, there's no denying about the increase in premature burials."

"Jesus, Lord . . ."

"And sooner or later, Bobby Babcock will have to be held to account for it. It's a disgrace, Jube. Meanwhile, every Chambless hearse going in *and* out of Custard Air Force Base should be searched. Thoroughly. I hope we can agree on that much."

"Listen to me, old buddy. No one is being buried alive. Okay? No one. And Harry is not taking orders from the fucking Kremlin. When are you having these brain tests?"

"Jube, I would love to be wrong about all this. Meanwhile, let's talk tactics for tonight."

"Tactics?"

"In case I start yapping about what great tits our concierge doctor has and ask you how she is in the sack. You're going to need to be ready to hit the silk."

"The what?"

"Do you not know that expression? Paratroopers in World War II used it. It's metonomy, a metaphor for jumping. Their parachutes were made of silk. The villagers around the drop zones would gather up the chutes and use them to make clothing. In fact—"

"No, no, never mind all that. Look here, old buddy, I'm thinking this dinner is a bad idea."

"Wasn't mine. Your wife's. Anyway, I don't mean to make you uneasy."

"Uneasy? You got me wanting to shoot myself."

"I'm probably exaggerating. But if I head in that direction, don't hang back. Hit the silk. Start yakking about some record fish you caught, or how someone's poodle got eaten by an alligator on the golf course. Actually, you know what you could do? You could say, 'He's choking' and Heimlich me. Do you know about the Heimlich maneuver?"

"Yeah, I know about the damn Heimlich maneuver. What are you suggesting?"

He sounds very stressed, Jube. Did things not go well with Dr. Paula last night?

"You make a ball with your fist, over the sternum, then hug, hard and suddenlike. Don't break my ribs, now. Hey, speaking of Heimlich, here's a weird one for you: Did you know that was the name of the German commando Hitler sent to kidnap

Roosevelt from Hobcaw in 1944? Hell of a story. Ask me about it at dinner tonight. That'll keep me off Dr. Paula's tits. Okay, gotta go, I'm pulling into the driveway. And there's my darling. See you tonight."

"No, no, no. Do not hang up!"

"Sweetheart. Great to be home."

Peaches stares at the front of the car.

"Babe. Your car is . . . all smashed in."

"What? You're kidding."

"Take a look for yourself."

He gets out and examines the front. "Holy camoly," he says.

Peaches peers through the window.

"Babe?"

"Yes?"

"The air bag has deployed. It's in . . . shreds."

He walks over, looks and sniffs. "I wondered where that smell was coming from. Boy, this is completely unsatisfactory."

"What do you mean?"

"Wouldn't you call that lousy valet parking? And I gave the guy a really nice tip, too."

CHAPTER 29

It *is* good to be home, surrounded by familiar things. He disappears into his study and emerges hours later with a masterpiece.

His darling is in the kitchen. She looks at him with concern.

"Everything okay, my sweet?"

"I'm kind of weirded out by the car, babe."

"You're not the only one. Here, see what you think," he says, handing her the five-page diatribe he's just composed, addressed to the management of the Congaree Inn, with quotations from Shakespeare, Dr. Johnson, T. S. Eliot, Henry Kissinger, Yeats, Thomas Paine, Dorothy Parker, and Yukio Mishima.

Peaches reads. Her brows furrow. She starts to skim, turning the pages.

"Ought to get their attention," he says. "Don't you think?"

"It's, uh, great, sweetheart."

"I'm kind of pleased with it. I hesitated about the Yeats quote, the one at the bottom of page three. 'The best lack all conviction / While the worst are full of passionate intensity.' It's been quoted to death these last four years. But it's so apropos."

"You should show this to Dr. Bhong."

"You think? At three-hundred and fifty dollars an hour, is it worth bothering him about a valet parking matter?"

"I think he'll be very interested. I'll make a copy."

"No need. I printed out a dozen."

"Why?"

"One each for the president, vice president, and general manager of the hotel. The Congaree's owned by a private equity firm in DC. So, a copy for them. Won't they be thrilled to know what's going on at their Charleston 'luxury hotel collection' property. Then one for the *Post and Courier*. One for the *Charleston City Paper*. One for WCSC-TV. One for *Plant and Pistol*. I googled to see if there's a trade journal for valet parkers, but I couldn't find anything. You don't happen to know, do you?"

"I don't, sweetheart."

"Plus a few copies for local media. The *Weekly Pimentoan*. *Grand Strand Today*. Folks here will be interested to know that their cars are being demolished while they're having dinner at the Congaree."

"Why don't I mail the letters for you?"

"Would you? Thank you, sweetheart. I do need to get back to work on the screenplay."

"Happy to."

"By the way, do you know, someone told me the Congaree is where people go to have affairs."

"Better not be why you've been staying there."

He loves that his darling is jealous.

"There was something I wanted to tell you, but I've forgotten. I can't remember anything anymore. Speaking of which, Dr. Bhong gave me a cognitive function test. I crushed it."

"That's wonderful, sweetheart. I did your shopping for dinner tonight."

"You are the best. Pancetta-not bacon?"

"Um-hm. And grated-not shredded Parmesan."

"Who's my cleverest girl? You get a kiss. Mmwah."

"I got some hideously expensive Barolo."

"*Bravissima.* I regret never having learned Italian. '*Nel mezzo del cammin di nostra vita, mi ritrovai per una selva oscura, ché la dirrita via era smarrita.*' Great stuff. What time are Dr. Paula and the others coming?"

"Who?"

"Dr. Paula. Concierge doctor to the rich and famous."

"Babe, Angie and Jubal are coming. Why would you think she's coming?"

"Hmm. Odd. No idea. But I'm glad. Frankly, I'm starting to have doubts about her."

"About time. Why—is she insisting on being paid in bitcoin?"

"Dr. Bhong seems a little skeptical about her. So, what time are she and Jube coming?"

"*Angie* and Jube, sweetheart."

"Right. I want to prep my carbonara so I can join in the cocktail chitchat."

"I told Angie six thirty."

"I'm starved. I've been subsisting on Congaree bar food. Though I will say, the Congaree does a better job with food than valet parking. Should I even ask if Angie and Jube got a Covid test?"

Peaches sighs. "I tried to think of a polite way to ask for proof, but I couldn't. We're going to have to take it on faith."

"Swell. I'll get started on our obituaries."

He wishes he could remember what he wanted to tell Peaches, but all he can remember is that it was important. Another thought gone with the whoosh of an email launching into cyberspace.

Angie/Angina arrives at five thirty, alone. Nothing unusual. Angina regards all time after 5 p.m. as pointless unless accompanied by drink. And she likes to have a bit of "girl time" alone with Peaches. Jubal will be along, she says. He had to go to Itchfield to deal with an electrical issue in the slave quarters. Most of the plantation owners are deemphasizing "the slave aspect" these days. They don't even call them "plantations." They certainly don't put up signs that say Old Slave Quarters. But Jubal feels it's important, as he puts it, "not to sweep heritage under the rug."

"Candidly," Angina says, "I was not bereft to see him go. He's been in *the* foulest mood since he got back from Charleston this morning. He managed to wrench his neck. I asked him, 'How does one wrench one's neck in Charleston?' He's wearing one of those collars that make you look like a sixteenth-century nobleman."

He's loved Angina from the get-go. They bonded the second time they met, ten years ago, when she showed up on the set of *Swamp Foxes* one broiling forenoon, looking, as they say down here, "rode hard and put up wet."

"You wouldn't happen to have any cocaine, would you?" she asked.

"No," he replied. For some reason, he felt he should add, "Sorry."

"I do not normally partake. I only ask because you're a member of the film community. I hope you won't take me for a reprobate. It's just that I have, arguably, the worst hangover of my adult life, which is saying something. And I have to chair a PTA luncheon in forty-five minutes. Death would be a mercy. Do you have any cyanide?"

Angina, like him, is not from here. Their sensibilities formed in cooler climes. They married into the South and, love it as they do, share eye rolls when the bourbon's been flowing and someone starts banging on about what a barbarian General Sherman was. The Irish have a term for it: *anam cara*—soul friend.

Only once did she open up to him about Jubal's infidelity, and if he'd blinked, he might have missed it. They were sitting together on a garden bench while everyone else was down by the dock, oohing and aahing over the sunset. He can't remember how it came up, but it did. "He and I have discussed it," she said. "On numerous occasions. There isn't an object in the house, including mother's Steuben polar bear, that I haven't thrown at him. He's gotten better at ducking." He thought she was about to laugh, but her face crumpled. She then pulled herself together and did laugh, about the smudge of mascara on her cocktail napkin. "I look like a raccoon. My happiness is now complete."

Angina is at her usual station on the upholstered highboy stool at the other end of the kitchen island. She takes out her smoking items—cigarettes, gold lighter, sterling silver ashtray— and arranges them before her, as a doctor does his surgical instruments. It's understood by Angie's friends that if you desire her company—which everyone does—you might as well resign yourself to secondhand smoke. There's no point tut-tutting, tsk-tsking, stamping your feet, or reading aloud from the Surgeon General's Report on Smoking and Health. She doesn't blow it at you, but she is going to smoke, so you might as well put on your big-girl panties and suck it up.

"How did your Covid test go?" Peaches asks pointedly.

"It was without doubt the most excruciating physical pain I've experienced since I last gave birth. I thought the swab would come out the top of my head. I have seen shorter telephone poles."

"Poor you," Peaches says. "And?"

"They told me I have the nasal passages of a twenty-year-old. They were most impressed. I'm being featured in the next issue of *Ear, Nose, and Throat* magazine. On the cover."

"How nice. Did they mention if you have the virus?"

"I didn't think it polite to ask."

Peaches groans. "Well, I hope you brought a warm coat," she says, "because that being the case, we'll be dining outdoors tonight, on the porch."

"Wonderful. I prefer to dine al fresco."

"Good. It's going to be real fresco tonight. Mid fifties."

Angina knows this is a hollow threat. They have those mushroom-type outdoor heaters, enough to raise the temperature on the porch to Death Valley levels.

He hands Angina her vodka and soda with lime.

"I saw someone on the television say that smoking kills the coronavirus."

Game on.

"Dr. Fauci, was it?"

"I couldn't tell you, but he was beautifully tailored, and I always take that as a sign that the person knows what he is talking about."

She exhales languorously. She's a beautiful smoker, Angina. He loves watching her smoke. At a distance.

"Of course," she goes on, "they don't *want* us to know that smoking neutralizes the virus."

"Oh? Why is that?"

"Because then people would throw away their masks and start smoking. Wouldn't they? And then where would the 3M company be?"

"That hadn't occurred to me."

"And the other corporations, which are making fortunes manufacturing . . . I don't like to call them 'face diapers.' Nonetheless."

"What unique perspective you bring. To any discussion."

"You do grasp, do you not, that the reason China was able to flatten its curve is that they *all* smoke."

"I read somewhere—was it in the *Lancet*?—it's even more effective if you soak your cigarettes in Clorox."

"Yes. I believe it was in the *Lancet*," Angina says. "But there was an awful lot of tippy-toeing in the article about how on earth one is then supposed to light one's cigarettes. Being all soggy."

"No, they've solved that."

"Have they? Oh, that *is* good news. Pray, tell."

"You put them in the microwave."

"The microwave! What will they think of next? The solution was there the whole time, right in front of us. In the kitchen."

"There is the risk of explosion."

"Yes, but they don't want people to know about that, either. Do they?"

"No."

"Because then people would stop buying microwaves."

"Exactly. And then where would the Deep State be?"

"In deepest doo-doo."

Peaches's tolerance for this jibber-jabber is finite.

"Y'all want to wake me when you're done?"

"So," Angina says, twiddling one of her earrings. "Who did I see today in the parking lot at the Publix?"

"Who?"

"Your husband's and my husband's *concierge* doctor." Angina stretches the word so far it snaps when she lets go.

He senses what she's saying has significance, but for the life of him can't think why.

"Charging seventy-five hundred dollars a year to 'Say, ah.' Nice work if you can get it. So, there she was, high heels, groceries in one hand. With the other, she's aiming the car key at the trunk of her car. Click. Click. *Click*. But the trunk was having none of it. And no wonder. The entire rear of her car was smashed in. Violence had been done to it. But she was not about to give up. No. She just stood there and kept clicking, getting madder and madder and madder. Poor thing. I almost went up to her and said, 'Darling, I don't mean to intrude, but I think the problem might be that your car appears to have been in a collision."

Angina is snorting with laughter. Between gasps, she takes sips of vodka and soda. Peaches, too, is doubled over in mirth. Why?

"So . . . finally," Angina continues, "she became so *enraged* that she flung open the back door and threw—*hurled*—her poor groceries into the back seat."

Heightened peals of laughter.

"If there were *eggs* in there . . ." Angina must now pause, for this scenario is for some reason so hilarious as to be crippling. She and Peaches are honking like geese at the prospect of broken eggs oozing into the rich Teutonic upholstery of Dr. Paula's Mercedes. They can barely remain upright. Their foreheads are nearly touching the island.

Enter Jubal, looking the very picture of a sixteenth-century noble person, head propped upon the neck brace. He frowns.

"Hi, Jube," he says. This is the only greeting Jubal receives, the ladies being too far gone in hysterics to notice his arrival. He stands, taking in the scene. He looks at his old buddy, who shrugs and smiles, as if to say, *I'm as confused as you are.*

Jubal goes to the bar and pours himself a heroic portion of bourbon.

"Appears I'm four drinks behind y'all. Maybe five." Jube is in no good humor. Why? he wonders. The electrical issue in the slave quarters? And what's with the neck collar?

Angina and Peaches are now nearly upright, but are still experiencing after-tremors.

"Anyone going to fill me in on what I missed?" Jube asks.

"Angina was telling us that she saw our doctor in the parking lot at the Publix today."

Jubal's eyes widen.

"Uh-huh," he says. "And what is the hilarious part about that?"

"You'll have to ask the girls. I don't get it myself."

"Ladies? Anyone care to enlighten me?"

The ladies again convulse in laughter.

"Angina said Dr. Paula was trying to open the trunk of her car. To put away her groceries."

"Uh-huh."

"But the trunk wouldn't open. Because the rear was all bashed up."

Jubal's foot is involuntarily tapping on the wooden floor.

"Uh-huh."

"So she put the groceries in the back seat."

"Uh-huh."

"That's pretty much it. Angina, did I omit anything?"

Angina mimics Dr. Paula pointing her key at the trunk.

"*Click. Click.* Open, you motherfucker!"

She and Peaches howl anew.

"Is there a punch line?" Jubal asks. "Or am I ten drinks behind?"

"Come give me a hand with the heaters," he says to Jubal. "We're eating outside, in honor of you and Angina not getting tested for Covid."

On the porch, Jubal whispers, "What the fuck was that? Why are they wetting their panties about Paula not being able to open her damn trunk?"

"No idea. But I'm inferring that our girls are not fans of our doctor. That said, why her damaged trunk should be a source of hilarity is beyond me. Are you familiar with the term *schadenfreude*? It's one of those interminable German compound nouns. *Schaden* means—"

"No, no, no. Fuck that." Jube seems not in the mood for etymology. "Look here—do they *know*?"

"Know what?"

"God in heaven, give me strength. The hell do you *think* I'm talking about? Last night."

"What about last night?"

Jubal stares. Then puts a hand on his shoulder. "Come on, old buddy. Let's light these 'shrooms and go join the ladies. See what the hell they're cackling about now."

His carbonara is a great success, as always. And the hideously expensive Barolo is the perfect complement to the egg, pancetta, and Parmesan, and cleanses the palette. Something about carbonara just makes people happy. The writer Calvin Trillin conducted a campaign to replace the national Thanksgiving turkey with spaghetti carbonara. If ever he finds himself facing the firing squad, this is what he'll request for his last meal. (Do they actually do that? He must look it up.) He's been making carbonara for years, but only recently learned it's a legacy of the American liberation of Italy in World War II. The GIs were always asking for bacon and eggs. Conditioned by thousands of years of being invaded and occupied, Italians shrugged and accommodated the gustatory cravings of their current occupiers. (What did Hannibal request? He must look that up, too.) They tossed bacon—pancetta—and eggs in with the pasta, added grated Parmesan, and *eccolo: spaghetti alla carbonara*. It was a huge hit. His uncle Gerry, who was wounded in Italy while serving with the fabled 10th Mountain Division, said that carbonara made it all worthwhile.

He goes inside to get another bottle of Barolo. They're three bottles in—on top of the cocktails—and the atmosphere is merry. Jubal's foul mood is gone. Listening to the laughter on the porch as he uncorks the wine makes him happy. Isn't this what it's all about? Friends, food, wine, laughter. Mushroom heaters. When he returns to the table, Peaches is regaling Angina and Jube with the saga of Colonel Ptarmigan's statue.

"Atticus is still in hiding. DIY witness protection. He calls us from pay phones. Won't say where he is. Momma is about frantic."

"What do these fools call themselves?" Angina asks.

"Oaf Keepers."

Angina shakes her head. "Do they have nothing better to do than hound your brother to the ends of the earth? Do they not have jobs?"

"Would you hire them?"

Jubal says, "I've got a few of them working at the plantation. I wouldn't give 'em anything too complicated to do, but they're good workers."

"Keep them away from the nuclear launch controls, do you?" Angina says.

"Aw, they talk a lot of shit, but it's just talk. You ask me, this statue toppling has gotten way out of hand."

"I didn't ask you," Peaches says sharply. "These yahoos tried to kill my brother. They chased him on the highway and tried to run him off the road."

"That's it!" he says.

"What?" Peaches asks her husband.

"What happened last night in Charleston. It's been driving me nuts."

Jubal freezes. The forkful of carbonara en route to his mouth stops like a cable car in a power outage.

"I was following Jube and Dr. Paula, in my car. And suddenly I hear 'Police! Freeze! Show me your hands, motherfucker!' I almost pooped in my pants. It was *The . . . The . . . The . . .*" Themistocles is an unusual name that does not trip from the Anglo tongue. But it's a word with which he's well familiar. It's just catching in his throat because of incipient laughter.

Jubal shouts, "He's choking!" He leaps from his seat with the alacrity of an eland suddenly aware of a lion. He knocks against the table with such force that everything on it topples: wineglasses, candles, floral centerpiece. Then, in his Samaritan haste around the end of the table, he bangs against one of the mushroom heaters, toppling it in a clatter of red-hot aluminum and propane.

"I gotcha, old buddy! I gotcha!" Jubal shouts. He pushes him forward, away from the chair back, clasps him about the torso with both arms, and jerks him with such force that he's nearly lifted out of the chair.

"*Uhhhhh,*" he gasps with what ccs of air Jubal's Herculean Heimlich has left in his lungs.

"I gotcha, old buddy! Again! One-two-*three!*" Jube gives another mighty heave, and again old buddy's rib cage is crushed. Jube must be working out.

"Can't . . . breathe . . ."

"It's okay! I gotcha! Again! One, two . . ."

"Nnnnhh . . ."

"*Jubal!*" Angina says in a commanding voice. "What are you *doing?*"

"Heimliching him! What the hell do you *think* I'm doing?"

"Well, stop! Now! This instant! You're *killing* him! Can't you see he can't breathe? What's *wrong* with you?"

Jubal releases his death grip. Old buddy slumps into his chair like a collapsed soufflé.

"Y'all right, old buddy?"

"Urrrhhhh . . ." His ribs feel like they did the time he was going forty miles an hour downhill on a bicycle and suddenly the bike was going one way and he the other.

"That was close," Jube says in a tone of humanitarian self-congratulation. "Thought we were gonna lose you there."

The table that minutes ago had been a bower of merriment and contentment now looks like Ostrogoths and moles have ridden through: puddles of Barolo, broken glasses, splatterings of candle wax, orts of carbonara, a reek of propane.

"Shall we have our coffee and dessert inside?" Peaches says.

"You know, sweetie," Angina says with a castrating sideways glance at her husband. "I had so much of the *delicious* carbonara I don't think I have room for anything more. I think we'll just be getting on home. Thank you for a delightful evening."

CHAPTER 30

"A re you all right?" Dr. Bhong asks.

"Fine, fine," he grunts.

"Why are you hugging yourself?"

"Helps with the breathing."

"Do we need to get you to the ER?"

"No, no."

"Have you seen Dr. Paula?"

He laughs, which makes it worse.

"You're in pain," Dr. Bhong says. "We need to get you seen."

"It only hurts when I laugh. How's that for a cliché? I don't think I've ever said that before."

"Was it my mention of Dr. Paula? I've left several messages for her, but she hasn't returned my calls."

"She called *me* this morning," he grunts. "To tell me she's sending me a bill. She's offering to make it look like a bill for a procedure not covered by Medicare. So my wife wouldn't know what it was for. Say what you will about concierge doctors, they do go the extra mile for you."

"A bill for what?"

"To make her Mercedes great again."

He explains about seeing Jubal and Dr. Paula canoodling as they exited the Congaree, about following them, about the crash, about Jubal nearly Heimliching him to death. He leaves out Jubal's name, not that Dr. Bhong would repeat it to anyone. He refers to him as "the Friend," which makes his narration sound like a police report.

Dr. Bhong says, "An eventful weekend."

"These tests, Doc," he says. "They're about dementia. Right?"

Dr. Bhong shakes his head. "That's putting the cart *miles* in front of the horse. I want to eliminate various possibilities. Meanwhile, on the assumption that Dr. Paula will no longer be continuing as your primary physician, let's start weaning you off all these meds she's got you on."

Peaches is waiting outside, to drive him back to Pimento. She's revoked his driving privileges. His car is in the shop, undergoing extensive body work and having a new air bag installed: $3,500.

She conducted a thorough debriefing after Angina and Jubal left. He was able to recall most of what happened in Charleston, but he was at a loss to explain why he followed them.

"It just seemed like the logical thing to do."

"The logical thing to do," Peaches said, "would have been to not drive after drinking four Negronis."

"I stipulate—"

"Stop saying 'stipulate!'"

"It's a perfectly good English word."

"I hate it."

"All right, but if you don't mind my saying, *that's* not very logical."

Peaches finally had no more questions. They cleaned up the wreckage on the porch and got into bed.

"Babe?" he said.

"What?"

"You won't forget to mail those letters, will you? About the valet parking at the Congaree?"

He felt her body tighten alongside his, then untense. She reached over and kissed him and said, "I'll take care of it, sweetheart. Go to sleep."

CHAPTER 31

Peaches shuttles him back and forth between Pimento and Charleston for his brain tests. Uber has yet to establish a presence in Pimento. His darling drives faster than he does. Much faster. He thinks this is because she grew up in the South, where people start driving at fourteen and by eighteen are competing in NASCAR. Having grown up in suburban Connecticut, his driving is of the more law-abiding variety. In a half century behind the wheel, he's gotten three tickets. Peaches has spent an aggregate of six nights in jail for her moving violations. One night when they were going out to dinner and she'd put on an orange dress, he quipped that this would save her the trouble of changing later in the evening. Peaches likes to hug the rear of the car in front, at high speed. She learned this from her brother Atticus, currently on the run from the Oaf Keepers. It pulls your car along in its slipstream and saves you gas. Atticus holds the record for most moving violations in South Carolina history.

He tells Peaches that the harrowing two-hour drives to Charleston might be skewing his test results.

Peaches replies that there are one thousand things she would rather be doing than "hauling your ass" back and forth.

"Fair enough," he says. "Nonetheless, do you know about the amygdala?"

"What about the amygdala?" Peaches says, sensing a trap.

"There was a booklet in the waiting room before the PET scan the other day. It said that the thalamus takes in sensory data and forwards it to the amygdala. Wonderful word. I looked it up. It's from the Greek for *almond*. Must have to do with the shape, wouldn't you guess?"

"Is there a point to this story?"

"The amygdala determines if the incoming data warrants a 'holy shit!' or 'fuck it, let's have a beer.' It's called the fight-or-flight response. If the amygdala decides it's a holy shit situation, it starts pumping adrenaline and cortisol, which make your heart rate go up. So I'm wondering if being in the car with you for two hours might be affecting the test results. It's not a criticism, darling."

At the end of the week, his car comes back from the shop. Peaches is tired of being his (unappreciated) chauffeur. She proposes a deal: if he promises to abstain from Negronis, she'll restore his driving privileges. Deal. He drives himself to Charleston without stressing his amygdala.

Dr. Bhong has all the test results.

"I have good news. And one or two questions, but there are always questions. Your cerebellum and brain stem are tip-top."

He senses Dr. Bhong is putting some spin on the cue ball.

"There's no evidence of intracranial hemorrhage, mass, or hydrocephalus. English translation—it's all good. Your sinuses are a thing of beauty. How's your sense of smell?"

"Fine, I think."

"Your skull is nicely intact. Indeed, I would go so far as to

call it solid. And here's more good news: your cortex is normal."
Pause. "Now, there does appear be some confusion going on in
and around your amygdala. The synapses—you know about
those—don't seem to be picking up neural messages as efficiently as they should. They're being a bit lazy, we might say. So.
That's something I'd like to look into more closely."

Dr. Bhong chides. "Why the long face?"

"I'm just a bit tired, Doc."

"That could be because we're titrating Dr. Paula's meds.
How's your frame of mind?"

"Medium-cool, I'd say."

"I can give you something to help with that. But let's wait
until Dr. Paula's meds have left the building, so to speak."

The funny part is that his appetite finally does seem suppressed. He hasn't been to Hippo King in over a week. He
wonders if this has affected HK economically. He can see the
headline: "HK 2Q Profits Off by One-Third." Do they miss him?
Is the guy who hosed him with nasal matter saying to his fellow
workers, "Remember the fat Yankee dude I honked on? Haven't
seen him around. Hope I didn't kill the motherfucker."

On his way home, he sees the sign for Lock 'N' Load, the
local gun shop. He's driven past it a hundred times but has never
been inside. He has fond memories of Bob's Sports, in his Connecticut hometown, where he used to buy .22 caliber ammo for
his squirrel gun. Bob's guns were mounted on the wall behind
the counter: rifles, shotguns, pistols, some of them made in the
next town over by the Ruger company. Next to today's high-tech
weaponry, those guns seem quaint today.

Lock 'N' Load is a survivalist's wet dream. They seem to
have everything except grenade launchers. On the counter is a

stack of brochures for a law firm with a niche clientele: people who've shot other people. "Home Invasion-Related Legal Problems? We Provide Solutions."

The two young men behind the counter have an ex-mil vibe: brush cuts, biceps, tats, bright eyes, clipped diction, holstered Glock 9s. One wears a tactical vest. The other has on a ball cap emblazoned *Molon Labe*. What *can* that mean? He googles it on his phone. Aha. Greek for "come and take them." Yes, of course: Thermopylae, the three hundred Spartans. It was the reply of their commander, Leonidas, to the Persian demand that they surrender their weapons. Google notes that the quote is "famously laconic." Doubly laconic, actually, as Spartans were laconic by virtue of hailing from Laconia. But whatever.

"Yes, sir. How can I help you?"

"I'm thinking of killing myself, and I'm wondering what kind of handgun you'd recommend."

"Sir, I'm not in a position to advise you as to something of that nature."

"I'm sorry. That came out bass-ackward. Let me start over. I'm a writer. I live in Aqueous Acres."

"Okay."

"I'm writing a screenplay for a movie."

"Okay."

"The main character is contemplating suicide. He goes to the local gun store and asks what type of gun he should use. I should have explained that at the top."

"Sir, I'm still not comfortable discussing something of this nature."

"I understand. I just want the scene to be realistic, you see. Authenticity is important. Viewers can always tell if you're faking it. I was hoping you and I could have that conversation. As if we're characters in the screenplay."

"I'd like to help, sir, but I can't."

"Tell you what." He points at the glass-top counter. "That one there. What's the price on that?"

"Six hundred and seventy-nine dollars."

"Fine-looking gun. Could I see it?"

The guy takes it out and lays it on the glass countertop, keeping his hands close to it.

"Help me out, and I'll buy it from you. Five minutes of your time, for a sale of six hundred and seventy-nine dollars. What do you say?"

"Well . . . okay."

"Excellent. Thank you. So, tell me about this bad boy."

"This handgun is an American classic. Smith and Wesson .357 Magnum."

"Impressive. What kind of exit wound would this make?"

"That would depend on the range and the load."

"Range? Let's assume point-blank. Shooting myself from across the room would be kind of a challenge, wouldn't it?"

The young man smiles. "Yeah, I guess it would."

"So, point-blank. Now, as to load. What's that about?"

"The amount of explosive powder."

"And what load would you recommend?"

"I'd go with a Hydra-Shok jacketed hollow point. Hundred and thirty grains."

"Ouchy."

"Yeah, it would do the job."

"Is this the gun Clint Eastwood had in *Dirty Harry*?"

"No, that was a double-action Smith & Wesson Model 29, .44 magnum."

Simultaneously they recite: "The most powerful handgun in the world. And would blow your head *clean* off."

They chuckle, all tension dispelled. He's made a gun buddy!

"Sold. And I'll take one of those Hydra-thingies."

"Box of fifty?"

"I really only need one. I'm no sharpshooter, but how can I miss?"

"We don't sell ammunition by the individual round."

"Then fifty it is."

The young man hands him a clipboard with forms to fill out, takes his driver's license, and goes off to the back office to find out if his customer is a member of ISIS.

He reads the label on the box of Hydra-Shoks. It boasts "better terminal ballistics than traditional cup-and-core projectiles."

Terminal ballistics? That's funny.

Sale approved. He signs the credit card and is good to go, in every way, so to speak. He heads to the door.

"Sir?" The young man holds out a bullet, smiling. "How about a round on the house?"

He laughs. "Very good, young man. That's going in my screenplay, for sure."

"Really?"

"You bet. That's good dialogue."

"What's the name of your movie?"

"*Heimlich's Maneuver.*"

"Okay."

"But now I'm thinking *A Round on the House* might make a better title."

"Really?"

"Tell you what, if it ends up called that, you get a front-row seat at the premiere. Two seats."

"Cool. Thanks."

"Thank *you*, young man."

Peaches calls out an affectionate greeting as he walks in. He does not present himself for a hug, inasmuch as a large handgun is stuffed into the waistband of his trousers at the back. But uh-oh: his darling approaches, wiping her hands on a dish towel, wanting to give him a hug. He feigns urgent urinary need and ducks into the powder room.

He looks around for someplace to stash the pistol. The powder room is small. It wasn't designed as an auxiliary storage area for firearms. The gun is laughably too big for the dainty little pink plastic wastebasket. Nor will the copy of *Coastal Living* magazine atop the toilet suffice to cover it. Perhaps between the toilet tank and the wall? He gropes, like Michael Corleone in the restaurant WC prior to assassinating Captain McCluskey and Sollozzo. Alas, there is insufficient space to accommodate a Smith & Wesson .357 Magnum. Maybe inside the toilet tank? He replaces the heavy ceramic lid carefully, so it won't clank and arouse curiosity as to why he is dismantling the toilet.

He washes his hands and regards himself in the mirror. He asks it: "How did it come to this?"

The mirror says, "Leave the gun, take the cannoli." What does that mean, for heaven's sake?

He emerges, smiling, feigning the relieved expression of a man with a drained bladder. "How'd did it go with Dr. Bhong, sweetheart?" she asks.

"Aces. I have the skull of an eighteen-year-old."

"Oh? Well, great."

"Inside the skull, it's all pure, unadulterated stable genius.

Dr. Bhong didn't use those exact words, but that was my take-away."

"Babe. C'mon. I've been worried sick all day."

"I know you have, sweetheart," he says, giving her a kiss. "It was a good report. On a scale of one to ten, a solid nine."

"Did he have the PET scan results?"

"He did."

"And?"

"I have the PET of a seventeen-year-old."

"I'll call him myself."

"Sweetheart. He was thrilled with the results. My synapses are crackling like Rice Krispies. By the way, did you know that the brain generates enough electricity to power a forty-watt light bulb for twenty-four hours? Bet Einstein's could run your hair dryer. He wants to have a second look at something or other. So we're doing another test next week."

"What does he want to have another look at?"

"My amygdala. The almond, remember? Mine's acting more like a pecan. Not a big deal. When it starts acting like a walnut, then you worry."

"You okay? You look kind of beat."

"Fine, fine. Bit tired from the drive. Had to outrun another pickup truck full of sodomite hillbillies on Dead Horse Road. You'd think the park police would be a little more proactive. It can't be helping tourism. 'Welcome to the Francis Marion National Forest. Squeal like a pig.'"

He goes to his study to work on the screenplay.

A half hour later he hears Them's voice calling, "Mom? There's something weird with the toilet." He thinks, *Them, dude, you're twenty-seven. Do you really need your mother to fix the toilet?*

The door to his study opens.

"Babe," Peaches says, "could you come here, please?"

"Sweetheart, I'm working."

"I need you to come and look at something."

He sighs. Why is he being wrenched from the arms of the muse to deal with a plumbing issue?

Them is standing outside the powder room with an amused look.

The top of the toilet tank is lying athwart the toilet seat.

Peaches points.

"Why is there a pistol in the toilet?"

He looks. Odd. Indeed, there is a pistol in the toilet. A large one at that. The chain connecting the lever and the flapper valve has tangled itself around the gun's trigger. Not ideal. But more to the point, why is the pistol in the toilet?

"I think I see the problem," he says, reaching in.

Peaches intercepts his hand.

"Leave it," she says sharply. "Do not touch it."

"I'm not sure that's a good idea, sweetheart. The chain's wrapped around the trigger. That could make for a nasty surprise when you flush."

"Sweetheart. Look at me. I'm asking you: Why is there a gun in the toilet?"

"It's a perfectly good question. Has the plumber been, recently? Maybe it fell in while he was replacing the bulb. A bit careless if you ask me. I'll call him."

"No. I'm calling the police."

"Really? Do we want to be an item in the *Weekly Pimentoan* police blotter? '*Deputies were summoned to a residence in Aqueous Acres by a homeowner who found a .357 Magnum in the powder room toilet.*'"

"I don't care how it sounds," Peaches says, heading to the kitchen to summon agents of law enforcement.

Suddenly, he remembers. *He* put the pistol there. *Fuck!*

"Okay," he says, raising his hands. "I surrender."

Peaches glares. "You put it there?"

"It was supposed to be a surprise."

"Oh, it was."

"It's a present," he says, putting his hand on his stepson's shoulder. "For Them's birthday."

"His birthday is in October."

"Well, excuse me. I didn't realize we have a rule that we can't buy presents for each other ahead of time."

Peaches groans. "My head is about to explode. Why is the gun in the toilet?"

"If you'll stop screeching at me, I'd be happy to explain. I bought it at Lock 'N' Load. When I came in earlier, you and Them were standing right there. I pretended I had to pee so I could hide it. But there's not a lot of extra space in there. I was going to retrieve it."

He gives Them a hug.

"Happy birthday, buddy. Hope you like it. It was hideously expensive."

That night in bed, Peaches says, "Why would you buy him a gun? He smokes pot all day."

"For protection."

"Against what?"

"Sharks. If he insists on continuing to surf, he might as well be armed."

"How is he supposed to surf holding a pistol?"

"Good thinking. I'll buy him a holster."

CHAPTER 32

He hasn't wasted much time over the years fretting about whether he'll be remembered. But now that he's made his decision, he finds himself thinking about it. Seems kind of preposterous. In the larger scheme of things, who really gives a shit? But it would be nice to think some of his work might last. As Hilaire Belloc put it,

> *When I am dead,*
> *I hope it may be said:*
> *"His sins were scarlet,*
> *But his books were read."*

One or two of his movies could hang in there. *A Bubble Off Plumb* might have a shot at Netflix immortality. Legacywise, that's not quite on the level of Ozymandias's "Look on my Works, ye Mighty, and despair!" or Christopher Wren's "If you would seek my monument, look around you." But it's not nothing.

He probably faces posthumous notoriety for *Swamp Foxes*. At one point he was going to preorder a gravestone inscribed:

HIC IACET

FACTOR ILLE AQUILONIUS

CINEMATOGRAPHEUM OBSCENUS

Latin, as best he could manage, for "Here Lies That Yankee Pornographer." But what's eating at him now, at his desk in his study, is the prospect of a Wikipedia entry: "Cause of death: suicide by firearm." There, as Mr. Shakespeare put it, lies the rub. Where *did* he say that? He looks it up, and what do you know, it's from his most famous soliloquy, where Hamlet is moaning about whether to plunge a bare bodkin into himself.

He remembers the back cover of his paperback of *The Sun Also Rises*, with the photo of Hemingway—handsome, burly, pecking away at his typewriter—and the brief bio that ends, "He died in Ketchum, Idaho, in 1961." Died. Okay, but as everyone in tenth grade knew, it was a little more complicated than "died." He blew his brains out with a shotgun. Someone in class had an uncle who lived in Ketchum, so he had all sorts of gory details. No matter how much you admired Hemingway—and who didn't?—there was always that S-word lurking around the corner like a mugger. It was a Catholic school, so the fact that he killed himself wasn't entirely extraneous. In the eyes of Mother Church, Hemingway was eternally damned. This was a depressing thought if you wanted to grow up to *be* Hemingway. Someone in class raised his hand and asked Father Damian, "Is Hemingway in hell?" You could see that Father Damian didn't want to get down in those weeds. Hemingway's location in the afterworld was not the reason he'd assigned *The Sun Also Rises*. He wanted to teach his pimply pupils about good, clear writing. "Notice how few adjectives he uses? Buckley, pay attention." Father Damian also had to tiptoe around the specifics of Jake Barnes's tragic wound. "Father?" "Yes, MacGuire?" "Did Barnes's penis get blown off? Or was it his testicles?" Titters. Sniggers. "It doesn't *matter*, MacGuire." "Bet it did to Barnes." Raucous laughter, and a week's extra study hall for MacGuire.

As for the S-word, Father Damian didn't have much wriggle room. On the other hand, Mother Church is nothing if not legalistic, and often provided loopholes. The loophole here was that killing yourself was *eo ipso* evidence of insanity, which could get you off eternal damnation. *But* your insanity had to certified by something like three priests and two psychiatrists. And the verdict had to be unanimous. The certification process was—as it were—hellish (get it?) and the paperwork endless. Suicide—"the sin of ultimate despair"—was pretty much at the top in the hierarchy of no-nos. About the only worse sin would be assassinating the pope or ravishing a nun. (Groping altar boys was never mentioned in those days, oddly.) Later, when he and MacGuire and the others moved on to Dante's *Inferno*, the location of suicides could be fixed as precisely as a GPS marker: Ring 2, Seventh Circle of Hell—"The Wood of the Self-Murderers." *I don't think we're in the Hundred Acre Wood anymore, Pooh.*

It's been years since he believed in all this. It's not the prospect of Saint Peter directing him to the Express Down elevator, where an usher with horns and forked tail looks at your ticket and says, "Ring 2, Circle 7. This way. Watch your step, *loser*." What troubles him is the indelible Scarlet S—on you and the loved ones you leave behind.

Stigma. He's never looked up that word before. He does. What an awful etymology: Greek for "a mark made by a pointed instrument." How nice for Peaches. "*Thanks, babe. I'm so looking forward to people staring at me and whispering, 'She must have been a horrible wife for him to have killed himself.' I think I'll tell them you did it because you couldn't go on living with the shame of having written 'that titty movie.'*" He hears himself telling her from beyond the grave: "*Sweetheart, I did it for you. To spare you having to care for a demented husband. Did you really want to*

*spend years spoon-feeding me and changing my diapers? I stip—
sorry. I admit that yeah, I also did it to spare myself all that crap.
(Literally.) But I mainly did it for you."* Why does this ring hollow?

Don't they cut you some slack if you were the artsy type?
Isn't Hemingway proof of that? It made him even more of a
legend. It didn't get him banned from Catholic school curricula.
Suicide hasn't hurt sales of David Foster Wallace's books. And
the guy who wrote *Confederacy of Dunces*. Suicide sure as hell
didn't hurt him. It made his career. It got him published.

There are suicides, and there are suicides. There are troubled artistes, and there are people no one is going to miss. The
embezzler who jumps out the window, landing (poetically) on
his Maserati. The person who came up with the idea of separat-
ing migrant kids from their parents and then realized what an
awful human being he was and drank the entire bottle of Clorox
he found in the White House briefing room. Is anyone going to
say of them, "Thank heavens his suffering is over. Let's hope he
found some measure of peace"?

Artists are supposed to be troubled souls. Okay, maybe in
his case, "artist" is a bit of a stretch. Still. *A Bubble Off Plumb*
was an art house hit, a sweet little story about a carpenter in
small-town Maine who thinks he's Jesus. He's low-key about it.
Even has a sense of humor. He tells people, "Believe me, this
wasn't what *I* had in mind for a Second Coming." He does nice
things for the townsfolk, and when he does CPR on a lobsterman who's been pronounced dead, the guy revives and everyone
goes, *Whoa.*

Wait. He's got it. Why didn't he think of this before?
Dr. Bhong will attest to the fact that he had dementia. No one
can get morally huffy about his shooting himself. He was nuts.
End of discussion, case closed.

He googles "writers who committed suicide." Holy moly. There are so many Wikipedia breaks them down into subcategories. "Writers who committed suicide, by nationality." "Male writers who committed suicide." "Female writers . . ." "Peruvian writers . . ." "Malagasy writers . . ." Malagasy?

And it's once more into the breach and down the old rabbit hole. Here comes the Google Noodge, going *psst* like a lowlife skulking in a dark alley wanting to sell him *feelthy pictures.* "Which band singer killed himself?" Fuck off. What does that have to do with writers who killed themselves? He hits the back arrow. Now Google Noodge hisses: *What about painters who killed themselves? You* know *you want to know.*

No, I don't. Well . . . okay, but only one. Van Gogh? Thanks. I already know about him. Rothko? Hmm. This actually is of interest. When he was a kid, they lived a few doors down from Mr. Rothko.

"He was found on the floor of his studio lying in a pool of blood, which was reminiscent of his work." Reminiscent how? Because he used red paint? Honestly. A half hour later, he's spelunked so far down the rabbit hole that he's now reading about someone named John William Godward, who departed this vale of tears in 1922.

"Reportedly, he wrote in his suicide note that the world was not big enough for him and Pablo Picasso."

Really? So now another hour is spent trying to find out Picasso's opinion on this. Did he feel the world was big enough to accommodate himself and the painter of *Violets, Sweet Violets* and *Portrait of Harriet (Hetty) Pettigrew in Classical Dress*? Alas, Picasso's opinion on the matter is nowhere to be found, which makes poor Godward seem even more pathetic. He was criticized for "painting Victorians in togas." He finds his paintings rather fetching. Downright erotic, in fact. Godward left England and moved to Italy with one of his models. His family was so angry they broke off all contact with him and even "scissored his face out of the family photographs." What lovely parents. When poor Godward killed himself rather than live another day in a world also inhabited by the painter of *Les Demoiselles d'Avignon* and *Musicians with Masks*, they burned all his papers. Only one photograph of him exists. But if the model he ran off with to Italy was anything like the babes in his paintings, weep not for John William Godward. Life wasn't all bad.

He finally emerges from this mine shaft of a rabbit hole dazed and blinking at the light, trying to remember what he was looking for in the first place. He's pretty sure it wasn't to compile a list of painters who killed themselves rather than share the planet with Picasso.

He stares at the screen. Here comes that asshole Google Noodge. What's he hawking now? "People We Wish Were Still Alive." Honestly. Like, say, Abraham Lincoln? Marilyn Monroe? Hannibal? Fuck *off*.

Writers who committed suicide—that was it. Okay, but let's not spend the next decade on this. Narrow it down. Start by eliminating "Male Bulgarian writers who committed suicide" and "Female Swedish writers who committed suicide." May they rest in peace.

Psst. What? Google Noodge wants him to check out "Sculptors Who Committed Suicide." No! Absolutely not.

He compiles a top-thirty list of writers who wrote their own "The End." It's subjective, skews American, and it is no doubt insufficiently woke, but it's fairly catholic (small *c*) despite excluding male Bulgarians and female Swedes.

Hemingway, Virginia Woolf, Hart Crane, Seneca, Petronius,

Richard Brautigan, John Berryman, Harry Crosby, Robert E. Howard (author of the *Conan the Barbarian* books), Abbie Hoffman, William Inge, Fletcher Knebel (coauthor of *Seven Days in May*), Hunter S. Thompson, John Kennedy Toole, David Foster Wallace, Sylvia Plath, Thomas Chatterton, Kenneth Halliwell, Brian Howard (one of the models for Anthony Blanche in Evelyn Waugh's *Brideshead Revisited*), Sir John Suckling, Arthur Koestler, Yukio Mishima (by full Monty ritual seppuku), Romain Gary, Berton Roueché, Gérard de Nerval, Nicolas Chamfort, Primo Levi, Gunther Sachs, and Stefan Zweig. He hesitates about Hitler (author of the runaway best seller *Mein Kampf*) and hears a voice telling him, "Hitler. Was. Also. A. Writer."

He remembers that Evelyn Waugh, the author whose novels he most returns to, once almost committed suicide. He recently reread Waugh's funny but somewhat harrowing autobiographical novel, *The Ordeal of Gilbert Pinfold*. Pinfold, a past-his-prime novelist, unwittingly poisons himself by overloading his system with sleeping potions and other drugs—without telling his doctor—and goes bonkers aboard a passenger ship to Ceylon.

Where did he read about the suicide attempt? Another rabbit hole beckons, but this one is of the old-fashioned kind, where instead of clicking and scrolling, you climb a ladder and pull books from shelves. And by gum, a half hour later he's found it, on page 142 of Humphrey Carpenter's *The Brideshead Generation: Evelyn Waugh and His Friends*.

Waugh was twenty-two, finished with Oxford, and teaching at a dreary boys' school in Wales. He was madly in love with a girl in London who was not in love with him. He'd written a novel and sent it to his Oxford chum Harold Acton, also a model for the louche but wildly entertaining Anthony Blanche of *Brideshead*. Acton's reply: "Too English for my exotic taste.

Too much nid-nodding over port." Not the reaction Waugh was hoping for.

So, wrote Carpenter, Waugh "burnt the manuscript in the school boiler. His spirits lifted when [his brother] Alec managed to fix him up with a secretaryship to 'a homosexual translator' in Florence—C. K. Scott Moncrieff, who had rendered Proust into English." Waugh gave notice, "whereupon he heard that Moncrieff did not want him after all." His gloom was compounded when all his chums embarked on exciting trips. "It looks rather like the end of the tether," he wrote in his diary. Carpenter continues:

> One night he went down to the sea without a towel, having chosen a quotation from Euripides, which he left on his clothes: "The sea washes away all the evils of men." He swam slowly out but met a shoal of jelly-fish and was stung into some sense. Afterwards, he could not tell "how much real despair and act of will, how much play-acting" had prompted the suicide attempt.

Thank heavens for the jellyfish, without whom we wouldn't have *Scoop, Black Mischief, A Handful of Dust, Brideshead, The Loved One*, or *Pinfold*, among other works.

Water. Hmm. Hart Crane leapt off the stern of a steamer between Havana and Florida. Virginia Woolf put stones into her pockets and waded out into the River Ouse. Drowning is a gentler way of saying goodbye than splashing your brains all over the place. Close your eyes, exhale, inhale a lungful of water, and that's that. No doubt the reality isn't pleasant, but "he drowned" sounds so much nicer than "he shot himself" or "he hurled himself into the path of a subway train."

Classy, leaving a quote from Euripides on his clothes. Brits. Such style. He looks up the quote. It's from *Iphigenia in Tauris*. He tells himself, *Do not spend hours on this! You need to find your own valedictory quote*. But he can't resist at least a quick look. Tauris was what is now called Crimea. He did not know that. Did Czar Nicholas I, who started the Crimean War, know that? Did Queen Victoria? What about the six hundred poor bastards in the charge of the Light Brigade? They probably did know. They all went to Eton.

He must find just the right quote. You don't want people at your memorial service muttering, "I can't believe he chose 'I must go down to the sea again, to the lonely sea and the sky.' You'd think he could have come up with something more original. Him being a writer and all."

He's tempted by the last line of the first paragraph of *Moby-Dick*: "If they but knew it, almost all men in their degree, some time or other, cherish very nearly the same feelings towards the ocean with me." Epitaph-wise, you can't do better than good old Melville.

He writes it out in neat longhand on his best writing paper. He rereads it. Perfect, and very to the point. But wait. Does it imply that everyone has thought about drowning themselves? Not really, but some wiseass at the memorial service might harrumph that he likes the ocean just fine, but not so much he's going to go drown himself in it. What fun for Peaches as she's passing around plates of Congaree Inn–catered devils on horseback—"These were his favorite"—while hermeneutic arguments break out over whether his suicide note misappropriated Melvillian ontology.

He feels weary. Why is it so complicated? Can't a man choose a quotation for his farewell from a venerable work of literature without everyone getting their knickers in a twist? It's enough to make you yearn for the peace of the grave.

But hold on. What is he thinking? Leaving a quotation, on the beach, with his pile of XXL clothes? *The whole point of drowning, you idiot, is to make it look like an accident. To spare Peaches getting stuck with the stigma. And now you're leaving a quotation from* Moby-Dick? *Brilliant! People who go for midnight swims* always *leave literary quotations behind on the beach with their clothes.* He can hear Coroner Babcock: "*It appears the deceased went for a swim in the middle of the night and drowned. There is no indication of suicide. However, he seems to have left behind an ornate statement to the effect that he, along with other folks, liked the ocean. So, we are looking into that.*"

The smart thing to do would be *not* to leave a quote from Melville. Or any note, for that matter. Remember Maureen O'Hara, insisting to the press that Brian Keith couldn't possibly have killed himself? "*Er, Miss O'Hara, what about this suicide note he left?*"

Tap-tap on the door. Peaches sticks her head in.

"Dinner's almost ready, babe."

The sight of his beautiful, darling Peaches, whom he's about to leave forever, is more than he can bear. He looks away, pretending to focus on his computer screen.

"Gonna pass on dinner, sweetheart."

"You don't want dinner?"

"I'll grab something later. Screenplay's on fire. Can't break off."

"Sure?"

"I'll be there in a bit. Love you."

"Love you, too. I'll leave a plate in the oven."

The screenplay. That's it! If he dies while writing *Heimlich's Maneuver* that's what he'll be remembered for, not for that piece-of-shit *Swamp Foxes*. But can he finish it tonight? No matter. The fact that he was working on it at the time of his death—"his *accidental* death"—will be proof enough that it wasn't suicide. His agent Winky will spin it (she's *very* good at that) as "especially tragic, as *Heimlich's Maneuver* may well turn out to be his masterpiece." Unfinished masterpiece. There's always buzz when someone leaves behind an "unfinished" work. And who would kill himself in the middle of his own master-piece? Winky will find someone to finish the screenplay. In the right director's hands—and with Donald Sutherland as Bernard Baruch—it could actually turn out to be his masterpiece.

CHAPTER 33

Interior. U-322 German submarine.

Camera follows Heimlich as he makes his way along a long passageway through watertight hatches, balancing a tray. He arrives at a door and knocks gently.

From inside, we hear a familiar, patrician voice: Yes? What is it?

> HEIMLICH: It is myself, Heimlich, Herr President Roosevelt. I have your breakfast.
>
> ROOSEVELT: Very well. Come in.

Heimlich opens the door to a surprisingly spacious suite for a submarine, decorated in tasteful nautical accents: oil paintings of German World War I battleships; portrait of Frederick the Great; brightly shined brass clock-barometer; and banner: "Welcome Aboard U-322, USA President Franklin Roosevelt."

Roosevelt is propped up in bed with comfy pillows, smoking a cigarette and reading Hitler's Mein Kampf *with an expression of revulsion. As Heimlich approaches, FDR tosses the book into a wastebasket.*

FDR: That is without question *the* worst book since the invention of movable type. Gutenberg must be rolling in his grave.

HEIMLICH: Good morning, Herr President. I hope you have had a rest. Again, I am regretting to you the circumstances under which you are becoming our guest.

FDR: Save it for the war crimes tribunal, Fritz.

Heimlich sets the breakfast tray on FDR's lap.

HEIMLICH: Heimlich is my name. At your service. So. Here we have a lovely juice of orange. *Kaffee.* Milk, with one sugar, is your preference, I think, yes? Here we have bacons, two pieces, of course crisp. And here we have two eggs of hen. Scrampled lightly, to your preference. And here, two toasts of wheat. Here is butter, and here is a most tasty jam from plums. A specialty, from Aachen. So, all will be your pleasing, I am hoping, yes?

FDR tucks into his breakfast with relish. They converse as he eats.

FDR: What was that dreadful business with the flaming pigs? Can't get the sound of them out of my head.

HEIMLICH: An unfortunity, I am stipulating. But as you witness, tactically, a success. I conceived the idea from the manual of Hannibal, the great general of—

FDR: Yes, thank you. I know all about Hannibal. Read about him at Groton. In Latin. Where'd you say this jam is from? It is good, I must say.

HEIMLICH: Aachen. This is a town near the border with Belgium.

FDR: Not that you Germans pay much attention to borders.

I take it your plan is to use me as a bargaining chip, to get the invasion called off.

HEIMLICH: Not my plan, Herr President. As we accustom to say in Germany, I am only following orders. But yes, a great honor to be choosed for to ... to ...

FDR: I think the word you're looking for is "kidnap."

HEIMLICH (*blushing*): I prefer "escort." To escort your illustrious personage from Hopcow—

FDR: Hobcaw.

HEIMLICH: Indeed, so. A strange name. More *Kaffee*?

FDR (*holding out his cup*): Just a splash. Tell me your name again.

HEIMLICH: Heimlich, *mein*—Herr Roosevelt. At your service.

FDR: Look here, Heimlich, you don't seem like a typical jackbooted, sadistic, mass-murdering Nazi. Which you may take as a compliment.

HEIMLICH: I am a simple soldier, Herr President. Who is having time these days for politics?

FDR: Especially when you're busy invading Poland, Austria, France, Hungary, Romania, Greece, Africa, and the Low Countries. (*Chuckles*) And let's not forget Russia. That one didn't go quite as planned, did it? But assuming *the* plan is to use me as leverage to cancel the invasion, I'm afraid you're too late. What's the date today?

HEIMLICH: March 28.

FDR: Pity. The invasion's set for March 30. At Dunkirk. Ideal spot. Lots of sand. Oh, damn. Careless of me to have revealed that. Forget I mentioned it.

HEIMLICH (*smiling and wagging a finger*): I think you

are—how is the expression?—"fucking with me," Herr
President.

FDR (*sniffing*): I guess we'll find out, won't we?

HEIMLICH: Thirty of March is a special day.

FDR: Oh?

HEIMLICH: Is the natal day of my auntie Gerta. It was she
who gave me the jam from plums, to give to you.

FDR (*skeptical*): Your *aunt* knew about a top-secret operation to kidnap the president of the United States?

HEIMLICH: A infortunate discretion on my part, I stipulate to you. Indeed, very. It popped from my mouth,
like a burping. But I told her most severely, "Auntie, you
must promise not to tell anyone, or it will be nasty for
both of us."

FDR: There's a bit of an undistributed middle there. Why
on earth would you tell her such a thing?

HEIMLICH: Auntie Gerta thinks that you walk on water,
Herr Roosevelt.

FDR: I can't walk on land, never mind water.

HEIMLICH: Yes, this is true. But for Auntie, this makes you
even more wonderful. Such a fan of you is she. All week
she would sit by her radio, waiting to hear your fire talks.

FDR: Fireside chats?

HEIMLICH: Yes. These. Not one—ever—did she miss. And
if should anyone speak while you were fire chatting?
Ach. Woe to that person. More tempestuous than a
Valkyrie she would be. She would shout, "Silence, you!
The great Roosevelt is speaking! *Such* a beautiful voice
he has. What a fortunate woman is Lucy Mercer."

Heimlich blushes with embarrassment, realizing that he has spoken out of school. FDR stares, somewhat dumbstruck.

HEIMLICH (*briskly changing the subject*): But then is coming the Gestapo, in the black leather coats, for to confiscating the radios from everyone. Then was no more fire chatting for Auntie. Which make her very sad. Like she is losing her best friend.

FDR: I must say, your auntie doesn't sound like a very good Nazi.

HEIMLICH: No, no. Auntie is no Nazi, this I am very assuring you. (*Whispering*) In her attic have been living—since 1938—sixteen Jews. Two families. Three generations.

FDR (*suddenly uncomfortable*): I wish we could have taken in a few more ourselves.

HEIMLICH: Herr Roosevelt, would you be consenting to make for Auntie a signaturing? For memento.

FDR: An autograph?

HEIMLICH: Yes. Here is the word. Thank you. Yes.

FDR (*flustered*): Well, if you think she'd . . . yes, all right, very well.

HEIMLICH: Such a generosity is this.

Heimlich pulls out a dossier marked Streng Geheim (*top secret*) *and rummages, pulling out papers and an eight-by-ten black-and-white photograph of Roosevelt with his dog, Fala, on his lap.*

HEIMLICH: If Your Honor would be autographing this photograph, Auntie will have an attack of the heart, from happiness. She, too, has a doggie. Not such a beautiful Scotty like your handsome Fala. A Schnauzer. Lucy is her name.

Close-up on faces of the two men. The moment is intense between them as FDR realizes that his captor's aunt has named her dog after his "special friend," Lucy Mercer.

The president is visibly moved. He removes his pince-nez to wipe his eyes. He inscribes the photograph at length and hands it back to Heimlich, who reads it, tears brimming in his eyes.

> **HEIMLICH:** Herr Roosevelt, how am I locating wordings for which to express my gratitude?
> **FDR:** No need, Heimie old shoe. But you'd better tell Auntie Gerta not to hang it in her window.

They laugh heartily. We discern in their mutual delight that they may be from different worlds, but if it weren't for Hitler, they might have been the best of friends.

Suddenly, the warm, indeed fuzzy, mood is shattered by an explosion—a loud whoompf-boom *followed by another* whoompf-boom. *And another. The presidential suite is violently rocked. Items sail through the air. The president's* Kaffee *spills.*

> **FDR:** I take it we're not alone on the bounding main?

Heimlich grabs the intercom handset.

[English subtitles]:

> **HEIMLICH** (*to the captain*): What the fuck is going on?
> **CAPTAIN** (*voice-over*): What the fuck do you think? We are being fucking depth-charged!
> **HEIMLICH:** Well, fucking *do* something!

CAPTAIN: What the fuck do you think I'm doing? Fuck off!

HEIMLICH (*to FDR*): It seems we are being depth-charged. But captain say everything is good. Everything hunky-dunky good.

FDR (*smiling slyly as he lights a cigarette*): I find myself between the proverbial rock and hard place.

Heimlich looks puzzled, then grasps the president's meaning.

HEIMLICH: Yes, of course. You are expressing irony. Well, Herr President, with respect, we shall see how you are feeling when the proverbial water is up to our proverbial armpits.

Both again laugh heartily.

He has to get up and pace. The screenplay actually *is* writing itself. And Auntie Gerta. Where did *she* come from?

This'll make them forget *Swamp Foxes*. Too bad he won't be around to see it.

What time is it? Ten forty-five. From his window, he can see their bedroom. No lights. Peaches will be in bed, emailing or asleep. He's exhausted, but he can't leave FDR and Heimlich 150 feet beneath the surface of the Atlantic, being depth-charged.

But why is the U.S. Navy trying to sink a submarine the president might be aboard? (Good question.) More pressing is how to get Heimlich and FDR out of this watery pickle.

You can do this, he tells himself. *Before the sun rises, you'll type the two sweetest words in the screenwriter's vocabulary:* FADE OUT.

Saving them may require torpedoing the American ship. Boy, war really is hell. But if U-322 sinks an American ship, Roosevelt will be furious, and something else will be torpedoed: the bond between him and Heimlich. And that could sink the most important thing of all—his screenplay.

U-322 will have to do something clever short of sinking the American ship. The U-boat captain can do it. He's up to the task. Karl Dönitz, Grossadmiral of the German navy, wouldn't have given him an assignment this important if he wasn't the real Kreigsmarine deal. He just has to figure out how to do it without loss of American life.

CHAPTER 34

Interior. U-322 control room. Captain Kreeg, various officers, crew, Heimlich.

We can almost smell the tension, to say nothing of the body odor.

Captain Kreeg peers intently through the periscope. All eyes are on him.

[English subtitles]

> **KREEG:** It worked. The Americans are taking the bait. They are disengaging.

Murmurs of "phew," "fucking A," "I think I shat myself."

> **HEIMLICH:** Allow me to offer my congratulations, Captain. A brilliant piece of submarining.
> **KREEG:** Brilliant piece of luck, you mean.
> **HEIMLICH:** Did not Napoleon say, "I don't want good generals. I want lucky generals." Not to imply that you are not also good.
> **KREEG:** If that giant squid had not suddenly appeared from out of nowhere, we would now be on our way to the bottom of the Atlantic.

HEIMLICH: The way you enticed it to swallow the noise-making device that tricked the Americans into thinking the squid was us was . . . I can only repeat myself. Brilliant.

Hearty jawohls! *from the crew.*

HEIMLICH: The führer will hear of your genius from my own lips when I present him with our captive. Speaking of whom, I must go and see how he is doing. That last depth charge was a real bowel emptier.

Roosevelt's suite. Heimlich and FDR, who is mixing martinis in a large brass shell casing.

FDR: Do you take yours dry or drier?

HEIMLICH: Dry is good.

FDR: Olive or twist?

HEIMLICH: I regret to say I have not read much Dickens.

FDR hands him a martini. They clink glasses.

FDR: Down the hatch.

HEIMLICH: Prost.

FDR: Proust? Haven't got 'round to reading him. Just never seem to find the time. The gunpowder residue gives it a nice kick, doesn't it?

HEIMLICH: I hope we will not explode.

They both laugh.

FDR points to the copy of Mein Kampf *in the wastebasket.*

FDR: Read much of that, have you, Heimie?

HEIMLICH: Candidly, I must inform, no. My tasting in books is more for the work of the great Zane Gray. And the great Owen Wister. Are you perhaps knowing of these excellent literatures?

FDR (*laughing*): Heavens, I could probably recite the whole of *Riders of the Purple Sage* and *The Virginian*, word for word to you, from memory.

HEIMLICH (*swooning*): Truly yes? How felicitious is this making me. These are my most favorite books.

Close-up FDR's face. We see from his expression that he's up to something.

FDR: You know, old cock, you really ought to give your führer's book a look. I know, I know—no time for politics. Yet here you are, implementing his politics. Don't you think you owe it to yourself to see what's on Herr Hitler's agenda?

Heimlich picks Mein Kampf *out of the wastebasket and regards it pensively.*

What time is it now? One thirty-five. Man, is he tired. He doesn't have the energy he used to, ever since Dr. Bhong took him off Dr. Paula's appetite suppressants. He needs to wrap this sucker. He tells himself sternly: *Do not start adding flashbacks to young Heimlich hiking in the Alps in lederhosen with his Jewish buddies. And no FDR and Lucy Mercer flashbacks, the two of them cozy and alone in the Lincoln Bedroom, FDR reading to her from* The Virginian *while Eleanor is off drumming up support for her cockamamie United Nations.*

Flip-card montage showing Heimlich reading Mein Kampf—*in his cabin, on the crapper, in the torpedo room, etc.*

His expression grows more and more disgusted. Subtitles reveal what he's reading in each scene:

[English subtitles]

"*I use emotion for the many, and reserve reason for the few.*"

"*All effective propaganda must be limited to a very few points and must harp on these slogans until the last member of the public understands what you want him to understand by your slogan.*"

"*Humanitarianism is the expression of stupidity and cowardice.*"

"*If you tell a big enough lie, and tell it frequently enough, it will be believed.*"

"*The recent forest fires in Prussia and Lower Saxony were caused by Jewish lasers in outer space. When I tell people this, they roll their eyes. But the day is coming when the eye rolling will cease, and the head rolling will commence!*"

In the final scene, Heimlich is asleep and snoring. Mein Kampf *is back in the wastebasket.*

———

Interior. U-322 radio room.

The youthful Aryan radio officer stands to attention as Heimlich enters and closes the door behind him.

Heimlich shows him a piece of paper that looks like it might be Hitler's personal stationery. The radio officer's eyes widen. Ach du Lieber! It is the führer's personal stationery.

HEIMLICH: Do you recognize the signature, Lieutenant?
Radio officer nods. He's very impressed. And very terrified.
HEIMLICH: Take this down. Wait ten minutes and bring it
to the captain.

[*No English subtitles*]

Heimlich dictates to him in German.

[*English subtitles*]

Interior. U-322 control room. Captain Kreeg, officers, crew, and Heimlich. Heimlich looks like he's up to something. And indeed— he is.

The radio officer enters. He glances nervously at Heimlich and then hands a piece of paper to Captain Kreeg.

RADIO OFFICER: Message from Berlin, *Kapitän*. Highest
priority.

Kreeg reads with a "WTF?" expression.

HEIMLICH (*feigning mild interest*): Anything . . . interesting?

Kreeg mutters furiously. He goes to the map console and plots a course with parallel rulers and compass.

KREEG (*grimly*): We have just been ordered to make for the
mouth of the Chesapeake Bay.
HEIMLICH: Oh? Is that the shortest route to Bremerhaven?
KREEG (*exploding*): No, it is not on the fucking way to fucking Bremerhaven. It is where the fucking headquarters
of the American fucking Navy is located.

HEIMLICH (*pensively*): Hmm. *That* doesn't sound good.

KREEG (*seething*): And from there—assuming we have not been blown to pieces—we are to proceed up the Potomac River to . . . Washington, DC. The American capital.

Crew exchange looks of scheisse! *("shit") and "That can't be right."*

HEIMLICH (*shrugging*): Well, we are Germans. And Germans follow orders. May I see the message?

Kreeg hands it to him with disgust. Heimlich reads it aloud.

Elite unit American Negro commandos have seized the führer. Threaten execute him unless Roosevelt immediately returned to Washington unharmed. Essential you comply without delay. For security reasons do not, repeat do not reply to this message. Oberkommando der Marine Dönitz. End message.

HEIMLICH (*affecting indignation*): American swine! How dare they! They will regret this. We will crush them!

KREEG: Yes, but meanwhile we have a more immediate challenge—not being sunk by the entire fucking American fleet. And we dare not depend on more giant squid.

HEIMLICH: Agreed, my captain. I see the problem. But perhaps there is a . . . solution.

Interior. FDR's U-322 stateroom. [We cannot hear what is being said.]

Heimlich speaks intently to FDR, who listens intently. FDR's eyebrows suddenly rise and his eyes go wide. He shakes his head, as if to say no. But then he nods, appearing to acquiesce to whatever Heimlich has proposed. He takes a pencil and writes a single word on a piece of paper. We cannot see what the word is, much as we want to.

Interior. U-322 radio room.

The radio operator sits at his station, chewing his fingernails to the nub.

Heimlich enters with the piece of paper FDR has written on. Heimlich writes on it and hands it to the radio officer.

> **HEIMLICH:** Send this message to Admiral Daniel Murphy at the U.S. Navy Atlantic Fleet Command.

Radio officer looks like he's about to faint but starts tapping on the transmission key.

Sometime later.

Interior. U-322 control room. Captain, crew, Heimlich. The atmosphere is beyond intense.

> **KREEG** (*pointing to their position on the chart*): We are at the mouth of the Chesapeake. Sonar reports over a dozen American warships, directly above us. They know that we are here. And do nothing.
>
> **HEIMLICH** (*casually*): Perhaps our plan is working.

FDR rolls up in his wheelchair.

FDR (*cheery*): Permission to enter?

KREEG (*hissing*): *Shh.* Yes. But *quiet*, please, Herr Roosevelt.

FDR (*whispering*): Sorry. Are we in the English Channel? You've made very good time, Captain.

KREEG: No. But *shh*, please.

FDR screws a cigarette into the holder.

FDR: It's all quite thrilling. I must say. Permission to smoke?

KREEG (*groaning*): *Yes.*

————————

Sometime later.

Exterior. Day. Washington, DC, Potomac River. In the background we see the Washington Monument and Capitol building. It's a beautiful spring day. Cherry blossoms are out.

The entire U.S. military appears to be present: troops, tanks, artillery, planes circle overhead. The tension is so palpable we can touch it, but happily doesn't smell of BO because we are outdoors and Americans are notably fastidious when it comes to personal hygiene.

We hear a strange sound. Gun turrets swivel, soldiers cock and aim their weapons. The moment is intense.

The surface of the Potomac churns as the conning tower of U-322 breaks the surface and rises, like an oddly shaped yet insistent whale.

The scene seems to freeze. Eerie silence.

A deck hatch opens with a clang.

President Roosevelt appears in his wheelchair, looking marvelously jaunty with cigarette holder and fedora. Heimlich is pushing his wheelchair.

A lusty, all-American cheer goes up. The submarine is swarmed with military brass. Admirals and generals salute the president.

FDR: Nothing like a sea cruise to lift the spirits, eh? Good to be back, gentlemen. Good to be back.

Interior. U.S. Navy Atlantic Fleet Command, Norfolk, Virginia.

In background, furious activity amid maps and boards showing ship positions.

In foreground, two extravagantly decorated admirals speak in subdued tones.

ADMIRAL MURPHY: Thank God they transmitted that message or U-322 would be at the bottom of the Chesapeake.

ADMIRAL #2: With the president of the United States aboard.

ADMIRAL MURPHY: Another five seconds and the *Gridley* would've sunk them. (*Shuddering*) On *my* orders.

ADMIRAL #2: Real career enhancer. What was her reaction when you called her?

ADMIRAL MURPHY: Her reaction? I would describe her reaction as surprised. That was one tough phone call, let me tell you.

ADMIRAL #2: Maybe we should leave this out of the official log.

ADMIRAL MURPHY: Affirmative. I need a drink.

_____

Interior. Day. Baruch mansion, Hobcaw.

In the foreground, Lucy Mercer sits at a writing desk.

Through a picture window behind her, we see Baruch and cartloads of charred pigs being wheeled away.

BARUCH (*grumpy*): Don't forget that batch over there. (*Muttering*) Guess we don't have to worry about overpopulation for a while.

Focus tightens on Lucy Mercer.

POV: Over her shoulder, as she writes a letter. She narrates as she writes.

MERCER (*voice-over*): *Dearest Bobo,*
I'm so very pleased to hear that you are safe after your terrible ordeal. I didn't feel that I could relate the details over the phone to you just now. But Commander Gilbert has kindly offered to deliver this letter to you personally. I told him not to give it to anyone but you.
On Tuesday morning, I received a telephone call from an Admiral Murphy in Norfolk. He was clearly mortified, poor man. He kept apologizing. He said, "Miss Mercer, I'm afraid I must ask you a very delicate question. But you

must believe me when I tell you that I wouldn't be asking if it were not of critical importance to our nation."

I said, "Well, Admiral, in that case, I suppose you'd better ask." He could barely get the words out. He said, "Does the president have a pet term for a particular part of your anatomy?"

Well! Now I was the one blushing. But clearly, it was important, so what could I do but tell him?

He sounded hugely relieved. Thanked me effusively, assured me it would be treated with the utmost confidentiality, etc. I sensed that he was in a great hurry, so I didn't keep him on the phone.

Well, there you have it. What an episode! I hope that whatever it was played some part in your safe return. I yearn to hear the details over our next game of mah-jongg. I might even let you win.

Your loving,
Lucy

P.S. "Foofie" sends her love, too. You old sea dog!

P.P.S. Bernie is in a foul humor over his burned pigs, but he's thrilled about your safe return. It may be a while before we're asked back to Hobcaw!

FADE OUT

He sits back in his chair and stares at the last two words. He's spent. But a good spent.

Whoever Winky hires to polish the screenplay will have a few blanks to fill in, including how a horde of flaming hogs got FDR aboard U-322.

He's very pleased with the "Foofie" device, an homage to Rosebud in *Citizen Kane*. No doubt it will be studied in future screenwriting classes at film schools.

CHAPTER 35

What time is it now? Four fifteen. Criminy. No time for preening. He hits print and goes about his preparations.

He tiptoes up the stairs, though given his heft, "tiptoeing" is euphemistic. He opens the bedroom door a crack. His darling is asleep, which she tends to be at 4:15 a.m. His objective is two-fold: swimming trunks and Xanax. The trunks are for show: evidence that he was going for a swim. Suicides tend not to bother with swimwear. But will they fit? He hadn't factored that in. He makes his way to the bathroom and opens the medicine cabinet. How many Xanax should he take? What is the plural of Xanax? Xanaxes? He must look this up. *No! No more looking things up!* Xanaxes sounds like a Persian emperor. It would make for a good—*Stop! Focus!*

If he takes all of them, and they find the empty bottle—which they will—that will definitely point to suicide. Best just to take a few. They're strong. When he needs a good night's sleep, he only takes half of one. But he'll need more than that to take the edge off thinking about drowning and sharks and alligators. Good to have some tranquilizer aboard, but not so much that the tox report will reveal he swallowed the entire medicine cabinet. Six should do the job.

He tiptoes out of the bedroom, forcing himself not to look

at his darling for fear of losing it. But on reaching the door, he does look back. He thinks of the hundreds of notes they left for each other under the pillow over the years, whenever they were apart. Sweet nothings. "Miss my girl already." "Peekaboo, I love you." If he would be gone for a while, he'd leave them where she wouldn't find all of them right away. Thinking about this, he starts to choke up. He kisses the tip of his finger and blows it at her. He thinks of the Larkin poem "An Arundel Tomb," about a marble effigy of a nobleman and his wife, lying side by side in an English church. The sculpture announces, *I was an important man. A big deal.* The poet notices amid the marmoreal pomp that the nobleman's hand is touching his wife's. "Our almost instinct, almost true / What will survive of us is love." The lines are on Larkin's slab in Westminster Abbey in Poet's Corner.

He goes to his study, praying his screenplay hasn't caused a paper jam: that would be a real pain in the ass. He can hear Coroner Babcock dictating into his recorder, "Traces of cyan, magenta, yellow, and black toner ink are present on the right forefinger and thumb . . ."

How did he get sucked into a fucking coroner election? Who gives a rat's ass who's coroner?

Good news. No paper jam. *That's a load offa* my *mind.* He sits and starts to write a farewell note to Peaches, then remembers Brian Keith and Maureen O'Hara and puts down his pen. *Better drown yourself before you do something else stupid.* He takes a last look around his fortress of solitude and leaves.

In the kitchen, he's tempted to down the Persian Emperor with a beer. But then that asshole Babcock will be muttering into his recorder, "Odor of alcoholic residue present in the salivary glands." He downs the pills with good old Poland Spring water and heads out to the beach.

A tantalizing thought now comes to him. Instead of a Wikipedia entry that says, "Cause of death: drowning," it might be even cooler indeed, the stuff of—dare he say it?—legend, if it said, "Cause of death: shark attack." Or even, "devoured by alligators." That would be way more attention-getting than "drowning." Imagine how much more famous Virginia Woolf would be if after pocketing those stones she'd been eaten by whatever there is in the River Ouse capable of swallowing an English novelist. Monster catfish, maybe, or giant carp? He must look this—*Stop!*

Okay, but if his body were to turn up with a shark bite or two, they'd have to put down "Death by shark attack." Wouldn't they? And that could really gin up interest in the screenplay. Winky's phone would be ringing off the hook.

"According to his agent, he had just finished what is now considered his masterpiece before his fateful decision to go for a pre-dawn swim in South Carolina's shark-infested waters."

Will his lifeless body be appealing to sharks? Why wouldn't it be? Sharks are scavengers, not picky eaters. *Another drowned writer. Borrr-ing. Let's keep looking for a live one.* But in the event, why not tempt them with an amuse-bouche, like they do at fancy restaurants—the little plate the chef sends out as a gift to whet the appetite?

He goes down the outside stairs to the basement-garage area and opens the big chest freezer. Holy cow, there's enough meat in here to fill Jaws. None of it is particularly suited to his purpose. How will it look if his body washes up with a pork loin or rack of baby back ribs duct-taped to it? What a field day Babcock would have with that: *"A 2.3-pound pork loin is present, attached to the abdominal section by means of adhesive tape."* What's Peaches supposed to say? *"He always duct-taped a pork loin to himself when he went for a swim. For ballast.*" Deeper diving in the freezer yields an ideal amuse-bouche: a string of Italian sausages, twenty or more links. They were made for this. He'll loop them around his torso diagonally, like a sash. What shark could resist? Should he stick an apple in his mouth as garnish, too? The thought makes him smile. Do sharks like apples? He must look that—*Just go.*

He takes his sausages and heads for the long wooden walkway to the beach. The steps should feel like a gallows, but don't. He's not scared or sad or depressed. On the contrary, he feels strangely elated, thanks to Emperor Xanaxes. Uh-oh. The sky's starting to turn orange. No time to waste. This needs to happen in the dark.

At the end of the walkway are the dunes where the turtles hatch, depending on the moon. He undresses. Now for the bathing suit.

Crap. No way it'll fit. He can barely get it above his knees. But no problemo. They'll find the trunks on the beach along with his clothes, proof that he was just going for a swim. It's all good.

Now for the sausages. And they do fit, nicely. He slings them across his torso, the way a mountain climber does his rope, and ties the ends together. If the sharks don't eat them, his body's going to look a bit odd, bandoliered with Italian sausages. Peaches can explain that he often wrapped himself with sausages in case he got hungry. "*He did love to eat.*"

Time to get this loco in motion. He takes a last look at the house. He and Peaches were happy here. It's nice to be able to think that at a moment like this. Imagine if you were doing it because you were miserable? That would be so sad.

He feels suddenly exhausted. As in barely-able-to-move exhausted. Emperor Xanaxes doesn't mess around. Molon Labe. *Come and take me.* He sits down.

He tells himself, *Okay, we're just going to sit here for ten seconds. No more. Hoping that baby turtles don't hatch and mistake our testicles for turtle num-nums. We'll gather our strength, then get up and walk to the water and become one with the ocean. It's going to be great. Ready? Okay. Let's roll.*

He tries to get up, but the sand is making it impossible. The more he exerts, the deeper he sinks. This must be what it was like for the dinosaurs in the final quarter of the Cretaceous era, when everything became gooey.

Okay, on my mark. One, two, three. Okay, that didn't work. We'll rest for five seconds. Then we're going to do this.

Something is tugging at him. What? Strange sensation. The sausages. The amuse-bouche for Mr. Shark. *Go on, then. Take a proper bite. What am I, chopped liver?*

He laughs. Wakes. Opens his eyes. It's a dog, not a shark, that's tugging at the sausages. And it's day. The world is illuminated, bright, whereas previously it was dark. Happens.

A woman's voice is shouting, "Ernie! *Ernie!* Come here! Stop that! Ernie!"

Why is she calling him Ernie? Ernie is not his name. Nor is his last name Hemingway. What's going on? He remembers: He has dementia. So it's natural that he would be confused. Nevertheless, he is 100 percent certain that his name is not Ernie. Imagine going through life with people calling you that. Did anyone call Hemingway Ernie? He must look this up.

He's on his back. A woman's face swims into his ken. He smiles at her. She does not smile back. She's looking at him with concern. Alarm. The dog strains at its leash. Aha. The *dog* must be Ernie. Sturdy-looking beast, English bulldog. It rightfully chafes at being denied sausage.

"Sir?" the woman says. "Are you all right?"

Rather personal question. He lifts his head to the extent he can and surveys the world about him. No hatching turtles are crawling toward his privy parts. There is only himself, the woman, and Ernie. He seems to be in a state of undress unless sausages could be considered a garment. More of an accessory, probably. The current rage in Aqueous Acres. Everyone is wearing them. As to the woman's question, it would depend on one's definition of "all right." Present evidence points to "not really." He suddenly feels very tired.

SWAMP FOXES WRITER FOUND ON
BEACH WEARING SAUSAGES

He suspects the source for the rather snarky item in the *Weekly Pimentoan* was the EMTs. He remembers them making rude comments about his weight as they lugged him from the beach to the ambulance. But it could have been Ernie's owner.

"I've gone from wife of that Yankee pornographer to wife of Sausage Man," Peaches says. "You're covering me in glory."

Peaches has been a proverbial trooper, tending to him as he detoxes on the sofa in the TV room. She and Dr. Bhong talk regularly by phone. The neurological mystery is solved: Dr. Paula's prescriptions of Contrave and Lysoloquine, in addition to alcohol—which, in fairness, she did not prescribe—produced what Dr. Bhong calls "a neuropsychiatric tornado." Peaches wants to sue Dr. Paula for malpractice. He himself prefers to move on. He'd rather lie on the sofa and watch submarine movies than be deposed by lawyers. Three times a day, Peaches brings him the only food he's allowed: cabbage soup. Yum, yum. But he's losing weight. It impossible to gain weight on three cups a day of cabbage soup.

Owing to Covid, the Oaf Keepers have abandoned their

vigil at the statue of civil rights icon John L. Lewis, which they have not detected was substituted for the one of Old Tar. Atticus found his way to Easter Island, which has since been closed to travelers, so he'll be spending many, many days communing with the stern-faced moai.

In other local news, someone has been shooting at Aqueous Acres's Do Not Feed the Alligators signs. The police are asking local residents to report any further shootings. He suggests to Peaches that this might be a good time for Themistocles to join his uncle on Easter Island.

Angina calls one morning at seven. The last time she was awake at this hour was when she stayed up all night partying. She's not calling to chat or report idle gossip. Itchfield has burned to the ground. Total loss. Seven—or is it eight?—generations of Puckett heritage, gone with the flame. Angina is delighted. Why? Years ago, when Jubal needed funding for a renovation, she loaned him the money from her trust fund. To secure the loan, he signed the deed over to her. He never got around to paying off the debt. Itchfield is insured for over $10 million. Angina is rich. She's especially pleased that it happened while Jubal and "his concierge slut"—that would be Dr. Paula—were off "fishing and fucking in the Florida Keys." To make Angina's happiness complete, Dr. Paula was arrested at the Key West airport for trying to board the plane home with a loaded pistol in her purse. In the rush to return, she neglected to put the gun in her checked baggage. Angina is eager to discuss this in all its delicious detail, but is off to Charleston to buy a complete set of Louis Vuitton luggage. She's planning on doing "a whole lot" of traveling.

He asks Peaches, "Do you think Angina had anything to do with it?"

Peaches replies, "Are you serious? Can you see Angina skulking about Itchfield with a can of gasoline? She'd set herself on fire."

He says, "If she writes her memoirs, the first sentence can be, 'Last night I dreamt I went to Itchfield again.'"

Between submarine movies and cups of cabbage soup, he reads his screenplay. Wow. Did he actually write this? Strange organ, the human brain.

Local TV reports that Itchfield's insurers have determined it was arson. "Are we *sure* it wasn't Angina?" he asks Peaches. They giggle at the image of Angina fleeing the country with her complete set of Louis Vuitton. The next day, the TV reports that someone has anonymously claimed credit—if credit is the right word—saying the fire was an act of "DIY reparations." Angina phones with the good news that this development won't affect her $10 million windfall. She's looking up charter yachts in the Mediterranean for next summer, trying to find the most expensive one. She wants them to join her.

The torching of Itchfield gets national media attention. A columnist for the *New York Times* writes that he is "experiencing a certain amount of guilty pleasure." Others in the wokestream media express similar views. Maybe HBO Max will add another public service announcement to *Gone with the Wind*, urging viewers to torch old Southern plantation houses. Owners of Low Country mansions are now hiring around-the-clock security. Good news for Officers Rusty and Not-Rusty. Everything is coming full circle. Hakuna matata, y'all.

The entertainment industry bible *Variety* calls. They're doing a story about how *Swamp Foxes*'s location has become "the new racial Ground Zero" and would like his comment. He tells *Variety* that he really has no comment. To keep him on the phone, the reporter asks what he's working on. He tells her about *Heimlich's Maneuver*, which he describes as "a piece of shit," adding, "I was on drugs when I wrote it." The reporter naturally quotes him. He learns from her story that *Swamp Foxes* has earned "substantial profits, mainly in the hotel in-room adult viewing sector." Needless to say, none of these profits have made their way to the movie's writer. He tells Peaches, "Seems the British weren't the only ones who got screwed."

Winky calls to discuss the article. She says that few of her clients describe their work to *Variety* as "a piece of shit." He tells her she would agree if she read it. Winky is now "morbidly curious" and says she must absolutely read it. She does and calls back and says, "You're right."

He chafes anew that Marvin, the producer, screwed him. Winky verbally shrugs, not because she is indifferent, but because it is the rule, not the exception, that the writer gets screwed. But she tells him that Marvin is "about to have his dick handed to him." He perks up at this, having spent much of the past decade fantasizing about lowering Marvin—and Brian, the director—into a pit full of starving animals. Marvin is a notoriously sadistic boss. An abused employee has been secretly taping his tantrums and inappropriate language. "He has him on tape calling Chadwick Boseman uppity," Winky says. This is even more inappropriate in the wake of Chadwick Boseman's death. Winky relays all this with relish, for she, too, has long fantasized about lowering Marvin into a pit full of ravening beasts. Many people have, really. A karmic tsunami is bearing down on Marvin.

He asks Winky if they should sue him. Suits are expensive, she replies. On the other hand, the last thing Marvin needs right now is more bad publicity. She says they could threaten to sue. "But we better move fast. At the rate he's handing out money to

Black groups, he soon won't have any left. He gave the NAACP a million bucks yesterday."

Marvin calls. He devotes less than twenty seconds to "How long has it been?" and "How are you?" before getting down to business. He saw the article in *Variety* and is "very excited" about *Heimlich's Maneuver*, which he says, "sounds like *Das Boot* meets *Airplane!*" He says he has been looking for "exactly this mix" for a long time.

He mentions to Marvin that Leslie Nielsen, who starred in *Airplane!*, played Francis Marion in the 1960s TV show *Swamp Fox*. Marvin demands to see the screenplay immediately.

He calls Winky, and they have a jolly good laugh, for they know that Marvin has no intention whatsoever of producing *Heimlich's Maneuver*. This is just a face-saving way of paying him off. Winky will send him the screenplay.

Next day, she calls back, and they have an even better laugh. Marvin loves it. He's offering $475,000, which Winky points out is "almost exactly what he owes you in back-end profits. What a coincidence, huh?" They have another good laugh.

She calls again and says, "You're not going to believe this." Marvin is offering an additional $250,000 for two rewrites and a polish. And an executive producer credit.

"He must be on drugs," he says. Is Dr. Paula his concierge doctor?

"He's actually serious," Winky says. "He's in talks with Donald Sutherland to play whatsisname."

He thinks of the line in Kurosawa's *Ran*. "In a world gone mad, only the mad are sane."

Marvin calls him the next day to report that Sutherland loves it. At least Marvin thinks he does. He's having a hard time understanding him over the phone. "I'm sending my doctor to check him out. He lives in Quebec. Who the fuck lives in *Quebec*? Meanwhile, I've been thinking. Does it have to be Roosevelt?"

"Who did you have in mind?"

"JFK. During the Cuban Missile Crisis."

"Okay. So . . . the Russians kidnap him? From the White House?"

"Palm Beach."

"Palm Beach. Okay."

"It's a little more glamorous than your fucking swamp in North Carolina." As always, Marvin is an attentive reader.

"The Kennedys have a mansion there. JFK is visiting."

"During the Cuban Missile Crisis. Okay."

"He wants to be closer to the action."

"And to the missiles? Okay. So, who is Donald Sutherland playing?"

"Baruch. He's visiting the Kennedys. He and Old Joe Kennedy are pals from way back."

There's no point in telling Marvin that Baruch loathed Joseph Kennedy.

"Baruch is shtupping Jackie."

He points out that Baruch would be ninety-two in 1962, but Marvin is unconcerned.

"It's how I sold it to Sutherland. He said, 'I get to shtup Jackie? I'm in!'"

"Okay. So, lose the flaming pigs?"

"Are you kidding? The flaming pigs are why I fell in love with this project. Hundreds of flaming pigs stampeding and squealing down Ocean Boulevard. What a metaphor, huh?"

"Metaphor for what?"

"You'll figure something out. The pigs reach the mansion just as the Russian sub pulls up at the dock. I'm getting a hard-on just thinking about it." Marvin adds that they need a Black character. "Not just a butler or chauffeur. A general or something like that."

"Why not the captain of the Russian sub?"

"I gotta take this call. Great to be working with you again."

He tells Winky to take the $475K and run, fast, to the nearest bank. He'll pass on the rest. She agrees this is the wise course.

"So," she says. "What's next?"

He tells her he's thinking of writing a novel.

"A novel?" she says dubiously. "About, like, what?"

He says he doesn't know, but he has a title: *Does It Have to Be a Novel?*

"Love it," Winky says.

The next morning, he gets on the bathroom scale. He looks down, and what do you know, there are the ten little piggies, wiggling at him. "Where have you guys been?" he asks. They wriggle back.

After a hearty breakfast of cabbage soup, he goes to his study and sits down and types

Has Anyone Seen My Toes?

May 2020–July 2021

Still with us? In 1756, during the Seven Years' War, the Duke of Richelieu laid siege to the capital of Minorca, Mahón, named for Mago, brother of Hannibal. The siege lasted so long the French ran out of butter and cream. The thought of a meal sans sauce being unthinkable, the duke's chef improvised one out of egg yolks and olive oil. He named it *mahonnaise.*

Acknowledgments

Thank you and then some to faithful first responders Katy Close, John Tierney, Greg Zorthian; His Eminence Cullen Cardinal Murphy; Douglas Bernon; and Robin Clements.

This was my first collaboration, and I hope not the last, with the splendid Robert Messenger of Simon & Schuster. Kind thanks, as always, to S&S generalissimo Jonathan Karp. A very big thank-you to Beth Maglione, Phil Metcalf, Lewelin Polanco, Emily Simonson, and Sherry Wasserman. And to Faren Bachelis for her sharp eyes and deft ear. Eternal devotion to Amanda Urban of ICM.

In addition to sources cited in the text, I'm grateful to the work of Mark Forsythe, John Train, Steve Bachmann, Joseph Epstein, Fred R. Shapiro, and the indispensable *Wikipedia* and *Britannica*.

No pigs were set on fire in the making of this book.

About the Author

Christopher Buckley is a novelist, essayist, humorist, critic, magazine editor, and memoirist. His books include *Thank You for Smoking, The Judge Hunter, Make Russia Great Again*, and *The Relic Master. Has Anyone Seen My Toes?* is his twentieth book. He worked as a merchant seaman and White House speechwriter. He was awarded the Thurber Prize for American Humor and the Washington Irving Medal for Literary Excellence.